GAYLE AND STEPHEN

PORTER

EX NATU

DIKAIÓ: Book III

ISBN: 978-1-957907-13-0 (Paperback)
ISBN: 978-1-957907-14-7 (Hardcover)
ISBN: 978-1-957907-15-4 (Ebook)

Library of Congress Control Number: 2025938955

Any references to historical events, real people, or real places are used fictitiously. Names, characters, and places are products of the authors' imagination.

Book design by Stephen Porter.

First printing edition 2025. Printed in the United States of America.

Porter Creative
3647 Oviedo
Brownsville TX 78520

www.portercreatives.com

Behold, children are a heritage from the LORD,
the fruit of the womb a reward.

Like arrows in the hand of a warrior
are the children of one's youth.

Blessed is the man
who fills his quiver with them!

He shall not be put to shame
when he speaks with his enemies in the gate.

-- Psalm 127

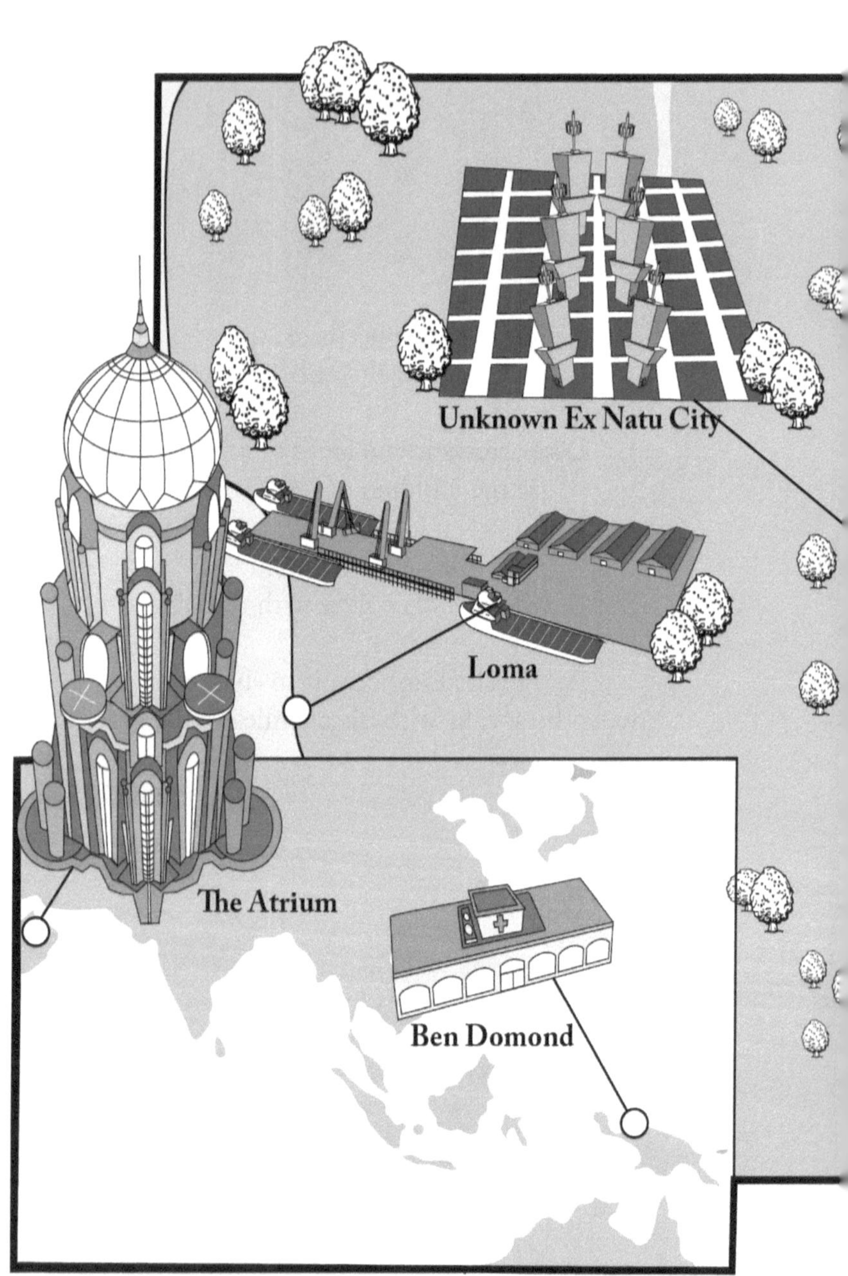

Unknown Ex Natu City
Loma
The Atrium
Ben Domond

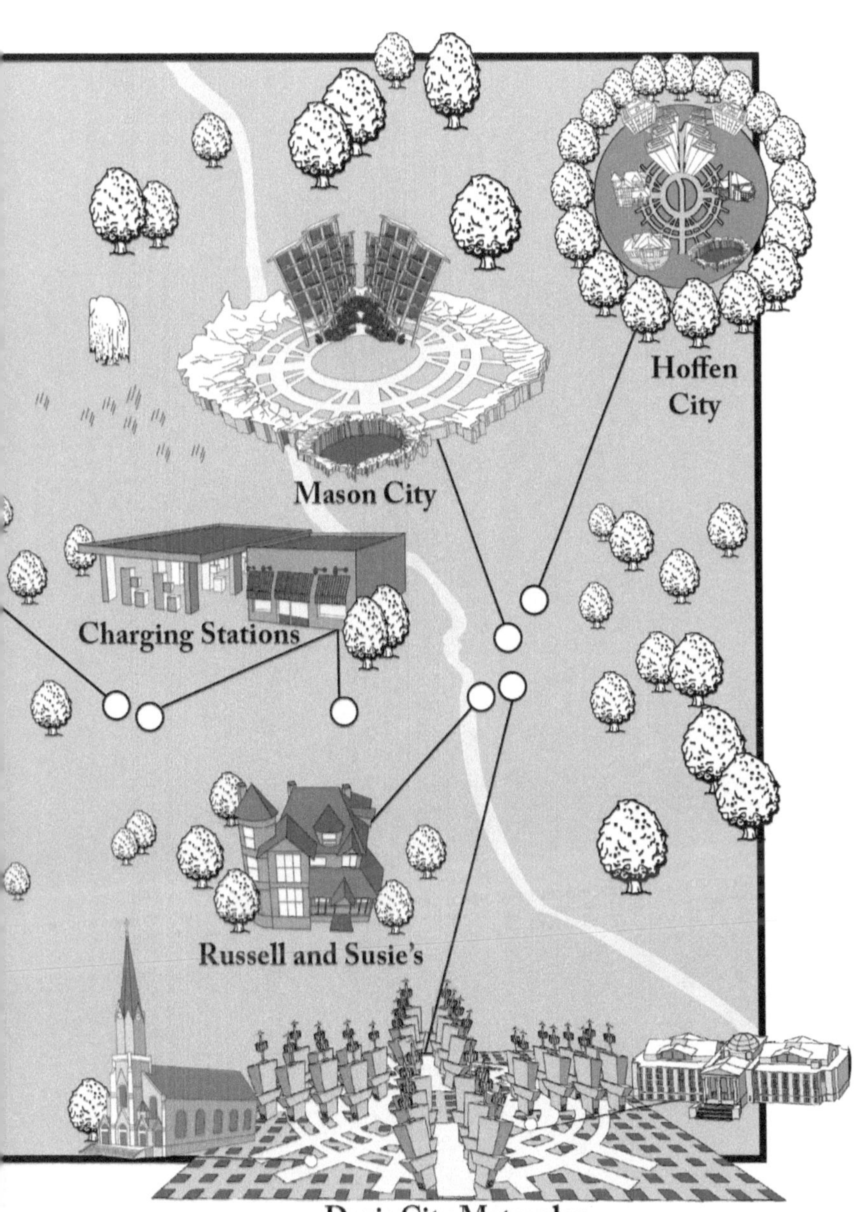

Hoffen City
Mason City
Charging Stations
Russell and Susie's
Davis City Metroplex

CONTENTS

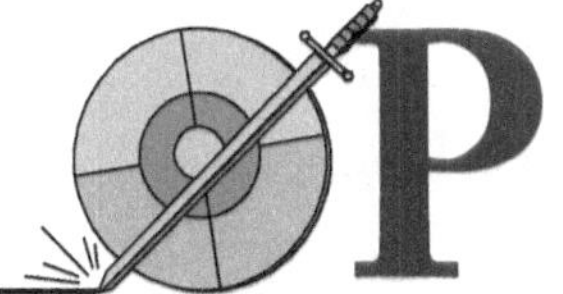

The small girl leaned forward in terrified rapture. She had been here eight times before, and yet her grayish-blue eyes barely blinked in the cool, evening wind, which whipped through her curly brown hair. Mosquitos left lines of unscratched welts on the skin exposed between her frilly white dress and her well-worn hiking boots. She pressed her hands into the shoulders of the two boys sitting in front of her, squeezing hard. Normally the boys, who were six and dressed in identical dark suits to match their nearly identical faces, would have brushed away their older sister's intrusion, but tonight, they did not notice. The twins had only been here six times. No matter how many years they had attended, all the children's mouths hung open, mesmerized by the storytellers on the stage.

Men and women danced in a circle around the theater with uncanny grace. They faced outward protectively as they spun, wielding rifles and blades, while a newborn baby in a small crib lay sleeping in the center of their defensive group. Outside the circle of warriors, several culture sprites twirled their whip-like arms in the air, making silver ropes dance like water fountains in the light. The sprites' arms swirled in sync with drummers lining the sides of the stage beating the rhythms of war. The drums paused. The dancers froze. The sprites' arms shot upward like spears: columns holding up the air. Then the drummers all struck their drumheads hard in unison while stomping one foot on the ground. With the explosion of sound, smoke and fire filled the stage.

The two boys screamed and turned quickly into the arms of the brown-haired girl, who closed her eyes and held the pair tightly. The trio trembled while they held each other. A middle-aged woman with dark hair and dark eyes, holding a baby of her own, gently inserted her free, rugged hand between the children and forced them apart. She pointed at the stage. "Watch!" she commanded.

One of the boys wailed, "No, mama! Please! It's too scary."

The others nodded in agreement, trying to clamber around their mother's hands back into their own circle of protective embrace.

The woman's eyes narrowed. "Watch!" she commanded again, unrelenting and wrenched them apart, forcing them all to face the stage.

The children turned their teary eyes back to the stage,

shaking violently in fear, but watching obediently. The rafters of the theater split apart revealing a large black aircraft hovering menacingly. Spotlights on its wings waved about across the stage and the audience, blinding them every time it crossed their eyes. Somewhere off stage, a collection of brass tubas warbled deeply mimicking the sounds of heavy engines. The sprites' spears went limp, and they quickly used their whips to whisk away the warriors guarding the child, gently setting them on the ground in haphazard clumps. The actors pretended to die agonizing deaths, throwing red ribbons in the air as if blood were squirting from their make-believe wounds. As they died, a door opened beneath the bottom of the aircraft emitting a red light and a gust of smoke. A long metal gangplank slowly extended from the opening. The edge of the gangplank landed inches from the sleeping baby in the cradle, who, without any acting ability whatsoever, had managed to stay asleep through all the cacophony of the performance.

A man with bronze skin, close-cropped brown hair, and gray eyes that looked quite a bit like the girl's in the audience, slowly began to descend out of the ship toward the child. His bluish-gray military suit seemed to suck in the brightness of the stage like a black hole eating light, which made the reflection of the medals on his chest even more spectacular and imposing. On his waist, he wore a white belt with a scabbard and a polished, golden handle swung from it as he walked. He slowly descended the gangplank. His eyes fixated on the cradle.

"Mama, I can't watch it again," the brown-haired girl

squealed and flung herself backwards into the folds of her mother's dress. The force of the girl's movements nearly toppled the woman and her baby, and she exhaled hard. She snatched the girl's wrist and spun her toward the stage. "You must watch, Vivian!" Then she softened, let go of the girl's wrist, and tenderly touched her cheek. "We all must watch."

Vivian grimaced as the man reached the bottom of the gangplank. The drums began to beat again, slowly, but growing in speed and earnestness. He reached down to grab the golden handle at his side and drew a brightly glowing saber from the scabbard. Violins began to sing with an intense vibrato. He held the sword high for a terrifying moment, and then plunged it into the cradle, as a loud cymbal crashed. The lights of the ship and stage immediately went dark. The instruments stopped. Dark stillness encompassed everything, heavy and expectant.

Vivian's mother broke the silence with a loud wail. Her cries were quickly echoed by other women in the audience: a loud mourning, more terrifying than anything that had been displayed on the stage. This was the moment that Vivian always hated most. Every year, she dreaded the wailing women at the end of the reenactment more than the story of the murdered innocent. But as she looked up at her mother screaming in the dark, she could see her terrified baby sister in her arms, crying in surprise and fear at her mother's sorrow, and something changed in Vivian. For the first time, she could see in her mind's eye her sister in the crib on the stage, and the glowing saber ending her life. Her fear was replaced with something else—something primal.

Anger? Hate? Loss? Loathing?

She could not tell, but she could hear it in the women's lament. Then her thoughts moved from imagining her sister in the cradle to imagining her own future baby at the end of the sword, while she lay on the ground covered in red ribbon, helpless to save her child. The feelings coalesced inside her, and she knew why the women wailed around her. It was love, or rather love lost. A powerlessness so intense that only a grieving mother could understand it: the pointless death of a child. Vivian's hands clenched into small fists. Tears burned hot in her eyes. She lifted her head skyward, and let her tiny voice join those of the other women.

The wailing continued in waves of ritualistic sobbing late into the night, and then one by one the crying mothers ended their lament, gathered their children together, and led them home. Soon Vivian's mother also ceased mourning, and Vivian took her cue, quieting herself as best she could. But the girl was not old enough to understand the ritual of the night. The deep emotions of the night's significance continued to wrack her small body with sniffles and coughs. The walk home in the dark was as much a part of the yearly festival as the food and the terrifying drama of the stage and the mourning mothers. The twins, who would usually run far ahead of their family getting into mischief, stayed close to their mother and sister. The natural night sounds of insects and birds were occasionally interrupted by howling coming from the trees and bushes around them.

"Beware the wilding wolves!" Their mother warned as they walked.

The children cowered. None of them had never seen a wilding wolf, and for some reason their calls could only be heard every year after the festival. But something was different this year, Vivian realized that this too was just more theater. The howling voices in the dark sounded more like the high-pitched calls her father made when gathering his flocks across the mountains than any animal she had ever encountered. And then to confirm her suspicions, several sheep crossed their path in the dark heading toward a cluster of trees to their left.

A large man dressed in gray and blue burst out of the trees yelling at the sheep, "No, no! Go back! You're ruining everything!"

Vivian's mother laughed. "You're a terrible wilding wolf, James!"

"Perhaps," the man said as he took a flashlight from his pocket and lit up his grinning face from underneath, casting his gray eyes, cropped brown hair, and olive skin in eerie, unnatural shadows, "but I make an excellent Knenne! Rawr!"

The twins screamed and clung desperately to their mother.

"James!" she chided. "They'll have enough trouble sleeping without you scaring them further. Here, take the baby," she ordered, holding their littlest out to him.

The large man handed the flashlight to Vivian and took the little girl from her mother. The baby snuggled deep into her father's chest, warming herself against the night. She yawned and closed her eyes. "Come now, my beloveds," James cooed. "Let's prove your mother wrong and see how fast you can go to sleep when we get home."

The group walked on in silence for a time, and then Vivian spoke. "Father?"

"Mhhmmm," her father answered absently.

"Why do you kill the baby in the play?" she asked.

While she could not see his face, she could hear his smile. "I would never kill a baby, my lovely girl, but General Knenne and his Ex Natu hated children. The massacre of the innocents in the great wars nearly wiped our people from the planet. We used to number in the hundreds of millions. There was no place on Earth where our people were not." He paused, and his voice took on a note of sadness. "But that was centuries ago."

"So, General Knenne is dead? He died a long time ago?" Vivian hoped.

Her father shook his head. "God grant us favor, I hope so, but the Festival of the Innocents reminds us to always be vigilant in case he is not."

"How could he not be?" One of the twins asked, suddenly interested in the conversation.

"Some say the Ex Natu discovered the secrets of immortality," his mother answered.

"So, they live a long time?" One of the twins asked, now even more interested in the conversation.

"Forever," his mother answered matter-of-factly. "Unless they can be killed in combat."

Her husband nodded. "And our warriors killed many of them."

"But not General Knenne?" the first twin asked.

"We don't know," his mother answered. "There's no record of it if he was."

Vivian did not feel like her original question had been addressed to her satisfaction. How could the Ex Natu and General Knenne hate children? She tried to go back to it. "So, he killed the baby because he hated our people?"

"Not our people, specifically. He killed the baby because the Ex Natu hate children," her father explained.

Vivian still could not believe that was what her father had said. "Children?" She thought for a moment. "Don't they have children of their own?"

The group reached the top of the hill they were climbing, and the light of their porch met them. "No," her father answered as he climbed the steps and opened their front door. The inside of the house was warm and inviting. The children trudged wearily into the foyer, hanging their jackets on the coat tree, and placing their shoes on the small shelves just inside the door before sliding on their house slippers. A panel with white translucent paper automatically slid open as they walked toward it, opening on a cozy cabin with rich-wood trim and white-painted walls. Her father handed the baby to her mother, and then walked to a bookshelf across the room. He pulled a large leather-bound volume from the shelf.

He opened the book to a page marked with a small red ribbon—no doubt placed there earlier in the day to answer any questions the children might have about the night's events. On the page was a photograph of a striking man with olive skin and gray eyes, who looked a little like Vivian's father, which was probably why he had been selected to play the part of General Knenne. Her father bounced the heavy book in his hand, and the pages waved about severely. "Our history books tell us that the Ex Natu sacrificed their ability to have children to extend their own years."

"So, they can't have any children?" Vivian shook her head, an unexpected feeling of pity washing over her.

Her father looked gravely into her eyes and said, "No, Vivian. Don't feel bad for them. What they've done is the greatest of evils. Their choice to do what is unnatural is also their punishment. Because of their great sin, there is not, and never will be, such a thing as an Ex-Natu child."

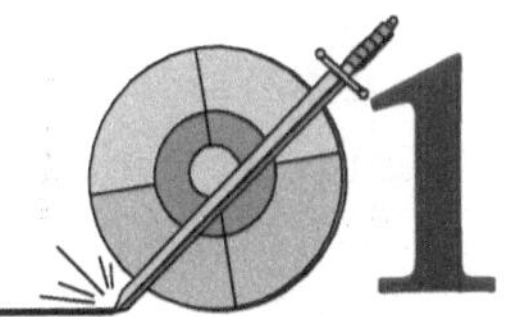

No matter which way Mallory swished her tongue around in her mouth, it stuck to her teeth, to her cheek, to the roof, and to her chapped dry lips. She tried to summon some saliva to swallow, but her salivary glands offered her little but thick sludge, which sat at the top of her throat, stubbornly refusing to go down. And yet, her dry mouth was the least of her discomfort. Sweat and other body fluids saturated the sheets on her bed, and like her dry tongue, no matter which way she writhed or turned, they clung to her skin. Her body odor, mixed with that of the coagulating fluids, roiled together in her nostrils like a dish of rancid cheese and week-old onion. Her brown hair, normally curly and dry, hung down in dripping ringlets all around her. Her throat was raw, both from dehydration and from screaming. For hours now, her body had been racked with spasming muscles. It was like a reoccurring leg cramp, but there was no option to walk it off. The cramps were in her stomach and lower back and came in rippling waves of pain. Those waves were getting closer to each other. Every one of them felt as if they were going to tear her apart from the inside out.

Her child was ready to be born.

In Hoffen City, as she had come to know her home city since being banished from it over a year ago, she had witnessed many births. The City's Matriarch was a familiar figure in labor and delivery at the hospital. Although her presence was more a formality than a function, the Matriarch was fully trained to act as a midwife and deliver a baby if the need should arise, and Mallory had watched her mother deliver several of the city's children when doctors were unavailable. As heir of the Matriarchy, she had even delivered two children herself under her mother's supervision: a boy and a girl, both named after her, Malachi and Mallory. She wanted to smile at the memory, but all she could think about was the pain that those mothers went through. She had had some empathy for them at the time, seeing the blood and the expressions of pain, but now she felt connected to those mothers—all mothers—on a different level. If there was an essence of womanhood, this experience defined it.

However, none of the births in Hoffen City were anything comparable to what she was experiencing. For one thing, the birthing rooms in the Hoffen City hospital were always bustling with people. There were doctors, nurses, the

Matriarch and her entourage, family members, and worried fathers. For Mallory's delivery, there was only a silver medic sprite hovering in a corner of the dark, dirty room. She had not seen another human being in days, or weeks. It was impossible to track time in the cell in which the Ex Natu had placed her. There was a small slit at the bottom of the door under which a tray of food was occasionally slid. Initially, she had tried to mark time by the arrival of the tray, but she remembered from the Archivist's *Chronicles of the Lost* that her captors no longer needed food the same way she did, and the arrival of the tray was intermittent at best. Mallory had often wondered if her baby would be healthy with the amount of time she had gone hungry in captivity. Surely, the little one was not getting the nutrition he or she needed to develop properly in the womb. Luckily, there was a sink in the corner opposite the sprite that offered running water, or they would have both died long ago.

But the Ex Natu did not want her dead. In particular Omaha, the leader of the Ex Natu who had attacked the Library and taken her, Caleb, and the Archivist prisoner wanted her alive. Mallory's eyes began to tear up at the memory. She corrected herself; she did not know that Caleb and the Archivist were prisoners. For all she knew, they could both be dead, and Omaha's only interest in her was the baby. She had no idea what he was going to do to her when the baby was born.

Her thoughts were interrupted by another series of agonizing contractions, and all she could concentrate on was the pain. She tried to breathe the way her mother and the doctors had instructed the women in Hoffen City: in, out, out, in, out, out. The breathing exercises were an exercise in futility, and soon she was not breathing at all, just grinding her molars in agony.

She screamed at the sprite, "Please, help me! I need something to drink! Medication! Anything!"

The sprite did not respond. It just hovered there silently.

She very nearly used the Dikaió to order the sprite to help her, but she bit her dry tongue to stop herself from invoking it. She looked at the mirrored wall to her left. Omaha could be standing on the other side of the wall watching her suffer. She had no idea what Omaha knew about her time at the Library—especially whether or not he knew that the Archivist had christened her a Dikaió Archivist. But she did know that Omaha could take it away from her again. The ancient weapons designer had invented the Dikaió, and he wielded a Dominus bracelet that gave him complete control of the technology that she had once believed was magic.

Mallory had considered that revelation in depth. All she had was time after all. No matter which way she turned over the Dikaió in her mind, Mallory did not truly understand how the Dikaió was technology and not magic. It gave someone christened to use it the ability to control almost any non-living thing with just a word, and those things could defy every law of physics she knew. If she wanted a drink, which she really did, she could order a glass of water to float to her lips and quench her thirst. The water across the room in the sink was a horrible temptation. But she also knew that her christening could be removed: a feat her best friend Alex had managed in Hoffen City, stripping all their people of the ability to use the Dikaió. When it happened, the light, a holographic plasma field that surrounded their city and protected it, had also vanished. They had assumed that Alex's words were the cause of that event, but it turned out that the light had been sabotaged by Reddy Lamarr.

Mallory screamed, partly at the thought of the old Sprite Master who betrayed them and partly because the contractions hit her again. Reddy Lamarr had turned out to be Omaha's old assistant—and an Ex Natu. The Ex Natu were immortal thanks to nano sprites injected into their bodies. Reddy Lamarr had not necessarily chosen to become Ex Natu, but just like Caleb, the nano sprites were necessary to save her life. She had been trapped by the light in Hoffen City for centuries, changing her identity every few decades, so the mortals there would not know she was an Ex Natu. Even though an Ex Natu could not be christened to use the Dikaió, Reddy Lamarr had taken Omaha's wife's, Dominus bracelet. Using it, she was able to blend in with the other citizens without raising suspicion. When Mallory knew her, she was the city's Sprite Master, responsible for birthing sprites at the city's rookery. After Mallory, Caleb, and Alex had been exiled, Reddy Lamarr followed them with a tracker she had planted on them, intent on killing the Archivist. Mallory was still not sure how the Sprite Master knew the Archivist would find them, or why exactly she wanted to kill her. Reddy Lamarr had sworn that the answer was in *The Chronicles of the Lost*, the Archivist's account of the events after she had been locked out of Hoffen City, but the Ex Natu's attack on the Library had interrupted them before she had gotten to that part of the journal.

And now, she found herself in this dingy Ex Natu cell, all alone, going over those events over and over in her mind, trying to find clues that she had missed. Another thing she did not completely understand was why she was here.

She had been injured in the attack, which is what led to Caleb's surrender on the condition of helping her. Omaha had promised that he would save her, but he also wanted to know if she had gotten pregnant before or after the clockwork sprite had saved Caleb's life by injecting him with nano sprites. Mallory did not understand how she could have gotten pregnant after the injection. Nano sprites were what gave the Ex Natu their immortality. They healed very rapidly, did not get ill, and would pretty much live forever. It took a wound that resulted in immediate death to kill them. To stop the world from becoming overpopulated with immortal human beings, the Ex Natu had also designed the nano sprites to sterilize the host. Caleb should not be able to have children anymore. They had both grieved that news. But Omaha had referred to Caleb and Mallory as his "experiment," and his comments seemed to suggest that he had done something to the nano sprites in Caleb to make him capable of reproducing.

Mallory had spent months wondering if the baby in her womb was an Ex Natu too. Would her baby and her husband both be forever young while she grew old and gray? Would they mourn her death, and then forget her in the centuries to come? Or was her baby just a normal human being? And what would Omaha do if that were case? Did he have any use for a mortal child? Or was that the experiment? In either case, she worried what might happen to her and her child after she delivered.

In the middle of that thought, the baby pressed hard on her cervix, and Mallory moaned in pain. The medic sprite in the corner must have been scanning her progress because it suddenly whirred into action, quickly positioning itself at the far end of her bed. Mallory kicked at it.

"Get away from me, you stupid piece of steel!" she growled.

Her bare foot connected with the sprite, but it did not budge. It just floated there maddeningly strong. Mallory's pain was intense, but instead of suffering, she felt a surging anger bouncing around in her head, as if her body were pumping her with a surge of adrenaline. She kicked at the sprite twice more, and then her eyes rolled toward the mirrored wall. "I know you're in there!" she shrieked. "If Caleb's in there with you, send him in. I'm going to kill him!"

She screamed again, and her eyes rolled back to the sprite. "I'm going to kill, you too! The sprites at the Library called me 'The Sprite Slayer,' you know." She snapped her teeth at the sprite threateningly.

The sprite seemed to regard her threat and responded. A tentacle slowly unwound from its body. There was a small spinning saw blade attached to it. Mallory's fight turned to flight instantly. She squirmed in her bed, trying to get away from the sprite and its saw blade, while simultaneously being racked with the worst pain she had ever felt in her life.

The baby was coming, and the sprite was waiting for it.

"No! No!" she screamed, trying to get out of the bed and away from the sprite.

Several other tentacles unwound from the sprite then and clamped onto her wrist and ankles, forcing her squarely onto the bed in a birthing position. Mallory strained against the cold, sprite steel and tried not to push the baby out. She might as well have tried to move the earth itself. She was equally powerless against both the sprite and her own body. Her baby was going to be born, and this sprite was going to do whatever it wanted to it. There was nothing she could do. Pain racked her body so hard that she felt it tingling like electricity in her teeth. Then the searing pain subsided into a smoldering sting. The baby was out. A sprite tentacle wrapped around the quiet infant and lifted it up into the air upside down. Mallory saw that her baby was a boy, and her heart stopped when the sprite's saw blade began to whir. She strained her hand toward the blade, but the sprite had her in an iron grip. It would have been a foolish move even if it did not. She would have lost her fingers. Mallory's brow furrowed, and she hissed, "Dikaió…"

But before she could finish the command, another tentacle sprang up and added a clip to the baby's umbilical cord, and the sprite used the saw to sever the infant from his mother. Then another tentacle slapped the baby's bottom, and Mallory's son announced to the world that he was alive with a loud and thunderous cry. The saw blade disappeared back into the sprite and was replaced with a nozzle that came out of nowhere, and the sprite sprayed the baby with warm water, cleaning her son off. The tentacles holding Mallory to the bed released her, and the sprite held the baby out to her still dangling upside down.

Mallory took the naked little bundle, gently checking him over for any damage the sprite may have done to him, or if his time of being starved in the womb had caused him any harm. His hands clenched in tiny fists, and he screamed loudly in indignation about being sprayed and slapped, but otherwise he was perfect: five fingers on two hands, five toes on two feet. He had Caleb's piercing blue eyes, but her wild mop of brown hair. It was wet but drying quickly and forming curls. His skin was darker like hers as well, but he had Caleb's nose. Mallory smiled down at the boy, and he screamed back at her in shaky protest. Mallory was sure the boy was unhappy about being evicted from his nice warm apartment too, despite how cramped it had become lately. And if he were anything like his father, he was already hungry. She quickly pulled up her soiled gown and pressed the infant up to her chest and lowered the gown over him. Her son latched onto his mother and soon, he settled into the two responsibilities he would have for the next year of his life: eating and sleeping.

Mallory's insides seemed to shift and slither about, and another cramp hit her, milder than the previous contractions, but not comfortable by any means. Pressure pushed up against her cervix again, and she felt her body needed to relieve it. The sprite quickly wrapped something else up in a towel, and then sped away to the room's only door. An invisible lock clicked, and the door slid open. As soon as the sprite was out, the door slid shut again, and the lock clicked back into place. They were prisoners once more. Mallory wondered briefly why the sprite would take her placenta, but the warm suckling babe in her arms had already begun to trigger hormones in her brain to make the whole experience foggy in her memory. She wished Caleb were here to name the boy. She wished her father were here to meet his grandson. She wished her mother could christen him with the Dikaió: an Athenos like his father—well, at least as his father once was. If Omaha had modified Caleb's nano sprites to allow him to have children, he had not made them so that he could use the Dikaió. While the Archivist's christening of Mallory and Alex had restored their ability to use the Dikaió in a limited fashion, Caleb was still a Dikaió Chorus, like everyone else in Hoffen City.

Mallory's childhood rushed back to her. Until the Archivist had replaced her christening at the Library, she had been a Dikaió Chorus for as long as she could remember. It had been her singular curse: The inability to use magic in a city full of magic users. Her grandmother had prophesied that a Dikaió Chorus would one day save the city, and then christened Mallory with the distinction. In the end, after Alex accidentally made everyone in the city Dikaió Choruses, it was Mallory's mother who had been the one that saved the city from Mallory and her friends. She had spent countless hours wondering what would have happened if they had just left well enough alone and not repaired the fire sprites they found in the dark woods. The obvious answer was that Alex's grandfather would have had Mallory put to death and used his small army of magistrates to seize control of the government. Without the Dikaió, how could anyone have stopped him? But the fire sprites in the woods turned out to be as dangerous as the old Administrator ever was. They certainly killed more people.

Mallory killed more people. She alone was the person who had the capability to repair the sprites. She had developed a knack for tinkering to get along in a city full of magic she could not use. The city needed saving from her, which is why her mother, along with the rest of the city council, exiled her, Caleb, and Alex. And now here she was, held captive by immortal monsters, and a new mother to boot. Alex and Caleb might both be dead. The Archivist and even Reddy Lamarr might be dead as well for all she knew.

The baby stopped eating, and Mallory absent-mindedly tickled the bottom of his foot, which got him started up again. She tried to regain her line of thought, but her eyes began to drift shut.

She was exhausted and very thirsty.

Her dreams took her back to the Library, to the room of art on the seventh floor, the one she had been studying just before finding out that she was pregnant. She was looking at the painting with the woman in the blue and white satin dress shimmering in light. Rather than forever perching on a stool with one arm resting on an open book on a tall table, and the other hand clutched at her breast, she was now climbing backwards up the spokes of her stool, kicking at the white and brown globe on the floor. The stool rocked back and forth, barely maintaining its tenuous grapple with gravity. The woman's eyes rolled up toward the ceiling, she was screaming about the dead snake below her with its protruding fangs and smashed head. In the background, the other woman, who also seemed to be upset, was writhing in grief. The man hanging on the tree was still obscured in shadow, but he was moving too, taking slow and ragged breaths. Mallory tried to focus in to see him clearer, and almost as if he could sense her gaze, his face slowly began to turn toward her, and Mallory felt her pulse begin to quicken. She was terrified that he would see her, and yet desperate to be seen by him.

A baby's scream came from another painting in the room. Mallory turned away from the man on the wooden beam to find the source of the cry, and as she did, the dream fluttered away, and her eyes blinked open. Her baby was squirming on her chest, crying for more food. Mallory laughed and cooed to the little man. "You're just like your father: always hungry." She repositioned the baby under her gown, and he settled in on second breakfast.

Mallory patted the babe on its rump and smiled. "You're going to need a name. What should I call you?"

The baby shifted his weight slightly and then smacked her in the chest angrily with his tiny fist while sucking furiously.

Mallory laughed. "A fighter, are you? Well, you come from a long line of fighters you know. You're great, great, I don't know how many greats, grandfather was a general. He was a general of the Ex Natu armies, and then he betrayed them and became a general of our people when his wife told him she had had his baby against every law. He chose family over power and nigh immortality. Without him fighting for us, you would not even have been born. His name was General Kirk Knenne." Mallory paused and looked down at her baby. "And that will be your name too. Kirk Knenne Aiworth."

The baby's eyes seemed to glance up at her as if he approved of her choice, and then his eyes rolled backwards, and he fell fast asleep. This time Mallory let the boy sleep. He had been through a lot.

Mallory was just about to go back to sleep herself when the lock on her door clicked. She tensed and clutched her sleeping baby a little tighter. The door slowly swung open, and a man with dark skin, a regal looking jawline, and bright blue eyes walked into the room followed by the silver medic sprite. Whatever the sprite had taken her placenta for had been enough to bring Omaha to visit. Living tattoos swirled and danced under his skin, making and unmaking images. A normal tattoo on an Ex Natu would be immediately healed by their nano sprites, ejecting the ink out from under the skin, so they had developed these moving tattoos that were constantly on the run from the nano sprites, shifting from one image to the next. One of the images that Omaha's tattoos kept repeating was the face of a lovely woman, who Mallory assumed was his wife, Melody. Melody had been killed in the Mason City explosion when the Ex Natu forced Omaha to remotely activate the city's holographic plasma field before it was ready. Mallory could not help but wonder why he would so happily serve the monsters that took his wife, and yet here he was. There were other images and words that came and went: doves feeding grapes to men and women dressed in togas, the words "ambrosia" and "nectar," but one image terrified Mallory. In it, a woman held her infant by the heel and dipped the baby's whole body into a flame.

Mallory tried not think about that image and instead focused on her visitor. It was always a mixed bag when Omaha came to see her. She knew she should hate the man, that she should be angry with him—maybe even try to use the Dikaió to kill him. But her captivity in this room had been a lonely one. The meals shoved under her door were pretty much the extent of her connection with the outside world. If not for her baby, she might have lost her mind in the solitude. She could count on two hands the times she had seen another human being's face while imprisoned, and for all of those encounters, Omaha had been present. She had come to look forward to and even long for his visits just for the sake of human contact. He smiled at her, and Mallory felt an immediate warmness and gratitude surge up unbidden inside her. She tried to stop it, but her lips spread into a desperate smile.

"Hello, Mallory," he laughed. "We have a new addition, I hear!"

He bounded over to her bedside, and Mallory was imme-diately struck by his body odor and bad breath. Outside of the Archivist and Reddy Lamarr, she had not met many real Ex Natu, but the ones who had come with Omaha were both filthy and stinky. She remembered her mother's preoccupa-tion with cleaning her wounds with stinging antiseptic to keep her from acquiring an infection, which was also something her mother often claimed as a reason for showering and keeping a tidy home. Since germs and infections were hardly a concern for the Ex Natu, they were rarely concerned with hygiene. Unfortunately, they were also unconcerned with her hygiene while she had been locked in this cell and having a baby. But she was not immortal with all-curing nano sprites coursing through her body. Predictably, Omaha did not seem to notice any of the filth. He hovered over her, looking lovingly at the baby's locks pooling out from beneath her gown. "Oh, he's a healthy fellow, isn't he?"

She wrinkled her nose at Omaha and responded, "Yes, and we're a mess. When can we get cleaned up?"

His eyes went wide in surprise. He looked her over, and his smile faded. "I should say you are." Then he waved his hand dismissively. "We'll make arrangements for that later. First, let me hold our little bundle of joy!"

Mallory hesitated. Why was he calling her baby "our" anything? Whatever feelings of human camaraderie she felt vanished. She clutched Kirk protectively and shook her head.

Omaha's eyes darkened. "Give him to me, Mallory. He belongs to me; I made him. He is the future."

"I don't know what you're talking about, but you cannot have my son," Mallory spoke quietly but forcefully.

Omaha sighed heavily and snapped his fingers and turned away from her. "I had hoped not to be here for this." Two Ex Natu soldiers entered the room, walking quickly around the sprite and Omaha. One drew his weapon, and the other reached for her gown, intending to lift it and forcibly take her son. "Bring the child to me when it's over," Omaha said, starting to walk toward the door.

Mallory was sure now. Omaha had no intention of leaving her alive once they had the baby. And she did not know if he intended to leave her child alive either. For all she knew, he was going to dissect Kirk for some sick Ex Natu experiment. Her eyes darted toward the door. She was weak, and she was not sure how far she would get, but this was her only chance. "Dikaió, defend me," she shouted.

Omaha stopped and spun on his heel, just as the medic sprite tentacles lashed out, grabbed the two Ex Natu guards, and spun them away from Mallory. Mallory's eyes darted to Omaha's wrist. His Dominus bracelet was there. For the moment, Omaha was too stunned to speak, and Mallory needed to make sure it stayed that way. "Dikaió, don't let Omaha speak."

Omaha's eyes went wide. He moved to run, but another tentacle from the medic sprite shot out and wrapped around his mouth, yanking him backward hard. He fell squarely on his rear end. His bright blue eyes darkened and narrowed in Mallory's direction. He reached into his coat pocket and pulled a weapon out, aimed it in her direction, and pulled the trigger.

The explosion was deafening, but the Dikaió was still protecting Mallory. The sprite quickly shifted position in between Omaha and Mallory, deflecting the projectile away from her and into one of the Ex-Natu guards. A whirring noise sounded from inside the man, and he squirmed in agony, straining against the sprite's tentacles. Mallory grimaced. Omaha was using the Ex-Natu-slaying ammunition the Archivist had written about in *The Chronicles of the Lost*. Part of her wanted to save the guard, but she did not have time for that. His body stopped struggling and went limp very quickly. Omaha must have improved the ammunition since his fight with the Archivist at the Ex Natu citadel. She turned her attention back to Omaha. "Dikaió, bring me Omaha's Dominus bracelet and his weapon."

The tentacle holding the dying Ex Natu dropped him as he was no longer a threat. It quickly wrenched Omaha's weapon from his hand and then reached for the Dominus bracelet. Omaha clenched his hand into a fist, and he grimaced as the sprite yanked hard on the bracelet, cutting deep rivulets into his hand, but the bracelet did not come off. A fourth tentacle unraveled from the medic sprite: the one with the saw blade that it had used to cut Kirk's umbilical cord. The saw blade began to whir.

Omaha's angry eyes widened in fear as he realized what the sprite intended to do. He quickly opened his fist and narrowed his fingers so that the Dominus bracelet could slip off. Mallory tilted her head and bit her lip. Was it possible that the Ex Natu's nano sprites could not regenerate a limb? Or maybe Omaha just did not want to go through the pain of losing his hand? Whatever the case, the medic sprite quickly slipped off the Dominus bracelet and then handed the bracelet and Omaha's weapon to her. They were both covered in blood, and Mallory felt her stomach roll as she slipped the bracelet onto her wrist.

She had been thinking about her next words very

carefully, and she was not entirely sure it would work, but she thought it was worth a shot either way. "Dikaió, christen Mallory Aiworth Dikaió Dominus." She hoped that now even without a bracelet, she could wield all the abilities of the Dikaió. If that were the case, she could give the bracelet to Caleb if she could find him, and together maybe they would survive the Ex Natu and carry their son to safety.

Omaha's eyes rolled in his head, and Mallory could not tell if he thought she was stupid for trying to christen herself as a Dominus, or if he was frustrated that she had done something really, really smart and unexpected. She was half tempted to tell the sprite to release his mouth to find out, but she had no idea what tricks the centuries-old monster had up his sleeve. And she doubted she would get another chance for escape if she did not act fast. With one hand, she clutched Kirk to her chest, and with the other she held Omaha's weapon at her side. She swung her legs out of bed and hopped out.

Her bare feet hit the cold floor, and she almost lost her footing in the filth coating the floor. But she held her balance and walked gingerly to the door. With every step, she felt her insides adjust themselves, trying to bring themselves back to their normal position now that there was not a baby crowding them. It was extremely uncomfortable, painful, and dangerous. Mallory knew that she should be resting, taking time to recover from giving birth, but that was not an option right now. In order to save herself and her baby, she needed to make it to the door and get out of this cell. She had no idea what she was going to do after that, nor what waited for her on the other side of the door, but she would deal with whatever it was when she crossed that threshold.

She scooted past the medic sprite, making sure to stay well out of the reach of Omaha, who was still sitting on the ground, glaring at her. His wrist that the sprite had injured was healing rapidly. Mallory lifted his weapon and aimed it at him. Once again, Omaha's eyes registered surprise. He held up his hands in supplication and shook his head as much as he could in the grip of the sprite tentacle wrapped around his mouth. He did not really need to beg. Mallory could not have brought herself to kill him if she wanted to; she was not a killer—but she wanted him to know that she could have—she wanted him to know that she was not like him.

She lowered the weapon and continued stumbling toward the door. It had swung shut behind the guards, so she tucked the Ex-Natu weapon under her armpit and tried the handle. It was locked. She pulled the weapon out and held it toward the door. If there were any more guards behind the door, she wanted to be ready. She did not relish the thought of firing at anyone, but she would do what was necessary to survive.

She took a deep breath and said, "Dikaió, open the door." The lock clicked, and the door slowly swung open.

Mallory stepped out into a dirty hallway. Crumpled papers, rusting sprites, and molding food were strewn along the walls. The smell of decaying compost hit her like a pungent punch in the nose. There were no windows—just several doors: some open, most closed along the dingy path. Long white lights overhead flickered on and off in irregular patterns. Her room was at the end of the hallway; the only path was forward. Mallory hovered there in the doorway. There was no way to know which door she should take: Which door led to freedom and which door led to more Ex Natu? Yet, she knew she had to move before Omaha figured out how to get free from his bonds. She tried to take her first step down the hallway, but a long-forgotten fear began to work its way through her senses. She suddenly felt claustrophobic.

She almost laughed at the old fear. She had been trapped in a small room for months and had not felt afraid of being in an enclosed space, and yet here she was making a break for freedom, with more than a few feet to stretch her legs, and she felt like the walls were closing in on her. For a brief moment, the fear gripped her sufficiently enough that she almost walked back into her cell, but then little Kirk twitched in his sleep, and her fear was burned away in determination. Parenthood had awakened something primal in her: something that turned fear into fire.

She stepped fully into the hallway and slammed the door behind her. "Dikaió, keep this door closed." The lock clicked, and the metal frame crumpled into the door, cold-welding it tightly shut. Mallory nodded and began walking down the hall.

Within two steps of the door, Mallory felt a sharp pang in her foot. She nearly fell over in pain. She stepped back and leaned up against a wall. There were several pieces of broken glass laying on the floor amidst the trash. She awkwardly balanced herself against the wall, holding Kirk and the Ex Natu weapon, while squatting with one leg to look at the bottom of her foot. Her body protested in pain in several places. She had just given birth after all. Eventually, she maneuvered herself into a position that she could see the bottom of her foot. A tiny trickle of blood oozed from a wound on her black sole, but it did not look like there was any glass stuck in her foot. Mallory sighed. If her mother were here, she would disinfect that wound. Mallory gingerly put her foot back on the ground being careful to avoid the glass. She would just have to hope that she would not get an infection from this mess.

She bit her lip and tilted her head studying the filthy hallway in front of her. "Dikaió, clean this mess up."

The debris in the hallway began to tremble. Even the dirt under her feet began to move, and Mallory nearly squealed at the ticklish sensation. All the strewn trash, glass, and dirt slowly lifted itself off the floor and began to float down the hallway. Mallory was not sure where the Dikaió was taking the garbage, but she hoped it would be outdoors, so she followed the trail down the hall. After a few steps, she noticed that the muscles in her arm holding baby Kirk were burning. She desperately wanted to switch him to her other side, but she also did not want to set the weapon down just in case she encountered any Ex Natu in her escape. "Dikaió, hold this," she said and then in an act of faith let go of the weapon. It hovered in the air in front of her, and she laughed out loud. If only her mother could see her now: no longer a Dikaió Chorus but a Dikaió Dominus. "Dikaió, keep this weapon near me and use it to protect me," she said and then switched Kirk to her other arm. He scrunched up his wrin-kled nose in protest, but he did not wake at being jostled. Mallory smiled. He was a heavy sleeper just like his father.

She began walking down the cleaned hallway again, trying to catch up to the floating trail of trash; the Ex Natu weapon kept pace with her, floating along like a loyal dog on a leash. The trash turned left at an intersection in a hallway, and Mallory heard several crunching noises coming from around the corner. The wound in her foot from the glass was really beginning to sting, but she rushed ahead to find what the noise was. When she turned the corner, she found the hallway blocked by metal bars. The larger pieces of the trail of trash were crushing themselves through the bars. Mallory studied the barricade and saw that there was a door handle and hinges attached to part of the bars. "Dikaió, open," Mallory called, and part of the bars swung open, letting the trash flow through freely. When the door opened though, a red light above them began to flash, and a siren began to wail.

Mallory frowned and hurried through the bars. Just as she got through, a large Ex Natu guard exited a door to her right. He pulled a weapon from a holster at his side but never got a chance to fire it. The weapon hovering at Mallory's side fired into his chest and sent him flying backwards. He lay against the door frame of the door he had exited, looking at her in confusion. Moving tattoos swirled about his face with images of growling wilding wolves and ancient lettering that Mallory did not recognize. The moment passed quickly when the whirring began inside him. Mallory clutched baby Kirk tightly and looked away not wanting to watch the man die. When the whirring stopped, Mallory looked back. The Ex Natu lay still and lifeless.

Mallory's frown curved further downward, and her chest physically ached. Even if it were the Dikaió that killed him, it had done so at her bequest. She had killed a man. Mallory looked away from the man's body, trying to focus on anything else. She found herself looking into the room he had exited.

There was a desk sitting across from screens glowing green. It looked a lot like the room they had spent the night in when the clockwork sprite was leading them through the tunnels of Clarington Station. But instead of broken boxes, these screens were lit up with scenes of different rooms. The sirens were still blaring, and she knew that she should run, but Mallory walked into the room.

On the desk, Mallory noticed a foot-long hoagie: the dead guard's lunch, no doubt. Her stomach growled. The sandwich had a couple of bites taken out of it, but she did not care. She picked it up and quickly took two bites. Her jaw muscles strained, and she nearly choked. Her mouth was still dry, and she had no saliva to break down the dry bread. Mallory set down the sandwich and chewed the dry mouthful slowly and deliberately. While she chewed, she looked at each screen individually. They seemed to display different parts of the building. From his position at the desk, the guard could see everything. She bit her lip and tilted her head, wondering how the guard had not seen her escape. She looked down at the sandwich she was holding and thought, "maybe he missed it when he grabbed his lunch?" She tried to swallow the dry sandwich, but it was like trying to swallow cardboard without saliva. A lump of bread stuck in her esophagus. It was not quite like choking: just a a burning, uncomfortable sensation in her chest. She swallowed again and again, hoping it would go down. There was a horrifying moment when she thought she would have to try to throw it up to get it loose, or that it would kill her like it had ultimately got the guard killed, but finally, the uncomfortable feeling faded, and the bread cleared.

Mallory turned her attention back to the monitors and saw the room where she had been a prisoner. Omaha and the surviving Ex Natu guard were still there. The guard had managed to free himself from the sprite's grip, now that Mallory was no longer in danger inside the room, and he was working on getting Omaha's mouth free, since her command to not let him speak still seemed to be active. How long would a Dikaió command last? It was something she had never considered before. When her mother ordered a sprite to make the family breakfast, she had never had to order it to stop making breakfast. At some point the Dikaió seemed to consider its task complete. She wondered how long the medic sprite would keep its grip on Omaha. She looked closer at the screen and realized she would not discover the answer to that question today. The guard had pried a piece of metal loose from her bed and was working on wedging it into a crevice in the sprite metal where one of the tentacles was connected. If he could get a big enough opening, he would be able to reach his hand inside the sprite and disconnect the sprite's heart. Mallory had done the same to an Ex Natu sprite near the Aiworth bridge. Because of that, the clockwork sprite started calling her the Sprite Slayer, though it had changed that title to Sprite Master when she had repaired its heart in the battle to save the Archivist from Reddy Lamarr.

Then Mallory froze. One of the screens showed an older woman in a cell very similar to Mallory's. She sat on the floor across from the door; her arms shackled to the wall. Her body looked remarkably fit for her age. Her white hair was longer and now covered her face, so there was no way Mallory could make a positive identification, but somehow, she knew it was the Archivist. She looked around the screens for some indication of where this scene was coming from. And then she saw another prison cell that made her heart skip.

The prisoner's blond hair was a lot longer, and his beard unkempt, but she would know Caleb anywhere. He stood shackled to the wall as well, but unlike the Archivist, he was standing and actively straining against his bonds. He looked like he was screaming, but the monitors in this room had no sound. Mallory could hardly believe it, but her husband looked more muscular than she had ever seen him. Her eyes darted around frantically for the key to finding this room. She noticed a repeating pattern of letters and numbers on every screen's corner. She clutched baby Kirk to her chest and stepped out into the hallway. Above the door was the label C-13. She ran back inside and looked at the screens. The Archivist was in B-7 and Caleb in C-10.

She stepped back into the hallway and looked at other doors. The doors advancing the way the trash had gone were counting down: C-9, C-8, etcetera. She stepped back through the barred gate and retraced her steps down the hallway: C-12, C-11, then C-10.

"Dikaió, open!" Mallory whispered.

An overpowering body odor washed over her, but she still walked quickly into the room, and Mallory stood in front of her husband for the first time in months. She wanted to dash into his arms, but his face was contorted in rage. He growled, twisting and turning wildly; his shackles tearing huge gashes on his arms, which immediately healed over and over. Blood dripped onto the brown-stained concrete below his arms. He had done this a lot, maybe for months. He snapped his teeth at Mallory and showed no signs of recognition. The Ex Natu weapon, still protecting her, floated up beside her, trained on the crazed man secured to the wall.

"Dikaió, not him," Mallory said, and the weapon turned away to face the door. Mallory breathed deeply and whispered her husband's name, "Caleb?"

Caleb growled in response, but it was a softer growl than before. There was a question in the utterance. His struggling slowly subsided, and his eyes brightened and focused on her face. The fire raging inside of him dwindled, and his deep voice grumbled back. "Mal? Is that you? Are you real?"

She leapt forward against his chest, sobbing. "Yes, Caleb! It's me; it's you!" This time baby Kirk woke up to see what was going on, and he did not like it. He screamed.

Caleb's eyes darted from Mallory to the baby she held. "Our child?" he asked hoarsely.

"Your son," Mallory smiled offering the baby to Caleb to hold.

He tried to reach for the child, but his shackles kept his arms spread open. He roared in frustration. "Aarrghh! If I should ever be free, I'll kill every Ex Natu I meet! I'll tear them apart with my bare hands!" He began to thrash against his restraints again in rage.

Mallory pulled away, holding her screaming baby protectively. "Caleb," she said quietly.

He paused and looked at her, immediately forcing himself

to be calm. "I'm sorry, Mal." Shame spread over his face, and he looked at the floor. "I don't know what I've become."

She again stepped up to him and pressed her cheek against his heaving chest. "You are Caleb Aiworth. My husband, our son's father, heir to the Governorship of Hoffen City. Nothing they've done to you can change that. But now, I need you, we need you, to be all those things and more." She shifted baby Kirk to her hip and maneuvered the Dominus bracelet off her arm. "We need you to protect us and get us out of here." She slid the bracelet over his hand.

His eyes were wide. "Is that?"

Mallory nodded.

Caleb's eyes narrowed. "Dikaió, release me," he growled. The shackles immediately sprang off his arms and legs. He stretched and groaned as his joints cracked throughout his body. Then he grabbed Mallory around her waist and pulled her body into his. He smelled terribly, but so did she. They kissed deeply for a long time.

When he finally let her go, she laughed dreamily. "We're filthy, smell awful, we've got a screaming baby, sirens are blaring, and we're probably about to die at the hands of immortal monsters. But this might be the most romantic moment of my life."

Caleb laughed and kissed her again. Then held out his hands for his son. Mallory handed the boy to him. "I named him Kirk Knenne Aiworth. I would've waited for you to name him, but I didn't know if…" Tears choked out the sentence before she could finish it.

"General Kirk?" Caleb smirked. "It's a perfect name, Mal."

He pulled him up to his chest and gingerly hugged the boy, who immediately began rooting around looking for his next meal. "I think he's hungry, Mal," he laughed handing him back to her.

"Just like his father," Mal smiled taking the baby back.

Caleb's face darkened. "Let's go." He moved toward the door, Mallory followed him, and the floating Ex Natu weapon took up the rear. Mallory was happy to see that the Dikaió command she had given it still seemed to be working, even though she had passed the Dominus bracelet to Caleb. She wondered if her self-christening had worked, but then she remembered that the Dikaió command to protect had worked before she put on Omaha's bracelet too. She would need some other test to know if she was more than an Archivist. Caleb could change her christening if Dominus was not an option. If she were an Administrator, she would have access to the military aspects of the Dikaió just like Alex's family. Caleb paused at the door, and lost in her thoughts, Mallory nearly bumped into him. He doubled over and growled loudly. His hand shot out and grabbed the metal frame of the door, crumpling it with the force of his grip.

Mallory stepped back in fear. "What did they do to you?"

He breathed out steadily, gaining control of himself. "I…I haven't eaten since we left the Library, Mal." His breathing quickened, and he straightened himself. "I should be dead, but these nano sprites keep repairing me. I can feel them taking me apart inside to feed other parts of me and then putting it all back together. I feel like I'm going crazy!"

Mallory touched his shoulder with her free hand. "There's

a sandwich on the desk around the corner in the guard's room."

Caleb shook her off and sprang into the hallway, hitting the wall across from the room, cracking the drywall, leaving a huge spiderweb of crumbling white rock. He barely registered the impact, sniffing the air like an animal and following his nose to the guard's room. Mallory followed quietly behind. She found him perched on the desk, greedily devouring the sandwich, barely breathing between bites. When he finished, he started laughing. "Oh, oh, oh, it's so good. It feels so good!" He sprung off the desk. "I wonder if there's more?"

Mallory pointed at the screens. "More will have to wait, my love." Several monitors showed Ex Natu soldiers moving through the hallways. Omaha's guard had managed to deactivate the sprite, and the two of them were working on breaking the door open. Mallory's finger stopped on the screen with the Archivist. She was still sitting on the floor, but she was no longer looking down; she was staring directly at them.

Caleb moved closer to the screen. He growled, "The traitorous witch! I've dreamed of killing her for what she did."

"You sound like Reddy Lamarr," Mallory chided.

"Was she so wrong? This," Caleb waved at all the screens. "All of this is her doing."

Mallory shook her head. "No, it was his doing." She pointed at the room with Omaha and his guard.

Caleb's eyes narrowed even farther. "Omaha. Let's get him."

Mallory again shook her head and started to cry. "I could

have killed him, Caleb. I have killed two men already." She thought about all the people who died when they rebuilt the fire sprites in Hoffen City and sighed. "Can we just get out of here?"

Caleb looked at his wife with a look of bewildered disgust and waved at the screens. "But they're both right here!"

Mallory bit her lip and tilted her head. "We don't know what Omaha is capable of when it comes to the Dikaió. I just managed to escape, and I just got you back. I don't want to lose you or my freedom." She grabbed the collar of his shirt in her fist and looked hard into his eyes. "Do you understand?"

Caleb softened, his rage somewhat contained by the euphoria of carbohydrates entering his brain for the first time in months. "And her," he asked hopefully pointing at the Archivist.

"She knows the Ex Natu," Mallory looked at the screen with him. "We need her if we want to live through this."

He sighed deeply. "Okay, Mal. Lead the way." He bowed and motioned with his hand, just the way he used to, and Mallory's heart beat hard in her chest. She had thought a lot about that moment when she found out the nano sprites made him nigh immortal, and how she had felt like her love for him had died—that somehow their marriage would be one of duty while she grew old and he never changed. But being without him for so long, suffering without him, giving birth without him—all of it made her realize that she would rather grow old with a young Caleb than without him. Her love for him was far beyond duty; it was that deep, heart-rending kind of love.

As she walked by him into the hallway, she tousled his hair playfully. "I missed you."

He followed after her. "I missed you too, Mal."

They walked down the hallway away from their cells until they came to an elevator. A sign hung beside the elevator that read "Level C". Mallory pushed the down button. "She's on Level B."

The elevator arrived with a ding, and Mallory realized she should have checked the screens in the guard's room to make sure there were not Ex Natu soldiers on the elevator. She pushed Caleb to one side as she spun to the other side, and just in time. The doors slid open, and the hallway was filled with weapon fire. The wall opposite the elevator was torn apart with spinning, whirring Ex Natu-killing ammunition. The guards started to move out of the elevator, but suddenly, their weapons were yanked out of their hands at the same time, and the firing stopped. Mallory's eyes widened, and she looked to Caleb: He was holding the Dominus bracelet up to his mouth the same way the Archivist used to when she used it. Mallory always wondered why she did that. Reddy Lamarr never had, and she was able to use the Dikaió just fine. When Mallory used it, she had not needed to either. Was it just an unconscious thing?

Whatever it was, Mallory saw the glint of hate in Caleb's eyes, and she screamed, "Caleb, no!"

But it was too late. Caleb said, "Dikaió alert alpha! Target the Ex Natu, except me. Attack!"

Mallory marveled that Caleb remembered Mari's exact words from *The Chronicles of the Administrator*. She did not remember the exact phrasing until he said it. She also could not help but notice the words he added to the phrase: "except me". How long had he been plotting to say that? But her wonder was short lived as the Ex Natu soldiers in the elevator began to dance in awkward motions, like marionettes on the strings of the Dikaió. The weapons that had been torn from their hands turned on them and began to fire. Mallory looked away quickly, but she could not escape the noises the soldiers made as their muffled screams echoed down the hallway. Part of her regretted that she had given Caleb the Dominus bracelet, but another part of her knew that baby Kirk and her survival were dependent on doing exactly what Caleb had done, and she knew that she would never be capable of it, even in defense of her child's life. The doors of the elevator dinged over and over as they tried to close, but something was stopping them. Mallory could not bring herself to look at what that something was.

Caleb must have noticed his wife's anguish. In a more tender voice he commanded, "Dikaió, clear the elevator."

Mallory kept her eyes closed, as swishing and clanging noises sounded all around her, and then there was just the sound of the elevator door chimes signaling that the door was still trying to close but not able to. "It's all clear, Mal," Caleb said softly.

Mallory turned to find him holding the doors open for her, and she nodded. She stepped into the elevator, and he followed her in. Together they reached for the button with the letter B on it. Mallory pulled her hand back quickly when it brushed against Caleb's, and she tried not to make eye contact with him, lest he know how utterly terrified of him she was in that moment. Instead, she moved her hand to baby Kirk's head and began to caress his brown locks in an attempt to quiet the boy. The baby nestled into her hand, rooting around her fingers looking for food.

The elevator dropped quickly to level B, and Caleb pressed Mallory and his son up against the wall, anticipating Ex Natu soldiers waiting for them. Mallory marveled at how his large hand covered baby Kirk's entire body. The doors dinged and then opened. There was only quiet.

Caleb let go of the mother and child and stuck his head out into the hallway. "It's all clear. They're probably all waiting for us on the ground floor." He stepped out into the hallway and said, "I hope you know what you're doing, Mal."

Mallory limped around him. "I have no idea what I'm doing. That's why we need the Archivist." She bounced the baby in her arms and looked for the alpha-numeric signs above the doors.

"You're hurt," Caleb observed.

"I stepped on some glass earlier. I'll live," Mallory said nonchalantly, pointing at the trash strewn about this floor. "These people live like animals." She cleared her throat and said, "Dikaió, clear the trash on this floor." The trash hovered into the air and moved past them, while a small bottle swooped down and pressed the up button on the elevator. When the doors opened, the trash loaded itself in, and Mallory marveled as the trash road the elevator to the top floor. "That's weird," she muttered.

"Which door?" Caleb was looking back and forth down

the hallways in a panicky sort of way. Mallory feared that his hunger might be rising again, and she was not sure how long before her quick-thinking husband would become a feral beast again.

She headed to the left, away from where their cells were on the floor above. "C'mon, this way."

The pair arrived in front of the door marked B-7. Mallory spoke quietly, "Dikaió open." The lock clicked, and the door swung on its creaky hinges. Mallory noticed that rust flaked off of them as the door opened. She wondered if it had been opened once during their entire time in captivity.

The Archivist did not move when they walked into the room. She just sat there, shackled and staring at them. Her eyes briefly acknowledged the baby Mallory was holding and then widened when she saw the Dominus bracelet on Caleb's wrist. Her voice was raspy when she spoke. "I always assumed it would be Omaha who would come through that door to kill me one day. I'm glad it's you instead. There's some justice in that."

Caleb growled low, but Mallory put her hand on his shoulder, calming him. "We're not here to kill you, Emily. We're here to rescue you."

The Archivist's eyes closed, and she dropped her head to her chest. "I don't deserve to be rescued, Mallory. Especially, not by you."

Caleb nodded. "She's right, Mal. We don't need her."

Mallory continued to nuzzle baby Kirk's head. "Archivist, look at us."

The ancient woman lifted her face to them again and

waited.

"What do you see?" Mallory asked.

"I don't understand," the Archivist responded.

"Look at us," Mallory insisted. "I just gave birth. My husband is a bundle of murderous rage. Compared to you, we're just babies ourselves. We know nothing about the Ex Natu. We know nothing about the world outside of Hoffen City. We're going to get ourselves killed here."

The Archivist really looked at them, and then again dropped her head. "What do you think I could do for you? I couldn't even save my own children when they needed me. I betrayed you; I turned him into a monster." She nodded in Caleb's direction. "All in a bid for revenge—and even that failed miserably."

Mallory bit her lip and tilted her head. She was not sure what the monster comment meant, but this was not the time for fact finding. She stepped gingerly forward and used her free hand to slap the Archivist hard across the face. The old woman's face barely registered the attack, but her eyes flashed angrily at Mallory. Mallory smiled. "I thought there was still some fire in there. Now, quit acting so miserable and help us."

The Archivist started laughing. "Fine! Let me loose, and I'll help you, you miserable girl."

"Dikaió, release her," Mallory commanded, and the Archivist's shackles fell off.

The old woman stood up and stretched and, just like Caleb, her joints cracked loudly back into place. Then she held her hand out to Caleb. He stared at her questioningly.

"What?" he asked.

"My Dominus bracelet," she pointed at his wrist.

Caleb shook his head. "Not a chance. I agreed to let you help us, but that doesn't mean I trust you."

The Archivist looked at Mallory for back up, but Mallory just shrugged. "He's only had one sandwich to eat in the last few months; I'm not going to wrestle him for it, are you?"

The Archivist looked back at Caleb, and he licked his lips then snapped his teeth at her. She moved her hand away in caution. "I suppose not. I'm not sure what help you think I will be without the Dikaió."

Mallory did not bother to answer. Instead, she walked out of the room toward the elevator and spoke over her shoulder. "First, we need to figure out where the trash went."

"What?" The Archivist looked at Caleb.

Caleb shrugged in response and turned to hurry after Mallory. The Archivist scowled but followed the pair to the elevator. She pushed the up button and said, "the Dikaió is dumping the trash somewhere on the top floor. That means there's a way out up there."

Caleb and Mallory stepped to the side of the elevator and pulled the Archivist over as well. She stumbled over and tried to shake them loose, but as the doors opened, a hail of weapon fire unloaded in the space where she had just been standing. Caleb ordered the Dikaió to dispatch the Ex Natu soldiers and clean the elevator, while Mallory buried her face in his arm, with her other arm covering over baby Kirk protectively. When it was over, she continued where she had left off. "Obviously, we can't go down, but they'll never expect us to go up." She stepped into the elevator. She pressed the button for the top floor but held the door for them.

The Archivist's eyebrows lifted. "And then what?"

Caleb groaned. "Mal, the last time we did this, we nearly died." He followed her into the elevator.

The Archivist hesitated outside the elevator. "What do you mean the last time? Did what?"

Just then a crash sounded around the corner along with the sound of heavy footsteps heading their way. Ex Natu soldiers had climbed the emergency stairwell and were coming for them. Mallory stepped back into the elevator next to Caleb and shrugged. As the doors started to close, the Archivist glanced toward the sound of the approaching boots and then back to Caleb, Mallory, and their baby. She sighed and then squeezed through the closing doors and joined them in the elevator.

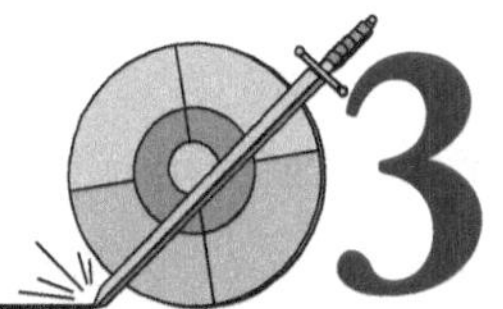

The Archivist used her finger to push Mallory's floating Ex Natu weapon away from her face and looked at the couple expectantly. "Well?" she asked as the elevator sped upward. "What's your big plan?"

Mallory tilted her head and bit her lip. "You have to know more about Ex Natu construction than we do. Why would the trash go up?"

The Archivist rolled her eyes. "I have no idea what you're talking about. What trash?"

The elevator stopped, and the group pressed up against the sides of the walls as the doors opened in case Ex Natu soldiers were waiting for them. There were none. Mallory made like she was going to walk around Caleb into the hallway, but Caleb grabbed her free arm and held her and baby Kirk back. "Let me check first." Mallory nodded, and Caleb stepped into the hallway, looked both ways, and then motioned for the women to follow him out.

Mallory looked up and down the hallway, unsure where to go next, but the hallway was filled with trash just like the other floors in the building. "Dikaió, clean up this floor." Just like before, the trash hovered off the floor, but this time instead of heading toward the elevator, it hovered away to their left, moving down the aisle like an enchanted army. Mallory switched the arm she was carrying baby Kirk with and started after the trash. The Archivist again rolled her eyes but followed after with Caleb taking up the rear. The trash turned a corner to the right, and the group gasped. At the end of the hallway, a double pained window was open to the outdoors, and the trash was simply lining up to throw itself out the window.

Mallory ran past the trash to look out the window. She had not seen the outdoors for months. She was not sure what she expected to see, but it was certainly not what she found outside the walls of the Ex Natu building. The sky was brilliant blue with speckles of cumulus clouds floating nonchalantly across it. Below them, a sprawling cityscape extended beyond the limits of her vision. Mallory could not count the number of Ex Natu citadels that lined the filthy streets, but what really excited her was that in between them there were smaller, more ancient buildings: gorgeously ornate. A few blocks away, she saw the Library. Except, it was not the Archivist's Library. It was the Davis City Library. The clockwork sprite had told them that the Archivist's dwelling was a perfect replica of the one in the Davis City Metroplex, which must be where they were. Mallory looked down the side of the building they were in. It was an Ex Natu citadel just like the others. As far as Mallory could see here was no way to tell them apart.

Caleb leaned his head out the window and took a deep breath. Then he turned to her. "Well, Mal. We don't have much time, and I don't see any rigging to get down with. What are we going to do?"

Mallory bit her lip and tilted her head. Then she turned to the Archivist. "You know how to ride a flying sprite, right? Is it hard?"

The Archivist shook her head. "It's not hard, but I don't see any flying sprite here either. I thought you had a plan, Mallory." She backed up and looked nervously down the hallway toward the elevator and stairway. "I should have stayed in my cell. You're going to get us all killed."

Mallory turned back to the window and yelled into the city. "Dikaió, bring me three flying sprites."

The Archivist laughed. "You can't be serious! Do you think the Dikaió works so easily?"

Mallory looked hurt. "I don't know. I had hoped so."

The Archivist rolled her eyes and held out her hand to Caleb. "Give me the Dominus bracelet, or we're all going to get killed."

Caleb shook his head and laughed. "That's never going to happen."

Mallory also shook her head, but asked, "Why? What

would you do with it? Help us escape? Or try to kill Omaha?"

"Why? Is he here?" A glimmer of hope flashed in the Archivist's eyes, and her body tensed.

Mallory had no doubt what the answer to her question was. Emily Carpenter had already shown that she was willing to throw all of them under the proverbial bus to kill Omaha.

Caleb interrupted the tension. "It doesn't matter. Mallory's plan worked, just like they always do." He pointed at the window; three flying sprites had swooped in and were hovering outside.

The Archivist's eyebrows arched in surprise, and she started walking toward the window. "It's not supposed to work like that. They must have been on the roof or some-thing—within the sound of your voice."

Mallory did not respond, but she did take note that the Dikaió was distance-bound in such a way. It was something that she had never really thought about and certainly did not have time to consider right then—not just because their lives were in danger, but also because she did not want to give the Archivist any more time to reconsider helping them. "Here!" she declared and handed baby Kirk to Caleb. Mallory then climbed up into the window. She managed to get one foot on one of the hovering flying sprites, and that's when her abdomen cramped in pain. She bent over to grasp her stomach, and her foot slipped off the flying sprite. The whole world seemed to slow down as Mallory fell out of the window.

The wind rushed by her, and she marveled at the goose bumps popping up on her body. She was still wearing a hospital gown, so the chill was hitting in her in places it normally would not. She was going to have to find some clothes. And then she wondered why modesty was even something she would worry about as she was plummeting to her death. It was better to focus on something more meaningful, like what exactly were her hands grasping for; there was nothing but empty air above her. Trying to hold on to the air was almost as useless as worrying about what she was wearing. She almost laughed seeing the Ex Natu weapon falling dutifully beside her. A lot of help that would be. She tried counting the floors that she had passed: seven, eight maybe, definitely not twelve yet, and that was a plus. Would she even be able to count the twelfth floor when she got there, or would she just stop counting? It was an interesting thought, but not one she wanted to focus on. She also thought it was immensely interesting to see the window and flying sprites above her getting smaller so quickly: all of them except one. One of the flying sprites was getting larger and coming toward her very quickly. Mallory smiled. Caleb was riding it. Her husband was coming to save her. Then she frowned. Caleb closed his eyes and turned his head away. Mallory had a split second to understand that he did not want to watch her die. Her eyes flashed to the side of the Ex Natu tower she had just fallen out of, and thought to herself, "twelve!"

The impact was sudden and not nearly as painful as she expected it to be. Instead, she felt as if she were enveloped in a blanket of soft mush, though there were some prickly bits here and there. The bright sky was swallowed up in a mess of moldy half-eaten food and crumpled bits of paper. The smell was almost unbearable, and Mallory held her breath trying to avoid it. She did not expect the life after life to be so disgusting, but she also did not expect to have to worry about breathing when she was dead either. Her mind was still in a surreal contemplative mode, and she wondered why neither she nor Caleb had thought to use the Dikaió to save her. It would have just been a few quick words, and she would not have had to die. That had not been a very bright way to end her life, and then she wondered if this was what the whole afterlife was going to be like, just laying around mulling over regrets. For example, she really regretted not having eaten every meal her mother had ever served her. She really missed her cooking. No one could order around a kitchen sprite quite the way she could. Mallory wondered if there would be food in the afterlife. She was starving. Hunger did not seem much like an afterlife feeling either. And neither did pain, but the cramps in her abdomen had not improved after falling to her death.

After a short time of nothing particularly supernatural happening, the cramps in Mallory's stomach made her eventually sit up and try to move to alleviate them. She found herself lying in a giant pile of garbage at the foot of the Ex Natu citadel—about three floors' worth of garbage, she estimated—at least she knew where the Dikaió had deposited it all. She reached down and touched her stomach, worried that the pain she was experiencing was because she had been hit by an Ex Natu weapon, but there was no spinning death inside her. The pain must have just been some post-natal cramping. She shook her head and grabbed a handful of decomposing food and threw it in the air laughing and happy to be alive. She looked up to wave to her compatriots and let them know she was alive, just in time to see the Archivist jumping out of the window above onto a flying sprite. She was holding a small bundle. Mallory gritted her teeth. Had Caleb handed her the baby to come save her? What if the old woman had betrayed them again and had taken baby Kirk to Omaha? How could her husband have been so irresponsible? She looked around for Caleb, so she could berate him properly, but she did not have time to find him in the sky as the windows of the top floor exploded outward.

The sound of weapon fire reached her ears an instant before the shower of glass. Mallory rolled face down in the garbage and pulled herself into a fetal position to limit her exposure to the falling glass. With all her various aches and pains, it was impossible to know if the glass cut her, but she knew that when it stopped falling, she was still alive, but she would not be much longer if she remained where she was. She pulled herself to her feet and started to run. Cramps besieged her with every motion, but she did not have time to acknowledge them. The trash around her started to pop up like tiny geysers. The Ex Natu above were firing down at her.

"Dikaió, protect me!" she screamed. Instantly, the garbage sprang up, creating a filthy ceiling above her head. She could still hear the weapons' fire raining down from above, but it was not penetrating the floating garbage shield protecting her—at least not yet. As soon as the projectiles hit the shield, they began to spin, tearing the garbage to shreds and piercing the barrier. Mallory bit her lip and slowed down. She stole a glance up at the spinning projectiles suddenly curious about how they worked. Just above her, a cardboard box and a plastic lid were being torn apart by a small bronze piece of metal with three tiny blades turning like a fan. Another projectile hit near her, and she saw its silhouette: just a black blob then it sprouted blades and began to spin. It was a fascinating technology, but too deadly to stand around studying. She picked up her pace and ran across a paved road, being careful to avoid huge potholes that the Ex Natu had not bothered to repair. There was another citadel on that side of the road, and Mallory ran behind it, out of the line of fire.

She peeked back around the corner of the building to see if she could see Caleb, the Archivist, or her baby anywhere. They were gone. She desperately wanted to run back to the building and look for them, but the weapons' fire was still tearing the garbage to shreds. Had they been shot out of the sky? Were they alive? If they had survived, did they know she was still alive? The Ex Natu certainly knew she had survived the fall. They thought she was still below the shield and were still firing into the garbage to kill her. Going back to look for her family and the Archivist would be a death sentence. If they were still alive, and she refused to believe otherwise, her death would be of no help to them.

Mallory looked around her. The Ex Natu weapon was somehow still following her doggedly. The sun was shining. The sky was blue. There were green plants growing here and there, and there were zero people anywhere that she looked. This city was massive. Where was everyone? Even though she was no longer trapped alone in the small room, the open emptiness of this unfamiliar city felt even more stifling than her prison. She did not know where to turn, where to run, where to hide. She was not even sure those things were possible here. Her feet were bleeding. Her hospital gown was covered in blood and other fluids. She would never pass for an immortal Ex Natu if she did run into one—not looking like this.

But she was no longer completely powerless, either.

"Dikaió, take me somewhere where I can find clothes and get cleaned up," she commanded the air around her. The paved street in front of her began to crack, and then the crack shot off to the right. Mallory hurriedly followed the path the broken concrete was creating to a somewhat cleaner part of Davis City. The cramps in her abdomen were subsiding as she walked, which was good, but she desperately wanted her baby back. She scanned the skies, hoping to catch a glimpse of the Archivist, but the city buildings obstructed her view. The path led her to an open-air plaza with a fountain in the center. The fountain was not ornately decorated like the ones in Hoffen City or the Archivist's Library. Instead, it was simply a large obsidian basin, with what looked to be nothing more than a rectangular block shooting water into the air. She hated the Ex Natu aesthetic, but the water looked clean enough. Mallory ran to the fountain. She was about to start bathing in the basin, when her dry tongue once again stuck to the side of her mouth, and she remembered that it had been a long time since she had had anything to drink. She cupped her hand and started to lift water to her mouth, but the water inside it was immediately covered in the filth of her palm. All the lessons she had had in school about microbiology came to mind, and she dropped the water back into the fountain. "Dikaió, give me clean drinking water that I don't have to touch," she said, and instantly a section of the fountain's wall crumbled. Then a pipe ripped itself out and snaked over to her. The fountain stopped flowing, as water sprayed out of the pipe. Mallory drank from it as she would a garden hose. It was cold and delicious.

When her thirst was quenched, Mallory looked around the plaza and wondered where the people were. While the city did not seem completely deserted like Mason City had been, there were not many signs of civilization either. She closed her eyes and listened intently. There were not any animal noises in the city that she could hear. It reminded her a lot of the dark woods where she, Caleb, and Alex had first set up camp after they were banished from Hoffen City. The only animals in the woods that she had ever seen were the wilding wolves, which would have killed them if not for the arrival of the Archivist's clockwork sprite.

Just like the dark woods, the whole city was eerily quiet. Even the weapon fire had ceased. She looked back the way she had come. The cracked path leading straight to her made her wince. She would not have long to get cleaned up with a trail like that leading the Ex Natu right to her. She quickly climbed into the fountain's basin began washing herself off. She paid particular attention to her cut feet, but the whole bath, makeshift as it was, felt glorious.

When she was finished, she was also soaked. It was

autumn when she had been captured, and judging by the temperature and the plants, it was currently early spring. It was warm enough that Mallory was not freezing, but the breeze in the air did leave her chilled. "Dikaió, take me to the clothes," She said.

A door slammed behind her, making her nearly leap out of her wet gown. She spun around and saw a door standing open. It looked like a boutique: one that had been abandoned for quite a few years by the amount of dust swirling around the door. Mallory stood up and walked gingerly over to the open shop. The place was dark and dusty, but it was also still fully stocked with clothing. There was not a vast selection in terms of style, everything was as drab as the Ex Natu's architecture, mostly black or dark navy blue, military-style clothing. Alex would have felt right at home.

Mallory shrugged and selected pants and a shirt that looked to be about her size. She held them up to herself and looked in a dusty mirror on the wall. She smirked and thought of the time she had put on her blue dress to show everyone how matriarchal she could look. That was the day she had nearly destroyed her people. Though, she did find some irony that just like that day, her feet were cut and trailing blood. She looked behind herself, half expecting an awkward, half-functioning fire sprite bursting into the window of the store to kill her, but there was nothing in the plaza except the broken fountain. She shrugged.

Changing into the Ex Natu garb required more effort than she thought it would. It was not just her feet that were still bleeding; she had just given birth, so she padded the pants with a pair of socks to help stem the flow. She also tore up several shirts to create bandages for the cuts on her feet. There wouldn't be any Chorus cart to whisk her around the city this time. She was just going to have to make the most of what she had. She stepped over to the dusty mirror and looked into the light gray eyes of a haggard woman staring back at her. The woman in the mirror was wearing dark blue pants with more pockets than she ever thought she would need; a black long-sleeved, v-neck shirt; and knee-high combat boots, which hurt her cut feet more than walking barefoot. She hoped that they would be more comfortable as she broke them in because they were the only pair of shoes in the whole boutique that had come close to fitting her. Then she saw a faded image of an Ex Natu woman on the wall near the door and noticed her bald head. Mallory's hair would be another quick give away here in Davis City. She found a stand with military caps and tried to tuck all of her quickly drying curls inside the hat. She barely accomplished the feat and knew that as soon as her wild hair dried, the hat would be resting on top of her fluffy hair instead of on her head, like a ship on an uncontrollable ocean. Even if she could shave her head, there was no way she could reproduce the moving tattoos they all wore, anyway. The hat would have to do for now.

Mallory looked around the room once again to see if there was anything else she might need. Near the counter there was a display of backpacks. She stuffed one with a change of clothing and more socks for pads. She grabbed the Ex Natu weapon floating in the air near her and said, "Dikaió, stop following me, now." The force holding the weapon let go, and Mallory shoved the weapon into her pack pack as well. She threw the backpack over her shoulders, and the straps rubbed against her breasts, which were full of milk. Tears sprung unbidden to her eyes. She needed to know where her baby was. Was Kirk even alive? Would he be for much longer if she did not get to him to feed him?

Mallory gritted her teeth and headed for the door. She had no idea where to even begin looking for her family and the Archivist. The Davis City Metroplex made Mason City look tiny. Plus, they were on flying sprites, meaning they could have left the city for all she knew. However, if the Dikaió could lead her to water and clothing, she figured that it could certainly lead her to her husband and child. "Dikaió," she began, but the word was barely out of her mouth before a huge mass of musty smelling fur hit her hard in the stomach, dragging her to the floor amid a blur of snapping teeth and scratching claws.

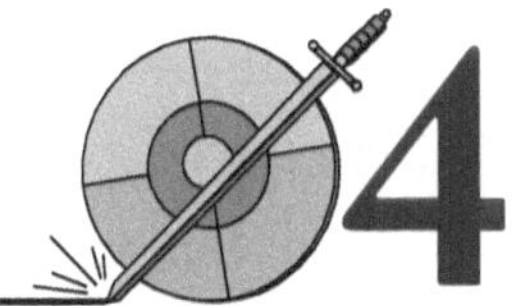

Mallory rolled and kicked at the mass attacking her. It was clear that the Ex Natu had let Davis City go, but she could not believe that wilding wolves were roaming the streets. She had assumed the Ex Natu hated the creatures they had created to control the human population, at least after what she had seen in Mason City when they set the trapped pack in the city's gorge on fire. Yet, one was attacking her in their capitol city. She kept waiting for the razor-like teeth to sink into her neck, or the claws to slash her chest open, but the death blows never came. Instead, the beast just jostled about on the floor with her. Some of the creature's fur tickled her nose in the struggle, and she unconsciously inhaled it into her mouth. It was loose and came right off.

The horrible taste and smell at once took her back to that day in the Library's foyer when she and Caleb had been bound to chairs with wilding wolf fur shoved into their mouths. She gagged. And then Mallory noticed the creature's claws scratching at her wrists.

What was it looking for?

Mallory's eyebrows knitted together in anger, and she bucked hard to her right, spitting the fur from her mouth while sputtering "Dikaió, protect me!"

Several of the clothing displays erupted: clothing spinning into the air. The creature jumped off of Mallory, backing away from her quickly, standing on its hind legs. It held its paws up in surrender, and Mallory noted the plume of red hair on top of its familiar face. It was not a wilding wolf at all. It was Hoffen City's old Sprite Master, Reddy Lamarr, once more dressed in the skins of the wilding wolves.

The clothing floated in the air between the two of them doing nothing. Apparently, the Dikaió did not see the older woman as a threat, standing there with her arms up. Mallory knew that was a terrible mistake. She slowly pulled herself to her feet. She felt very vulnerable having to turn her back to Reddy Lamarr to crawl up off the floor, but she hoped that the Dikaió would ward off any attack the older woman attempted. Finally, huffing and puffing, Mallory turned to confront her attacker. "I thought we were rid of you forever, Sprite Master." Mallory brushed herself off.

Lamarr lowered her hands and shuffled her feet. She did not say anything, but she did not leave either.

Mallory shrugged and held up her hands. "Well?"

Reddy Lamarr stood there between Mallory and the door, silently.

"Look, if you're not going to say anything, I need to leave," Mallory moved to the left as if she were going to go past her.

The Sprite Master matched her movements, still blocking the door. "You don't want to do that, little Matriarch."

Mallory paused and looked at her suspiciously. "Why?"

The older woman motioned toward her outfit. "I'm not wearing these because I like the smell. These streets are full of wilding wolves. Soon enough, they'll catch the scent of all that blood you left in the fountain and come for you."

"So, you're here to protect me?" Mallory asked touching her wrist. "That doesn't explain why you were looking for a bracelet. How could you have known I took a Dominus bracelet?"

Reddy Lamarr smiled. "You always were too clever for you own good, Knenne."

Mallory felt her lip curl in disgust. The old woman knew she was married to Caleb and that her last name was Aiworth now. Reddy Lamarr had always fancied that at some point the two of them would end up together: at first in Hoffen City where she would have stayed forever young and used him until he was too old for her, and then at the Library after he was injected with the Ex Natu nano sprites, she tried to convince him to leave Mallory to Omaha and the Ex Natu and run off with her. Using Mallory's maiden name suggested Lamarr still saw her as getting in the way of that outcome.

But Lamarr was still talking. "But you're not cleverer than

him. Not by half."

Mallory stepped backward, suddenly afraid. "Who? Omaha?"

"Who else? He's going to be very upset to find you've lost his bracelet." Reddy Lamarr grinned wickedly.

Mallory shook her head. "I don't understand. You were so sure the Archivist was wrong about Omaha. You kept insisting that he wasn't an Ex Natu." Centuries ago, Lamarr had been Omaha's assistant in the underground resistance. And at the Library, she had been reticent to believe he was still alive, or that he had betrayed their people and joined their enemy. She held the man up as some kind of saint. "Now, you're okay with it? You're okay that he betrayed us?"

The old Sprite Master spit. "The Archivist is the evil one, Knenne. Omaha is still on our side. He always has been."

Mallory's head hurt trying to follower her logic. "But—" the word was literally all she could respond with.

"After the Library, I followed you here to Davis City. It's a lot harder to fend off a bunch of wilding wolves without the Dikaió. I had the weapons I took from the Archivist, but there are always more of them. The things breed like rabbits." She grimaced. "Luckily, Omaha spotted me outside his building and sent some soldiers to check on me. They took me to his office.

"It was really Omaha. He looked different with his head shaved and those awful tattoos, but when I saw that one of them was Melody, it was hard to deny who I was looking at. He sat behind a large wooden desk with his hands folded just the way he used to when he was thinking, and he stared at me in my wilding furs. 'You look familiar,' he said. 'I used to know someone who looked just like you.' Then he waved away the old memories like they were flies. 'But that was ages ago. Maybe you're a descendant.' He paused and his eyes narrowed. 'A descendant from Hoffen City, perhaps?'

"'From Hoffen City, yes, but I'm no descendant, sir,' I said. I lifted one of my hands and bit my finger until it bled. Then I held it out for him to watch it heal.

"His eyes widened. 'Reddy? Can it really be you? But how?'

"I told him the whole story."

Mallory interrupted a little worried. "The whole story? Even the part about his son Alexander dying at the hands of the Ex Natu the day you injected the nano sprites?"

"Well, maybe not the whole story," the Sprite Master smiled. "I didn't want to ruin the opportunity, you know?"

"Opportunity?" Mallory wondered.

"To get my old job back."

"Your old job?" Mallory nearly screamed. "You used to work for the rebellion and now you work for the Ex Natu. I don't see how that's your old job."

"I used to work for Omaha, and now I'm his assistant again. I don't see what's hard to understand, Knenne." The old Sprite Master shifted her weight and looked away from Mallory's eyes.

"And the fact that Omaha is an immortal Ex Natu doesn't bother you?" Mallory pressed.

"Not all of us who ended up with the curse of immortality did it by our own free will. I don't know why you can't understand that, not after what happened to Caleb."

"The Archivist didn't get her nano sprites by choice either, Reddy," Mallory reminded her. "Omaha chose immortality."

"You only have the traitor's version of the story, Knenne!" Lamarr spat.

"Maybe," Mallory conceded. "But I do know that Omaha kept us all prisoners. I do know that he was going to kill me and take my baby, Caleb's baby! He didn't feed Caleb for months: tortured him and the Archivist. There's nothing you can say that will convince me the man is not the purest of evil."

Reddy Lamarr sneered at Mallory. "You're such a young fool, Knenne. You should have read *The Chronicles of the Lost* all the way through like I told you. The Archivist is the evil one. Yes, Omaha is still alive, but it doesn't change the fact that she betrayed our people, and she intends to finish us all off too. It will make what you and the Nelson girl did look like a minor inconvenience."

Mallory was getting angry now. "And what about what he did to us, Sprite Master!? Surely, you knew what was going on—what your master was doing!"

"It was necessary to undo what your Archivist set in motion," she paused and an emotion passed over her face that Mallory had never seen the Sprite Master exhibit before: pity. "I've never liked you, Mallory. There's no use hiding that, but what happened to you and Caleb was…," she struggled to find the wording, "difficult."

"Difficult?" Mallory almost laughed. "It was barbaric, Reddy. Barbaric!"

Reddy Lamarr did not answer. She quickly looked behind her into the street as if she had heard something. Mallory listened, and she could hear the roar of flying sprites approaching. She feared that the Sprite Master had just been wasting time with this conversation to keep her in one place until Omaha arrived. Mallory took a step toward her, menacingly. "Move out of my way, or I'll move you."

Reddy Lamarr did not move; the pity in her face vanished. She looked at Mallory in disgust. "Barbaric for someone else maybe, but not for a Knenne. Omaha may be brilliant, but he made a mistake choosing your family. I've always thought so, and I've seen a lot of Knennes come and go in my lifetime. You're cleverer than some, but…"

Mallory had heard enough. "Dikaió, move Reddy Lamarr out of the way." Instantly, Reddy Lamarr was airborne, picked up by her own fur camouflage and flung out into the street; her diatribe cut short by the motion. She rolled backward and landed on her feet as Mallory walked out the door.

The Sprite Master chuckled, and then bent down onto her hands and knees. Mallory did not understand why she would laugh and then bow down to her, but then the older woman's eyes glanced slightly to the left. Mallory followed her gaze and found herself staring at a pack of three wilding wolves. There was no mistaking them this time. The beasts had been drinking from the bloodied fountain and were now staring at the two women, their tongues lolling in their mouths over their razor-sharp teeth. Mallory stopped in her tracks, afraid to move and uncertain what to do. Two of the wolves crouched low and began walking: One moving to the right and one to the left. The third wolf walked slowly to Reddy Lamarr, smelling the fur she was wearing. It yipped questioningly and nudged her shoulder. She bowed her head low and gurgled in her throat. The wilding wolf sniffed her again, and then turned its attention to Mallory. Apparently, it had accepted the old Ex Natu as one of its own. Mallory again wondered how Reddy Lamarr knew how to deal with wilding wolves at all. She would have been inside Hoffen City behind the light when their people had first encountered them.

Mallory shook her head and whispered, "Dikaió, protect me," hoping it would be enough to ward off the wolves. Pieces of the broken concrete from the path she had created earlier and chunks from the fountain floated up and surrounded her. The wilding wolves danced through the floating rocks playfully as if they were puppies chasing balls. The Dikaió did not seem to see them as a threat as they played. Just like Reddy Lamarr earlier, they were not acting aggressively, so the invisible force did not strike them down, but they were drawing closer and closer. Mallory panicked and turned to run, but the two wolves that had gone right and left had hedged her in. The only way to run was backwards into the shop, but Mallory knew that was a death sentence. She looked to Reddy Lamarr in desperation, but the woman had not lifted her head.

Suddenly, the lead wolf's head snapped toward her, and it leapt off the ground, jaws and teeth wide open. Several stones blew through it, knocking it slightly off target, but it still smashed into Mallory's shoulder sending her spiraling. She hit the ground hard, knocking the wind out of her, and the lead wolf rolled onto the ground at her feet. She pushed up onto her forearm just in time to see the wolf stand back up, a large wound on its face healing quickly. Mallory remembered that when the culture sprites and the clockwork sprite fought the wilding wolves, every blow was not immediately lethal, and the wolves still died. But these wolves healed just like the Ex Natu. They must have nano sprites too. The other two wolves had danced within striking range, and Mallory knew she would have to act fast.

"Dikaió, kill the wolves," she ordered. The stones in the air responded accordingly, plowing into the wolves and spinning inside them just like the Ex Natu weapons. Maybe watching the Dikaió kill immortal wilding wolves had given Omaha the idea for their design? The wolves howled and yipped about, mad with pain. The one on the left dove for Mallory despite its agony, nearly biting her face, but the concrete spinning inside it dragged it away just before it snapped its mouth closed. Soon, all three of them lay dead.

The old Sprite Master was standing now, clapping. "Well done, little Matriarch. I honestly didn't think you had it in you." She paused and looked up in the sky. "It doesn't matter though. They're nearly here, and he'll have brought another Dominus bracelet with him. He has another, you know."

The roar of flying sprites was loud, so they were close, maybe just on the other side of the building. Mallory tried to stand and grimaced. Her ankle screamed in pain. The wilding wolf must have twisted it when it hit her in the shoulder and knocked her off kilter. She straightened, ignoring the pain and the stinging in the bottoms of her feet and started running across the plaza toward an opening between two smaller brick buildings that stood between Ex Natu citadels. There was a tight alleyway that she could just barely squeeze through. An old rusted-iron fire escape overhead would make it hard for the flying sprites to drop down on her. She had no idea where she was going, but she knew she needed to get away from Omaha and Reddy Lamarr.

Mallory checked the skies as she exited the alleyway. They were clear, but to her right, about 400 yards away, were four more wilding wolves sniffing the air. There was another alleyway that she could run across to in order to keep her cover from the skies, but if the wilding wolves caught her scent, she would be a sitting duck. She hesitated, but then sighed. "Dikaió, kill the wilding wolves," she whispered. Bricks from the buildings to her sides ripped free and flew at the wolves. Mallory did not wait to watch them die; she sprinted across to the next alleyway and continued for several minutes repeating the same actions. It seemed as if every new street she crossed, she ran into more wilding wolves. As a group of twelve or thirteen yipped and howled in their death thralls, Mallory paused. She bit her lip anxiously. It dawned on her that she was leaving a trail of wolf bodies, marking her passage through the city just as clear as the cracks in the concrete that the Dikaió had left on the way to the fountain, which is probably how Reddy Lamarr had tracked her to the boutique in the first place.

She listened carefully and sure enough the sounds of flying sprites were only a couple of buildings back. Mallory turned around, thinking that she would backtrack, only to find Reddy Lamarr standing in the alleyway she had just exited. The old Sprite Master leaned up against the side of a building, smiling. Mallory felt her face drop in defeat.

Lamarr laughed. "You look surprised, Knenne. Did you really think you could just run off?

Mallory ran.

And Reddy Lamarr ran after her calling, "You could kill me just like you killed all the wolves."

Mallory shook her head. She wished she could wake up from this nightmare. She did not know what to do. Her brain felt foggy, and her body felt exhausted. She should be spending this time resting, not running for her life, being hunted by predators and immortal monsters like Reddy and Omaha. She knew there had to be a solution, a way to escape, but she could not seem to formulate a plan. Caleb had such faith in her plans. Earlier he had even said that they always worked. Mallory could think of very few of her plans that had not resulted in someone getting hurt one way or another, but at least they accomplished something, gave her hope in whatever situation she found herself. But this prison break left her feeling nothing but hopelessness.

Then she saw the man from the painting in the Library— the man on the tree. A stone statue of the man hanging on a cross stood outside of an old, brick building. It had three wooden doors with arches over them and gables covering the arches. The green copper roof slanted on the sides in an A-frame, and several windows arched upward around the sides. The entire design of the building forced the eye skyward, toward a nine-story tall tower with arched windows and a green ionized copper roof pointing to the heavens. The tower had a broken clock set near the top, but the thing that really drew Mallory's attention was the peak of the tower where a crossed wooden beam just like the one the man hung on jutted into the sky. Mallory ran toward the building. It could not be coincidence that she would see this image again. Maybe she would find safety here.

She climbed the crumbling stone stairs and ran to the center wooden door. The door had large, ornate, wrought iron handles, and Mallory was dismayed to find them rusted and in disrepair, much like the building itself now that she was up close. She grabbed one of the handles and pulled hard on it. The metal broke off in her hand. Mallory threw it to the ground in disgust. "Dikaió, open the door," she said, and the door groaned under the invisible force of the Dikaió. A lock on the inside whined loudly and then clicked open, and the door slowly began to swing open on rusty hinges. Mallory was a little worried it might break off as the handle had.

A puff of dust accompanied the door as it opened, and Mallory waved her hand in front of her face. She looked behind her and was again dismayed to see Reddy Lamarr standing in the street with her arms folded. She hated the woman, and it briefly crossed her mind that she might do what she suggested and kill her with the Dikaió, just to be rid of her, but she worried what kind of mother she would be if she went down that road. Protecting yourself or your child was one thing—she was even responsible for people dying accidentally because of her actions (and those events hung heavy on her soul), but she thought she could still be a good person with those accidental deaths on her record. Murder was something else entirely.

Was there any redemption for murder?

Mallory was torn out of her introspection by the sound of flying sprites, and she saw them rounding an Ex Natu citadel. Two of them were coming in her direction. She stepped quickly into the building and said, "Dikaió, close the door." The heavy door swung slowly closed, and then two of the rusted hinges cracked loudly, and the door fell slightly askew, wedging itself into the door jam of the building. "Let's see Reddy Lamarr follow me through that," Mallory smirked to herself as she turned to explore the building.

Her breath caught in her chest, and not just because of all the dust she had stirred up: the building was massive on the inside. There were wooden benches mostly lined up in rows, and there must have been a hundred columns all extending upward to gothic arches in the ceiling. What windows where left unbroken were filled with a kaleidoscope of stained glass. Mallory immediately thought of the dragonfly window in her bedroom, which had once served as her grandmother's office. She had spent countless hours dancing, sitting, dozing in those warm greens and purples. The window in this building depicted unfamiliar images: a man in the water with a glowing bird on his head, a tiny boy in a tree calling down to that same man, an empty cave with a large round stone at its entrance, and of course the man on the beam from the painting. He looked a lot like the man in the other images, though more than half the windows were broken.

At the far end of the room, there was a raised dais, and Mallory found herself drawn to it. There was more statuary here too, or at least what was left of it. Mostly there was rubble and a few carved hands and feet that she could make out. There had once been a large statue of the man on the beam mounted to the wall, but it was laying on the dais in pieces. Mallory stepped over the crumbled mess, carefully. She found the face of the man and stared deeply into his marbled eyes. She felt an odd sense of peace, considering all the events of the day, and she sighed. As her adrenaline levels dropped, she became acutely aware of her twisted ankle and the cuts in her feet. On top of that, her chest was bulging uncomfortably with milk. She lowered herself onto what remained of the stone feet of a robed figure and again looked at the man's face.

"Well, here I am. Now what?" she said, hoping whatever ancient image this was held some old magic that could help her.

"Mallory?" a man's voice answered back.

Mallory startled so hard that she nearly fell off her seat. She whipped her head to her left, toward the sound of the voice, which was not coming from the statue's face on the dais. She was not sure who she expected to see there: Omaha or the man on the beam, but she did not expect to see Caleb. He was standing there staring at her as if he were staring at a hallucination. Her husband had found her. She looked toward the three broken doors at the entrance, but they were still closed. Her brow knit in confusion. "Caleb?" she asked. "But how?"

He ran across the dais to her, sweeping her off her make-shift pedestal into his arms. "Oh, Mal! I thought you were dead!" He kissed her again and again, taking breaths and mumbling between them. "I saw you fall. I saw you hit the ground, Mal. How can you be alive? I mean, I had hoped, and I had to come back to know for sure, but I—how can you be alive?" He spun her around looking her over for injuries.

Mallory laughed and then pulled back, getting dizzy. "It was all the garbage I cleaned up with the Dikaió. It broke my fall."

Caleb also started laughing, almost hysterically. He laughed until he cried, and Mallory felt herself grow afraid. There was something wrong with the way his emotions were swinging all over the place, but he did not give her time to study him. "The trash? Of course it was the trash! You brilliant woman!" He picked her up again and swung her around again. "Of course it was the trash!"

Mallory again felt sick with all the motion. She needed to change the subject and yelled over Caleb's hysterics. "Where's our baby?"

Caleb's eyes widened. "Oh right!" He set her down, grabbed her hand, and pulled her behind him in earnest.

Mallory's ankle twisted further, and she screamed. "Oh, Caleb! Stop!"

He paused, and Mallory collapsed to the floor, rubbing her ankle. "Mallory, what happened?" he asked, kneeling down and touching her ankle. It was very swollen.

"A wilding wolf. It twisted," she hissed in pain.

Caleb's face instantly snapped into solemness. He had control over himself once more. He nodded and gently picked her up. "It's okay. I've got you." He carried her across the dais into an alcove cleverly hidden from the view of the sitting area of the building by walls that overlapped just slightly with one another, creating a small hallway that turned into a large hallway. They passed a few closed doors, and then came to a staircase that went underground. Caleb began to descend the stairs carefully, and Mallory clung desperately to his neck. The small, dark, tight underground space felt like it was crushing her. He tried to say something, but it was muffled.

"What?" Mallory loosened her grip slightly.

"I can't breathe, Mal." Caleb smiled. "Also, Dikaió, lights," he commanded and Dikaió lights instantly illuminated the stairs.

Mallory stared in wonder at the lights. There had been powered lights in the Library and the Ex Natu citadel, but none of them looked like these lights. These were just like the lights the citizens of Hoffen City commanded when they used to be able to use the Dikaió. She had not really thought about the differences in illumination until she saw these, but the ones in the Library and that the Ex Natu used were uniformly lit with tiny glowing balls of light, each about the size of a grain of sand, whereas the lights in Hoffen City had a tiny metal filament stretched between two wires that glowed. It was an almost imperceptible difference, but it felt immensely comforting to see her people's lights again.

The staircase led into a tunnel made of concrete. Parts of the wall had crumbled with the passage of time, and Mallory could see rusted rebar poking out in many places; it looked twisted, almost making a solid line leading down the hallway and up the stairs. Mallory wondered if there had been an earthquake or worse in the tunnel. There were tiny squeaks emitting from places here and there in the broken walls. "Rats?" Mallory squeaked and again cut off Caleb's oxygen supply.

Caleb sputtered but kept walking. After about two minutes, Mallory heard the sounds of baby cries echoing down the tunnel. She released her grip on Caleb's neck and tried to scramble down him with the intent of running to baby Kirk, wherever he was. "Mal, your ankle." Caleb managed to say as he fought her from getting to the ground.

"Oh, right!" Mallory stopped struggling and let Caleb reposition her into a more comfortable position, cradled in his arms like a baby. "Please hurry, though. He has to be hungry."

Caleb nodded. "Okay, Mallory. Just hold still, and I will get you to him as fast as I can."

But it seemed as though no matter how far they traveled, the baby's cries never grew any louder. Eventually, they entered a room, where the cement walls were not cracked. There were a table and chairs in a corner, and three glowing screens with boards covered in letters sitting on the table. One of the screens had a crack in it, but text was visible on all three. Two other entryways to other tunnels split off in different directions from the room. Otherwise, it was empty. Caleb growled deeply in his throat. "I'll kill her!" he snarled.

Mallory looked at him in concern. "Who? What? What's wrong, Caleb?"

"The Archivist. She was supposed to wait here with the baby!" Caleb's teeth ground in his mouth.

Mallory felt her chest tighten. "Kirk?"

Caleb shouted. "Dikaió, take me to the Archivist!"

Nothing happened.

Pain shot across Caleb's face.

Mallory said, "she christened Alex and me Archivists too. You need to be more specific."

Caleb looked at her, emotional pain stretched across his face, this time mixed with a question in need of an answer.

Mallory understood immediately. He had not read much of *The Chronicles of the Lost* and had maybe only heard the Archivist's name once at the Library. He only knew to call her by her title. "Emily Carpenter," Mallory said. "Her name is Emily Carpenter."

"Dikaió, take me to Emily Carpenter!" Caleb called out. Immediately, the walls groaned, the concrete in one of the tunnels crumbled as rebar ripped itself out and wrapped around itself, creating a solid line to show the way. Mallory smiled, thinking of all the broken concrete in the hallways and staircase. Of course, that's how Caleb had found her. The same way she was going to use to find him up above in the city streets—at least before the Sprite Master showed up.

Caleb started to walk toward the path, still carrying Mallory. She touched his shoulder lightly. "Caleb?"

He looked at her with daggers in his eyes. "What?" he nearly screamed.

"You'll go faster without me." She nodded toward the chairs. "I'll be fine here."

Caleb's rage swirled about in his blue eyes, a tortured confusion. He did not want to choose between his wife and his child. "I just got you back, Mal."

"I'll be fine." Mallory assured him. "I have the Dikaió now. I fought off a whole ton of wilding wolves up there. I'll be fine."

Caleb hesitated still.

"Caleb, put me in one of those chairs and go rescue our child, or so help me—" Mallory did not know what she would do, but she was getting angry.

Caleb nodded and dropped her gently in one of the old chairs. "Okay. I'll be back. I promise!"

"You'd better!" Mallory said. "Now, go on before she gets away."

Caleb hesitated one moment longer and then said, "I love you, Mallory Aiworth."

Mallory felt her heart skip a beat. "And I love you, Caleb Aiworth. Now, go get our son!"

Caleb shot out of the room faster than Mallory had ever seen him move. He was moving so fast, Mallory could count an entire two seconds where his feet did not touch the ground between strides. When he reached a turn, he flew at it feet first and kicked off it at an angle to make the turn without slowing down. His impact left a small crack in the wall. The nano sprites that had been tearing him apart and rebuilding him while he was hungry had enhanced his speed and strength. The Archivist and Omaha had both moved like that as well, unnaturally fast. Could all the Ex Natu move that way? Mallory did not remember the Ex Natu soldiers moving that fast at the Library or in the citadel. They were much slower, human almost. Mallory pondered that while she sat at the table. She hoped that Caleb's new speed would help him catch the woman carrying her son away from them before she turned the child over to Omaha.

While Mallory did not trust Reddy Lamarr—at all—she could not help but think that the Sprite Master must be right about Emily Carpenter's betrayal of their people. What else would explain what had happened at the Library? After all, it was she who built the clockwork sprite that had injected the nano sprites into Caleb and brought Omaha to the Library looking for the baby. But Mallory hesitated. On the other hand, the Archivist had not betrayed them to Omaha. She had used them as bait and seemed intent on killing him— exacting revenge for the death of her husband and sons.

Mallory shook her head. She had had this same thread of thoughts running through her mind for months, and it had nearly driven her crazy. She instead turned her thoughts to baby Kirk. A ball of tension twisted in her stomach, and she began to cry: deep heavy sobs. She wanted her baby. She had never felt so hopelessly, helplessly desperate in all her life. She would have faced down a hundred magistrates, a thousand fire sprites, a million wilding wolves, and all the Ex Natu to hold him in her arms again. Then her despair turned to anger. That witch of a woman had taken her child. Mallory gritted her teeth in rage. Whether they needed the Archivist or not, Mallory was not going to hold Caleb back next time. Then she sighed. There was a good chance, Mallory would not be there when Caleb caught up with her. She hoped he would protect the baby if he chose to kill the old woman.

Mallory shook her head again. She was going to drive herself crazy, sitting her alone running through scenarios outside her control. She needed a distraction. Mallory turned her attention to the screens. She bit her lip and tilted her head, trying to concentrate on what they were. The light of the screens was very dim. They were made of glass and housed in a box of some very old material. It looked like it used to be white but had faded to a yellowish-brown, which felt brittle to the touch. She could make out lettering on one of the screens, contrasted in dim green compared to the black back-ground of the screen. She held her hands up to the screen to block out the ambience from the Dikaió lights. There were some sentences on the left side of the screen and some on the right, staggered like bricks in a house speaking to one another. The blocks of text were conversing: one calling, the other responding. Mallory started to read what was written on one of the screens and realized the text was a conversation, and what she read made the blood in her veins run cold.

Emily:

Are you there?

Zane:

I am, but you know the protocols.

Emily:

I don't have much time.

Zane:

Time is relative, isn't it?

Emily:

I don't have my codebook with me. Is
there any other way to prove my identity?

Zane:

How could you not have your codebook
with you? Were you compromised?

Emily:

I was. I only just escaped.

Zane:

This conversation is over.

Emily:

I have the child.

Zane:

…I'm listening.

Emily:

He's newborn. Today. But the mother was
killed in the escape, and I have no means
to feed him.

Zane:

How long has it been since it's eaten?

Emily:

Hours maybe.

Zane:

Has it eaten at all?

Emily:

I believe so; I wasn't there for the birth.

Zane:

Bring it to the compound in Ben
Domond. We'll see to it.

Emily:

I am in the Davis City Metroplex, and I
have no access to intercontinental transport. They'll be watching for me at the
transit stations.

Zane:

Can you make it to Loma on the West
Coast?

Emily:

Via flying sprite? Yes, but it's going to be
a long time, and I'll have to stop to charge
it. The sprites I have don't have that kind
of range.

The baby won't stop screaming, he's so
hungry.

Is there no chance for extraction?

Zane:

I'm breaking all kinds of rules even
offering transportation from Loma
without authentication, Emily, if that is
who I am speaking to.

If you get to the right place in Loma, we'll
waive level-one protocols. After that we
will run a DNA scan to authenticate your
identity and clear you for transport to Ben
Lomond. That's the deal I'm offering.

Emily:

Fine. What's the entry code?

Zane:

Stand outside with the baby. We'll be
watching.

Emily:

Fine.

Mallory jumped up off her chair. The Archivist had
stolen her son after all, but she was giving him to this Zane
character instead of Omaha. Mallory picked up the screen

with the letter board and examined it from every angle. The conversation just ended there; it had no pages to turn or anything. Mallory dropped the screen and quickly examined the other two.

The one with the cracked screen had what looked like an article detailing how long a newborn could live without food and water. Mallory's chest ached when she read that her son needed to eat every four to five hours, and in the most dire of circumstances, could only live two or three days without her. In Hoffen City, there was a formula that could be mixed with water for babies if they could not access their mother's milk, but why would they need that in an Ex Natu city where there were no children? She was the only thing here that could save her son, and now, the Archivist was taking him who knows where to some Ex Natu who could not possibly feed him. Her hands clenched the table in a vice grip, and she tried to scream. All that came out was a whimper. Then more sobbing.

Mallory hoped that Caleb would catch up to the Archivist before the old woman could leave the city to Loma or Ben Domond, wherever those were. They were clearly outside of the Davis City Metroplex. The Archivist had written something about intercontinental travel. Mallory was not sure what that even meant. She put the second screen down and turned to the third screen to look for clues.

The third screen showed a timer counting down. It was at 00:02:04 and rapidly going lower. That screen had two wires running out of it under the table. Mallory followed the wires down to a small brown box wrapped in cellophane, which was taped to two large white, rusted metal barrels with faded red stickers of fire on the front. Mallory's heart skipped a beat.

She turned to the tunnel that Caleb had run down and quickly limped after him following the path of exposed rebar. Her ankle throbbed, but her adrenaline was dulling the pain again—somewhat. Mallory had never seen a bomb before, but she had dealt with enough flammable liquid when repairing the fire sprites to understand the concept. She also knew that a large enough explosion could bring this whole tunnel system down on her head, she had nearly done that at the Library when she accidentally blew up one of the Archivist's fire sprites. Destroying the tunnel was no doubt the Archivist's plan—not to kill Mallory of course, the older woman already assumed she was dead, and maybe not even to kill Caleb, though she obviously did not care if he died. Clearly, the Archivist wanted to destroy the evidence of whoever Zane was and her communications with him. However, if Mallory was in this tunnel when that timer ran out, she would end up just the way the Archivist believed she was already: dead.

Mallory did not make it far before the world turned sideways, and she was thrown against the wall of the tunnel. Concrete cracked and rained all around her, and the tunnel was filled with a plume of thick smoke. Mallory's eyes stung in the gray fog all around her, but she could still somewhat make out the walls of the tunnel. On the wall across from her, the rebar path stuck out toward her, and Mallory was very thankful that she had not been thrown into that side of the wall, or she would have been impaled by the rusted metal. This thankfulness was short lived as a new terrifying sound came from behind her; the sound of hundreds of squeaks fleeing in terror. Mallory turned around to face a small army of rats running down the tunnel, followed by a column of heat and a ball fire that was swallowing them in its wake.

Mallory's squeak joined the frightened chorus of rodents behind her, and she started to run, pain in her abdomen, ankle, and feet completely forgotten in her dash for survival. She had no idea where she was going, but she kept following the broken walls and twisted metal. Behind her she could feel the heat growing and hear desperate squeals erupt in short fits as the fire took the rats. She turned a corner and nearly smacked her head on a low doorway. Ducking just in time, she entered another small room just like the one where the small screens and the bomb were. She barely noticed it as she ran, but there was an old wooden door wedged open on the inside of the room.

Where she found the breath, she had no idea, but she

screamed, "Dikaió, close the door!" The door ripped free from its years of disuse and slammed shut, cracking the ancient wood of the door in several places. Mallory considered slowing momentarily to see if the door would hold, but instead she continued to run along the hallway following the cracks in the wall. It was good that she did because very quickly she heard several thumps against the door behind her followed by muffled rat screams, and then the door exploded with the force of the fireball. Mallory was not sure if the door had done anything to slow down the blaze's momentum, but she kept running. Then she turned another corner and saw sunlight ahead of her. She quickly glanced behind. There was no way she was going to cover the distance before the fireball caught her.

Mallory screamed again. "Dikaió, stop the fire!" The ground below her began to shake, and she lurched to the side, twisting her ankle again. She fell to the ground hard. She tried to keep scrambling toward the daylight, but the rumbling ground made it hard to keep her balance even on her hands and knees. She looked behind her again expecting the fireball to be on top of her at this point but found the fire was gone. The tunnel had completely collapsed behind her, and it really should have collapsed on her too. The cement was cracked all around her—all the way to the exit—and was still trembling as if it could collapse at any moment. "Dikaió, keep the tunnel up until I exit," Mallory called, hoping that what she was asking was even possible. The rebar that marked Caleb's path began to unwind itself and shoot up here and there, enforcing the crumbling concrete. Mallory shook her head; this was temporary at best.

She slowly pulled herself to her feet and again began to make her way to the exit. Without the imminent threat of a fireball bearing down on her, Mallory moved a little slower. All of the pains—the ankle, cut feet, birth aftermath, trauma from the explosion—hit her full force. She started retching. There was nothing in her stomach to release, so it was just unproductive spasms. Despite all of that, she gasped for breath and willed herself to keep moving forward. The flat terrain of the tunnel floor was now a maze of sharp rocks and twisted rebar poles that she had to weave through and over. More than once, she had to use the Dikaió to make the rebar move out of her way and was nearly squashed by falling chunks of concrete doing it. Finally, she pulled herself free from the tunnel into the sunlight outdoors.

There was no way to know exactly where in the Davis City Metroplex she was because she had never seen the city before. The Ex Natu citadels and poorly kept streets looked identical to the ones she had used to flee Reddy Lamarr. The packs of wilding wolves who had been attracted by the rumblings of the tunnel collapse looked familiar as well, except now there were hundreds of them pouring around the bases of the Ex Natu citadels. All of them looked her way at once when she exited the tunnel.

Mallory froze in place.

She could not run anymore if she wanted to; the pain was too great, she was too exhausted, and there was literally no direction other than backwards available. She bit her lip and tilted her head. She was not sure even the Dikaió could handle all these wolves, but then she thought about baby Kirk dying somewhere out there, without her, and she gritted her teeth, bracing herself for what might be her last fight.

Then she noticed a flying sprite leaned up against the entrance of the tunnel. It must have been the third sprite that flew along with Caleb and the Archivist during their escape. Neither of them had needed it, so here it lay, just for her. Mallory climbed onto the thing. She was not sure where to put her feet, but there were two handles that seemed like natural places to put her hands. The wilding wolves howled and began to charge her. Somehow, they recognized that their dinner was about to evade them. Mallory scanned over the controls and grimaced. She had no idea how to work it; that had been the whole point of springing the Archivist in the first place.

She sighed and fell back on the Dikaió again: "Dikaió sprite, take me to Emily Carpenter."

Lights flashed on the front of the sprite, and it wobbled into the air. Mallory grabbed the handles and held on tight. The wolves were upon her, and she worried that it was all too late. Just as she felt their hot breath at her ankles, the flying sprite shot upward fast. Mallory felt her stomach in her throat, and she almost passed out from the blood leaving her head. She looked out at the massive city and marveled at its never-ending mass of cement blocks stretching out before her. The flying sprite slowly turned toward the setting sun, and then blasted forward.

Mallory could not help but remember the Archivist's description of traveling across the Davis City Metroplex via flying sprite in *The Chronicles of the Lost*. She said that it took nearly an hour to cross the city, and she was right. By the time the buildings started to thin out, Mallory thought she might go insane if she had to look at another boring Ex Natu citadel. Why had immortality destroyed these people's creativity? The city was just horrible to look at. She missed her childhood home with its eaves and large porch. Her ancestor Eva Knenne had designed it to meld into the flower gardens that wrapped around its base. Mallory also missed the giant oaks that stood like sentries guarding over their family. Mostly though, she missed her parents.

Normally, she would say that she missed her father the most, as his humor and understanding had always tempered her mother's exacting strictness. Her mother kept her hair so tight that not even a strand would slip out of place. But now that Mallory was a mother too, she wanted nothing more than to sit and pick her mother's brain about child-rearing. And that thought sucked Mallory into an unbidden depression. She was a mother, but her newborn son was gone—not even a day old and stolen from her. What would her mother think of that? Mallory had lost her grandbaby. Would her mother be glad that she had banished her from Hoffen City?

Probably.

Mallory's face grew hot, and she thought she was going to cry, but her mouth had grown dry in the wind from traveling via flying sprite. Her eyes were dry too; there were no tears to shed.

Mallory closed her eyes to keep the wind out and immediately felt the weight of the day overwhelm her. A deep aching pain settled into every muscle, every joint—even her head throbbed. Her insides seized up in cramps. The wounds on her feet screamed. Her foot, hanging limply over the flying sprite, dangled at an awkward angle and pulled on her injured ankle. But even more pronounced than the pain was a deep, deep weariness. Her head bobbed downward as sleep snuck up on her, and she jerked awake, leaning backwards and nearly falling off the flying sprite.

Mallory shook her head and looked down. She was several hundred feet in the air. Falling asleep up here was a bad idea. She repositioned herself on the seat, trying to get more comfortable, without getting too comfortable. On top of the pain and the weariness, the wind was chilling. Mallory's body began to shiver despite the long-sleeved clothes she had picked up in the abandoned Ex Natu boutique. She gritted her teeth and tried to think about something other than her body's various complaints. She thought about the wilding wolves' skins that the Sprite Master used. As awful as those things smelled, Mallory mused that they must have been pretty warm; plus, they seemed to be a good way to stay off the wolves' dinner plate. But why was Reddy Lamarr running around the city streets with the wolves if she was back in the good graces of Omaha? The man seemed to have quite a few resources at his command. The Sprite Master also had not shaved her head or gotten the living tattoos indicative of being an Ex Natu.

The last time they had spoken in the Library's armory, Reddy Lamarr had said the Ex Natu killed her family. She all but cursed them. Mallory could not begin to understand how the old woman had such a change of heart in such a relatively short time, especially if she now knew that Omaha was still alive, being an Ex Natu himself. Something about her story just did not sit right. One gnawing issue was that she still held the belief that the Archivist was a traitor to the people of Hoffen City. Mallory had just experienced the brutality of Omaha and the Ex Natu, and he had treated the Archivist even worse, more than once. She was the man's sworn enemy, lured him into a battle at the Library, and tried to kill him. How could she be a traitor to Hoffen City?

Surely, Omaha was the traitor, and yet, Reddy Lamarr defended him to Mallory's face. And the Sprite Master was now back in Omaha's employ, claiming that what happened to Mallory, Caleb, the Archivist, and baby Kirk was all necessary to undo the Archivist's betrayal—but Lamarr was not living like an Ex Natu. She might not even be living in the citadels with the Ex Natu, which would certainly explain the wilding pelts she was sporting. But she did know that Mallory had taken Omaha's Dominus bracelet, so Mallory had no reason to doubt her story of reconnecting with Omaha.

Still, something seemed off.

There was something bigger going on that she needed to understand: something her baby's survival depended on. She thought about the screens in the tunnel; the Archivist had written to someone named Zane that she "had the child," and they had spoken as if they were acquainted but did not trust one another. Yet, the older woman was taking her baby to this Zane. Were these more Ex Natu? And if so, how could they feed baby Kirk? Mallory knew one thing for certain: She intended to read page ninety-three of *The Chronicles of the Lost* as soon as she found paper and a pen. Perhaps when the Dikaió copied the rest of it, the story would get clearer.

Mallory yawned.

Maybe if she could sleep on it, things would get clearer? She looked around the flying sprite for some way to secure herself to the silver hull, so she could nap. There was no strap, no back rest, nothing that would keep her from plummeting to her death should she fall. The flying sprite was not made for rest. She thought back to the tall grass of the plains and what the clockwork sprite had told them. Flying sprites had short ranges and needed to recharge often, which would exclude sleep while driving even when automated by the Dikaió flying the sprite. She adjusted herself uncomfortably on the seat and tried to keep her eyes open without staring directly into the wind.

She looked down at the sprite's handles and noticed a small dashboard with a small lightning bolt. Next to the lightning bolt, there were ten bars of increasing lengths. Five were lit up, and the five largest were dark. The fifth lighted bar was blinking, and then as she watched, the bar went dark. The next bar began to blink. It was another countdown. Mallory looked up ahead of her. She knew that Caleb and the Archivist were probably traveling ahead of her at the exact same speed, and their flying sprites were probably losing power too, which would mean that they would need to recharge somewhere. Her heart began to pound, and adrenaline poured into her body. She was not sure how long it took to recharge a flying sprite, but there was a chance that she was not going to have to travel all the way to Loma to catch up with the Archivist. Both she and Caleb would have to stop to recharge their sprites somewhere, and the Dikaió would take her right to them.

She watched the blinking bar on her dashboard. It was mesmerizing. It was impossible to know how long it took for the fourth bar to go dark, but the sun was nearly set, and the dense cityscape was starting to thin out. Mallory could see a vast, dark forest opening ahead in the distance. She again looked at the blinking bar and worried: Would there be a place to recharge this flying sprite in the forest? Surely, the Archivist would have stopped to recharge here in the city if there were not charging stations in the forest, but what if her flying sprite had started out with more bars than Mallory's had? What if Mallory found herself in the middle of the forest, just like the Archivist and the others when they were locked out of the city by Mari Nelson and the activation of the light? The Dikaió did not work on living things like trees and plants. How was she going to defend herself against wilding wolves in the forest without it? She still had the Ex Natu weapon in her backpack, but it did not have unlimited ammunition.

Mallory bit her lip and tilted her head. She waffled back and forth on what to do. Her heart desperately wanted to keep going, take down the Archivist, and recover her son. Her head knew she would be no help to the child if she crashed out of the sky and was eaten by wilding wolves in the darkness of night. She sighed heavily and said, "Dikaió, take me to a place to recharge this flying sprite."

The flying sprite dipped sharply to the right, and Mallory had to hold on to the handgrips tightly, which proved difficult as her hands had gone numb from the wind and the cold. She descended quickly to the roof of what looked to be a two-story house in the outskirts of the city. In the purple-orange light of the setting sun, the house was not exactly beautiful, but it was certainly more interesting than the Ex Natu citadels. It was essentially two rectangular boxes set on top of each other with asymmetrical windows and a sloping roof. The yard was immaculate and well-tended. Several trees dotted the property, and a large, gated wall enclosed it. As Mallory swooped by one of the trees, she was surprised as several birds startled, chirping and flitting about, but they did not scatter and fly far away. Clearly, some animals had found shelter within the house's walls, and Mallory's arrival was not as threatening as the wilding wolves beyond the barrier's protection, so they did not flush when confronted with a human. Beyond the trees was a small circular pad where a pair of flying sprites sat motionless.

Mallory's own flying sprite lit quietly next to the others. These two were a lot smaller than the one she was riding. The seats had less padding, and the necks leading to the handles were just thin, chrome bars. Two thick, black cords ran from the house to the pair of flying sprites, and Mallory could see that the charging bars on these two sprites were completely full, lit green in the fading light. She climbed off her flying sprite and stretched her limbs, arching her back. Several cracks sounded up and down her spine, and Mallory felt waves of tension leave her body. She stepped unsteadily to the other flying sprites and felt about where the black cord connected to the sprite. There was a small lump in the rubber cord that depressed when she pushed it with her thumb. The cord clicked loudly and released from the flying sprite. The sun was sinking below the horizon quite quickly now, and the darkness made it hard to see, but there were six bronze-colored prongs inside the end of the cord, and six slots on the flying sprite that corresponded to them.

Mallory dragged the cord to her flying sprite and felt around in the dark for the slots. When she found them, she plugged the cord in. She waited, expecting the dark bars to begin lighting up immediately, but it took several minutes for the bars to change from three to four. Charging the sprite was going to take her all night, and who knew how far ahead the Archivist would get with her baby? Fear welled up in her. What if the Dikaió could not track her so far? She had said there was a limit for how far it worked. What if the Archivist got out of range while she sat there waiting for the flying sprite to charge?

Without warning, a bright light flashed, and Mallory wheeled around dazzled by the sudden change in illumination.

"What are you doing there?" a deep voice growled.

Mallory's eyes adjusted, and she could make out a rather large shadow of a man looming out of the door of the house. She had been spotted by the Ex Natu! She quickly began trying to pull her backpack around to the front of her to get to the Ex Natu weapon. The man was walking slowly toward her now. "I said, 'What are you doing there?'" he repeated louder.

Mallory backed up, stumbling over the cord attached to her flying sprite. "Dikaió protect me," she yelled as she fell.

Her head struck the edge of her flying sprite hard as it flew into the air defensively, and she tumbled into the other two on the platform, knocking them both over loudly. The man paused with his arms raised in the air incredulously. "Hey, those are expensive! Stop!" He turned his head back toward the house. "Susie, call the cops. Someone's out here messing with our bikes!"

Mallory managed to right herself and pull the weapon from her bag. She pointed it at the shadow. "Wait!" she yelled.

The shadow's shoulders slumped, and it quickly raised its hands. "I don't want no trouble. I didn't recognize you. I should have with that sprite, and those clothes, but I've never seen an officer with hair—not in a couple of hundred years anyway."

Mallory was uncertain what to do. Who did this man think she was?

Another shadow, more diminutive than the first, appeared at the door. A woman's voice called out: "What's all the fuss about, Russell? The last thing we need is the law out here; you remember what they did to the Stanleys next door." The shadow that must have been Susie froze and let out a small squeak when she saw Mallory.

"Stand behind me, love," Russell whispered.

Susie did not move. The pair were frozen in place, looking at Mallory with her weapon trained on them. A small sprite and bits of yard decorations floated around her defensively, but the Dikaió did not seem to consider these two a threat, and Mallory agreed with it this time. The couple did not seem dangerous. She sighed heavily and said, "I'm not looking for trouble. I just need to charge my sprite, and I'll be on my way." She lowered her weapon.

Russell nodded. "Oh sure, sure. Help yourself. Let's go, Susie." He turned and tried to herd her back toward the door.

Susie stepped around him and walked toward Mallory. "How come your head's still bleeding?" she asked and pointed at Mallory's temple.

Mallory reached up absently and found a tender gash on her head that she must have received when she knocked it against her flying sprite. She grimaced and tightened her grip on the weapon at her side. "I really don't want any trouble," she said again.

Susie did not seem to hear. "Is something wrong with your nanos, dear?" She stepped beyond the light, and her face came into focus. The woman looked like she was in her late fifties or early sixties. If the couple was not talking about centuries and nano sprites, Mallory would have never known this old woman was an Ex Natu. She did not have any tattoos. Her hair was white, about shoulder length, and tied back in a ponytail. She was wearing a white flowing silk pantsuit, like the ones the Archivist favored, and over that she wore a denim jacket.

The man walked out of the shadows behind her. He was a large man, at least three inches taller than Caleb and wider by half. He had a gray beard, and his head was balding, but not shaved like the other Ex Natu Mallory had seen. His skin was also free of tattoos. The man grabbed the woman's arm, "Susie, just let her charge her bike and go."

She looked back at him and then returned her gaze to Mallory. "Are you hungry? I've heard sometimes the nanos don't work right when they don't have anything to eat."

Mallory frowned and thought of Caleb, starving for months, but his "nanos" still worked fine, painfully keeping him alive the entire time. She was about to protest, but her stomach growled loudly.

"See!" Susie clapped. "The girl's hungry, Russell. You wait right there, and I'll fetch you a bite. We'll get you all fixed up." She turned and ran past her husband back into the house.

Russell stood awkwardly in the yard looking at Mallory. He reached up and ruffled what was left of the hair on top of his head. It stuck up in static columns as he pulled his hand away. "You don't have no nanos, do you?"

Mallory shook her head.

He nodded. "I thought not. I've heard rumors of your lot. Rumors of ancient wars brewing in the South Seas. Children's children, revenge, and all that."

Mallory did not know what to say, so she stayed quiet.

He shifted on his feet. "It's not that you don't have a right to revenge. Lord knows, you do. What the military did to your ancestors was terrible, but it wasn't all of us you know. We didn't all believe that Malthusian nonsense, killing babies like they were a virus on the planet. It was sickening." His hands migrated to his pockets. "We wouldn't have even took the nanos on principle, but Susie was sick you know. The cancer—there's a word I haven't heard in years—and our names came up in the lottery. I couldn't lose her. You can understand that, can't you?"

Mallory could not. She assumed Russell was referring to getting nano sprites to become an Ex Natu, and she could never imagine choosing that curse under any circumstances—to give up family for immortality. She glanced at the flying sprite charging. It had made it up to six bars now. She willed it to hurry up, so she would not have to listen to this man try to justify himself anymore.

The man seemed to read her mind. "We had six babies of our own. Six children that didn't get picked, you know? We had to watch everyone of them grow old and bury them when their time came. We know what it's like to lose our children, you know?"

Mallory did understand that part. Tears welled up in her eyes, and she again looked at the charging flying sprite: six bars.

Susie burst out of the house holding a plate full of meat and potatoes. "Here you go, dear. C'mon in and sit while your bike charges. Have a little something."

The aroma drifted to Mallory's nose, and it was intoxicating. She looked at Russell, and there was a deep sadness in his eyes. He closed them, and then stepped out of her way and motioned that she should go ahead. Mallory walked slowly and cautiously toward the house, her hand clutching the Ex Natu weapon stiffly at her side. She took a wide berth of Russell and then entered the couple's home. Mallory gasped.

The interior of the home looked almost identical to her parent's house. She had entered the kitchen door, which led into a dining room and a sitting area. Off the sitting area, stairs ascended to the second floor. Susie set the plate on the table in the dining room, and Mallory sat gingerly in front of it. She was tempted to eat it like an animal would, but she only had one hand—the other occupied with holding the Ex Natu weapon and all. She studied the plate. It looked like meatloaf and potatoes, but the meatloaf was off-colored. It looked yellow and dry, though the tangy-red sauce on top seemed right. She looked up at Susie, who stood over her expectantly. Mallory smiled and picked up a fork.

The meatloaf tasted as off as it looked. It was gritty, more like a corn tortilla than the meat from a cow. "What kind of meat is this?" Mallory asked between bites.

Susie's expectant expression was replaced with confusion. "Meat?" she asked. "Like animal meat?"

"Yeah. It doesn't taste like beef," Mallory took another bite, grateful for any food no matter how it tasted.

Susie turned to Russell, worry lines deepening.

He took her hand. "She's not going to hurt us. She's just passing through—a stranger in a strange land, and we're doing her a kindness like Rahab in Jericho."

Susie's mouth was aghast. "Is she an islander?" She shook her head and looked back at Mallory. "Her head's still bleeding, Russell. Maybe she's an islander?"

He folded her into his arms and nodded to Mallory. "Eat quick, young lady. Whatever charge you have out there when you're done, I'd ask that it's enough. We don't want no trouble, either."

Mallory nodded and shoveled the food into her mouth as fast as she could. When she finished, she thanked the couple and limped outside. She paused and turned back to Russell. "Do you have paper and something to write with?"

Russell raised an eyebrow. "A bit. How much do you need?"

"Just a few pages, please."

Russell stepped over to a buffet and opened the center drawer. He pulled out a pad of yellow-lined paper and a pencil. He held them up in Mallory's direction. "Will this do?"

"Yes, thank you." Mallory took the pad and pencil with the hand not holding the weapon. She tried to reach behind her toward her pack, but it was quickly clear she was not going to be able to put the writing materials or the weapon in the pack without setting one of them down.

The large man took a step toward her, and Mallory felt her heart jump. The hand holding the weapon shook, but Russell held up his hands. "Let me help you." He took the pad and pencil from her and placed them in her pack.

"Thanks." Mallory said shyly.

"You can thank me by leaving," Russell nodded. "You're going to get us in trouble if you're caught here. We've lived a long time and would like to live a bit longer, so if you don't mind," he pointed toward the landing pad.

Mallory nodded and continued out to the flying sprite. It was at eight bars now. She unplugged the cord and climbed back onboard. She looked back toward the house. The Ex Natu couple were standing in the doorway: silhouettes folded into each other's embrace. Susie's shadow was shaking and sobbing. Mallory looked down at the flying sprite and sighed.

She said, "Dikaió, take me to Emily Carpenter."

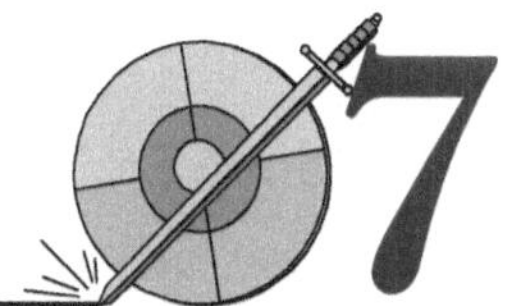

Shortly after Mallory left the Ex Natu couple's house, darkness enveloped her. The sun had set; it was a moonless night, she was far outside the city lights, and below her were the deep shadows of treetops. All the light that Mallory could see was the steadily blinking light of the power bars of the sprite, which were draining faster than Mallory had hoped they would. At the rate she was flying, she would need to recharge within two and a half to three hours max. She just hoped that she would find someplace to recharge before the flying sprite ran out of power and crashed.

On top of that, it was cold now that the sun had set, and the wind was not helping anything. She wished that she had thought to dig out another shirt from her backpack when she had stopped, but trying to do it while riding the sprite risked a fall to her death while she grappled with maneuvering the bag around to open it. She also needed to change her padding, her ankle was incredibly painful dangling off the sprite, and her fingers and toes had all essentially fallen asleep from the cold and lack of movement.

Mallory tried to take her mind off all her woes by focusing on what the couple had said about her: Southern Islands, ancestors, revenge. She bit her lip and tilted her head. She was not entirely sure what the word "island" meant, but she had heard it before. She started thinking about how Eva Knenne had begun *The Chronicles of the Matriarch*. There was a war in some "islands" where the holdout families had tried to avoid the Ex Natu birthing laws. The families had ultimately lost that war, butchered by Mallory's ancestor General Kirk Knenne. And then when he came home, he learned that his own wife had given birth to a baby girl, Mari, and that his own family would almost certainly be targeted by the Ex Natu for breaking those same laws. To save them, he started a secret resistance movement with Omaha to preserve their lines. But it sounded like they were not the only survivors: The couple seemed to believe that some of the islander families had also survived out there somewhere.

Mallory's eyes widened in dawning realization as to where the Archivist was heading with baby Kirk. Mallory almost immediately lost that train of thought and regretted opening her eyes so wide, as the wind pummeled the liquid out of them. She clenched her eyes shut and shook her head. She wished there was enough water in her body to make some tears to deal with the windburn. Just as she let go of one of the handlebars to wipe at her eyes, the flying sprite dipped down. Mallory quickly clenched her legs around the sprite and reached back toward the handle. She peaked with one eye to see where the sprite was going and at that moment a huge explosion blinded her, throwing her backwards. If her legs had not already been secured around the sprite, she might have fallen to her death. Mallory squeaked again, as the fireball loomed ahead of her, and the stupid flying sprite was aiming right for it.

She briefly considered jumping off anyway, but before she could do anything, the fireball was swirling around her. Heat and smoke batted at her eyes, forcing them closed again. She had trouble catching her breath in the midst of the flames: The oxygen had been sucked out of the air. The old burns from the fire at City Hall, long since healed, reared in a familiar searing pain. She popped one eye open to see if she was on fire. She was not, at least not yet. There was smoke rising off the sleeves of her shirt. Just then, another explosion went off to her left, and the flames around her blew out in a gust of wind. Her flying sprite shimmied in the second shock wave but did not alter its course, hurtling toward the ground and the second explosion.

For an instant, the smoke cleared just enough for her to get a glimpse of the ground below her. A rectangular building with an outcropping was illuminated by several bright lights. Under the outcropping, there were several charging stations like the ones at the Ex Natu couple's house. One flying sprite was plugged in to a charger. Another flying sprite lay half in and half out of one of the building's windows. The Archivist was hiding behind a pillar supporting the outcropping. She was holding a small bundle in her arms. About fifty yards away from her, Caleb screamed in rage. Three large white metal cylinders hovered around him. He spoke into his wrist and pointed at the pillar. One of the cylinders flung itself at the structure.

Mallory sucked in smoke as the cylinder crashed against the pillar and exploded.

A third fireball flew into the air, rocking Mallory's flying sprite. The Dikaió was taking her to the Archivist, who Caleb was presently trying to kill: thus, the flying sprite kept flying straight into the fireballs. She clutched the handles and tried to yell. All that came out was a weak cough. "Dikaió… dikaió…" She whispered her command and hoped the Dikaió would respond. "Land behind Caleb." The flying sprite shifted direction away from the Archivist and instead aimed for Caleb.

It landed a few feet behind him, and Mallory quickly jumped off. She was still having trouble breathing because of all the smoke. "Caleb!" She hacked. "Caleb!" She ran around to the front of him, and once again, she had to earnestly search his face for signs of the man she loved. He was lost somewhere in the rage. His eyes looked like they were on fire, reflecting the flames in front of them. The twin fires scanned the rubble for signs of the Archivist.

Mallory touched his chest gently. "Caleb."

His eyes darted down to hers, and the fire reflected in them began to slowly shift to a smokey blue. "M-Mal?" He stuttered.

"Dikaió, put down these tanks—gently," Mallory said. The remaining tanks gently dropped to the ground around them. "Let's get our baby first." She took her hand off his chest and turned back to the charging station.

The Archivist was on the the flying sprite, having somehow managed to dodge Caleb's explosive tanks. She was fumbling with the plug connected to the sprite, trying to free the sprite from the charging station. Mallory stepped forward and tried to yell, but her voice was still barely a whisper. "Dikaió, stop her from leaving." One of the tanks floated up into the air, and Mallory shook her head. "Dikaió, no not like that!" Her voice was louder now.

"Dikaió, detain Emily Carpenter." Caleb barked loudly. The Archivist had just finished disconnecting the cord from her flying sprite when the cord jumped out of her hand and wrapped around her. She struggled against the cord to keep the baby she was holding safe, which left her in an awkward position, barely holding the child by some folds of the blanket, and it did not look she was going to hold him there for long.

Mallory tried to sprint forward to save her son from falling, but her ankle was done letting her punish it, no matter how much adrenaline her brain sent its way. It buckled hard, and Mallory heard the snap despite the roar of the fires. The world seemed to slow down as she fell. She saw baby Kirk's bundle slip from the Archivist's hand, just as Caleb leapt over Mallory's head. Even though everything slowed down, Caleb was moving unnaturally fast. Mallory wondered if he would make it in time to catch their baby. He would have to cross two-hundred feet before baby Kirk could fall three feet. Then she wondered if Caleb intended to save their baby at all. He had just been throwing explosives at the child after all. What if he was just running over to kill the Archivist?

She closed her eyes, not wanting to see either way.

An eternity seemed to pass by in darkness, and as long as she kept her eyes closed, Mallory had a Schrödinger's baby. Kirk was both alive and dead, and if her son were really dead, she thought she would prefer to keep him stranded in that equilibrium than grieve his loss. On the other hand, she desperately wanted to hold her baby in her arms; plus, she really wanted to know what was happening. She bit her lip and tilted her head. Her mother's instinct mixed with her curiosity forced her eyes open.

Caleb was standing alone at the charger looking up into the sky.

The Archivist, the flying sprite, and baby Kirk were gone.

Mallory felt confused. "Caleb!" she coughed. "Caleb!"

Even at that distance, he seemed to hear, as his head sank, and he slowly turned toward her. Her husband walked to her in defeat. He knelt down in front of her and pulled her up to him in a crushing embrace. "I'm sorry, Mal. I didn't know what else to do. She was going to drop our son. I had to let her go. I had to."

Mallory understood what had happened. Knowing he was not going to make it, Caleb had used the Dikaió to release the Archivist, who had caught baby Kirk and flown off on the flying sprite before he could catch her. Mallory reached up and touched his face. "It's okay. It's okay. You did the right thing—you really did."

Caleb's face darkened, and he bared his teeth. "I should have killed her though. I want to kill her, Mal. So much."

Mallory's stomach rolled in fear, and she pulled back from him.

Caleb saw the fear in her face and shook his head violently. "I'm sorry. It's hard to concentrate. I feel so different, out of control."

Mallory reached and stroked his beard. "Is it hunger?"

Caleb's eyes flashed. "Why? Do you have any food?"

Mallory wished she had thought to bring some of the Ex Natu couple's food with her when she left, but she had not. "No, I don't. I'm sorry."

He looked like he was on the verge of anger again. Mallory was losing her husband to whatever the nano sprites had done to him, so she quickly changed the subject away from food. He seemed to need purpose. Mallory needed to direct whatever was happening toward their goal. "The Archivist couldn't have charged her flying sprite much, right? She'll have to try to stop and charge somewhere else. How many bars did your flying sprite have?" Mallory pointed toward the sprite in the building's window.

Caleb's eyes moved slowly in the direction she was pointing. Then they focused. "Two bars I think," he said.

"Help me up," Mallory pulled on his broad shoulders, and he easily pulled her off the ground. "Hers can't have much more than that. They take a while to charge. Let's get ours and charge them a little, and then we'll go after her and catch her wherever she tries to charge next." She heard herself saying it, and it was rational, but the mother bear inside her heart was screaming at her to go after the Archivist. Mallory looked at Caleb, whose face was twitching, and squashed her emotions. She was not sure what he would do if she exhibited anything but calm reason.

Caleb helped her limp to the building. There was a bench next to the door, and he set her down there. Then he pulled the sprite out of the window and looked at it quizzically. "How do we charge them?"

Mallory pointed at the flying sprite. "There on the left side just behind the seat. The holes match up with the prongs on the cords."

Caleb tilted the flying sprite looked at it quickly, nodding. Then he started to drag it toward the charging stations. Mallory called after him, "Caleb!"

"What!?" he snapped back at her.

Mallory smiled. "It will go faster if you use the Dikaió."

He growled and then raised his wrist to his mouth. Mallory could not make out what he said, but both flying sprites floated up off the ground and floated toward the charging stations. The cords at the station also floated up and plugged themselves into the sprite. Caleb's shoulders slumped. Mallory bit her lip and looked at him with concern. He needed to be doing something. She looked back at the building with its broken window. Inside were several shelves with small packages and cans lined on them. Through the light of the fires still raging near the chargers, she could make out some of the images on the packages and cans. There were pictures of pastries, pasta, crackers, and other food items she didn't recognize. Behind the shelves were what looked like four refrigerators that had small red lights on the top. She listened intently and could hear their motors humming.

She turned back to Caleb and hollered—this time without coughing. "Hey babe, there's food in here!"

He whipped around and started running her way, covering the space between them at superhuman speed. Mallory wondered if he had moved this fast at first whether the Archivist would have escaped at all. Caleb tried the door to the building, but it was locked. He grunted and pulled harder, putting all of his weight into prying the door open. Mallory rolled her eyes.

"Dikaió, open the door," she said smiling.

The door sprang open, and Caleb toppled backwards on the ground. He rolled around and pulled himself up onto all fours and snarled at her. Mallory's smile disappeared. His eyes were glazed over again, as if he were acting on pure animal instinct. Caleb jumped up off the ground and ran into the store, tearing open packages and dumping food into his mouth. Crackers, chips, powdered donuts, sausage sticks, cheese. He tore open the refrigerator doors, and lights inside them turned on. Mallory saw that the first one contained several gallons of milk. Caleb grabbed the nearest gallon and peeled its lid off. Within moments he drained the entire thing. Then he grabbed another. Mallory bit her lip and shook her head. She had seen him try to drink a gallon of milk before when they were younger: He had vomited. The Governor, Caleb's father, patiently explained that the human body cannot process that much cow's milk in one day. And yet, here Caleb was downing his third gallon of milk with no signs of slowing down. Maybe his nano sprites had removed the limits of a normal human?

The nano sprites were certainly doing some unexpected things to him physically. As her husband shoveled more and more into his mouth, his belly would begin to bulge. He would pause for a moment, and the bulge would vanish. Then Caleb would moan as if in pain, as another part of his body would swell, and then again diminish back to normal. Then more food went down his gullet. After what seemed an eternity of gluttonous abandon, his frenzy began to slow. He slowly began to drink his fourth gallon of milk, and then Caleb's face turned a funny shade of green.

Mallory tried to stand up and come to her husband's aid, but her ankle protested her movements. She would have never made it in time anyway. The air filled with the smell of sour cheese, and Mallory felt her stomach lurch. The weird Ex Natu meatloaf was acting like it was desperate to join the regurgitated milk on the floor. Mallory turned her head away and held her hand up to her nose to try and block out the smell.

Caleb spit and coughed. Then he looked at her and smiled with embarrassment. "Sorry, Mal. I was starving."

Mallory waved her hand dismissively and nodded without looking at him. "It's okay. It's okay." Mallory hesitated for a moment, and an awkward silence filled the air. Then Mallory bit her lip and tilted her head. She turned back to Caleb. "What exactly was happening to you while you were eating?"

Caleb shook his head. "It was like when I was chained up without food. I could feel my insides being pulled apart and put back together, but in a good way. I feel better than I have in long, long time." He paused and looked at her sadly. "I feel like myself, Mal. And I don't have to use all my strength to feel that way either. I'm just me again."

Mallory did not reply. She did not know what to say, but she did wonder why the Archivist did not act the same way as Caleb. Surely, she had been treated to the same starvation as he had. What was different between them? Was it just because he was a man, and she was a woman? Caleb definitely had more mass to feed.

Caleb put his hand behind his head and rubbed his hair awkwardly. "So, uh, do you want anything?" He pointed to the messy shelves.

Mallory looked at him with mock revulsion. "Uh … no!" She shook her head and shrugged. "Besides, I already ate."

Caleb's eyebrows crinkled. "You said you didn't have any food."

"I didn't … I don't, but I stopped and had dinner with a nice Ex Natu couple who let me charge up my flying sprite a little."

"A nice—an Ex Natu couple—dinner?" Caleb stammered in disbelief.

Mallory nodded and changed the subject. "We should check our flying sprites. They don't charge fast, but maybe they've charged enough to go after the Archivist. If our son takes after his father, he must be very hungry by now."

Caleb's face darkened. "Babies need to be fed every few

hours, Mal." He did not say anything more but rushed over to the flying sprites to check their progress. "Four bars!" he yelled across the expanse.

Mallory called back. "Let's wait until six, just to be sure, and then we'll go. I really don't think she could have gone far, but I don't want to get stuck in the woods with the wilding wolves."

Caleb glanced toward the trees, and Mallory saw the realization dawn on him. He looked down at the flying sprite's gauge and made hurry up circles with his hands. Mallory also looked out toward the trees, and as the fires around the charging station began to dwindle, she imagined she could see several pairs of glowing eyes looking back at her. She had nearly convinced herself she was imagining them when the howling began.

The sound was high-pitched and unnatural, and it sounded like it was coming from a long distance away, but it was growing louder—as if it was coming toward them at high speed. The eyes in the trees vanished. Mallory felt her stomach churn in worry. That was not the sound of the wilding wolves. It was the sound of sirens. "Caleb!" she screamed. "Caleb!" She again tried to get off the bench and managed to fall onto the ground. "Caleb!"

He rushed to her aid. "Mal, what is it?"

"Can't you hear them?" she clutched his leg and tried to pull herself up. "The Ex Natu are coming!"

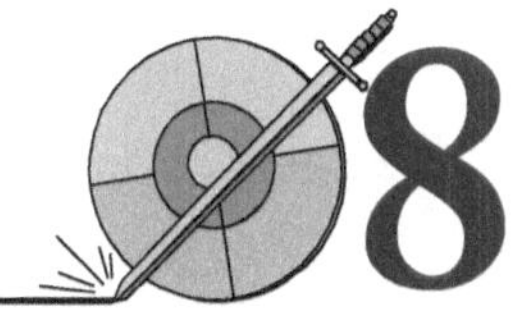

Caleb paused and listened to the air. The sirens were growing louder and nearer. He reached down with one arm, and without taking his eyes off the skies, lifted Mallory to her feet. She put her arm around his shoulders, and he helped her limp to the fire sprites. Caleb grabbed her by the waist and effortlessly lifted her onto one. He unplugged it. Mallory looked down at the charge bars and saw that that the fourth bar was flashing. She also saw that the flying sprite was quite scratched up. She looked over at the flying sprite still charging and saw that it had six bars charged and was in much nicer condition—almost like it hadn't been crashed into a shop window. "Hey, this one is yours," she waved at her seat.

Caleb did not notice. He climbed onto Mallory's

more-charged sprite and pulled up his wrist to his mouth. "Dikaió," he said. "Take us to the Archivist."

Nothing happened.

Caleb frowned.

Mallory rolled her eyes. "Which Archivist, Caleb? Remember?" Then she leaned forward and grabbed her handles. "Dikaió, unhook our chargers and take us to Emily Carpenter."

Caleb did not acknowledge her reprimand. Rather, he kept his eyes on the skies looking for the source of the sirens, but he did lean forward and grab his handles as the chargers began to uncouple themselves.

A voice shouted from behind them. "Hey, you can't leave! Who's going to pay for this? I called the police!"

Mallory looked over her shoulder and saw what appeared to be a middle-aged woman with a shaved head and shifting tattoos running toward them. She was wearing short, orange nylon shorts and a white tank top. Mallory wondered if she was the shopkeeper and felt bad for the damage they had caused. Mallory did not get anymore time to reflect on the shopkeeper's loss as her flying sprite shot into the air. Caleb was flying right beside her, shooting up into the night sky. When they cleared the tops of the trees, they nearly collided with two flying sprites sporting flashing red and blue lights with sirens blazing. Ex Natu riders clad in dark uniforms with badges were riding them, or at least trying to as they nearly fell off when Mallory and Caleb buzzed past them. Mallory noted that their uniforms looked very similar to the magistrates' uniforms in Hoffen City, and not at all like the

Ex Natu soldiers that had been with Omaha at the Library and the citadel. They were also wearing helmets with face shields. These must be what the Ex Natu shopkeeper referred to as "the police."

Mallory and Caleb's sprites kept moving forward at full speed aiming for the Archivist wherever she was, but Mallory could see from the red and blue flashing treetops below them that the Ex Natu police were in pursuit. The undulation of colors made her feel queasy, and her head hurt. She glanced behind her: the police's flying sprites were silhouetted by the bright flashes, but Mallory could tell that the pair's cycles were moving faster than hers. "Dikaió, go faster," she commanded, and the flying sprite shot forward at almost double the speed it had been moving. Mallory had to close her eyes and duck her head down because the wind felt like it was going to peel her skin clean off. Now she knew why the police behind them were wearing face shields.

Mallory tucked her head down and lowered her shoulder, so she could look behind without getting blasted by the air. The police were quite a ways back and so was Caleb. In fact, they were almost on top of him. Mallory could see her husband kicking at his flying sprite, trying to get it to go faster like a cowboy spurring a horse. "Use the Dikaió!" Mallory hissed.

Caleb did not, and one of the Ex Natu police managed to get up next to him. The Ex Natu pulled a hook with a spring-loaded clip off the police flying cycle and connected it to Caleb's handlebars. When the clip snapped shut, a spark jumped off of Caleb's flying sprite, and it began to fall. It only fell a few feet, and then dangled below the police sprite, as it was connected to a metal cord. Caleb's flying sprite was now dangling below the police sprite, being dragged underneath it just above the treetops. Caleb was waving his arms at Mallory and kicking at the lifeless sprite on which he was sitting.

The other Ex Natu police sprite had increased its own speed in pursuit of Mallory, though at best it had matched her current speed. Mallory looked down at her handlebars to check her power. The second bar was flashing rapidly. The flying sprite was draining a ton of energy at this speed. At this rate, she was not sure it would last until she reached the Archivist. For that matter, she was not sure that she could take back her son without Caleb there to help. Plus, she did not want to leave him with the Ex Natu, not after what they did to him. She sighed heavily and bit her lip.

Then she said, "Dikaió, stop!"

The flying sprite slammed on its brakes, and the Ex Natu police sprite chasing her flew past. Mallory yanked her backpack off, and slipped her arm through backwards, so that the pack was now in front of her. Then she grabbed the handlebars again. The Ex Natu flying sprite in front of her had stopped and was taking a short arc to come back her way; the one behind was approaching with Caleb in tow. Mallory unzipped the pocket with the Ex Natu weapon in it and pulled it out and aimed it toward Caleb. She really hoped this would work. "Dikaió, break the line holding Caleb's sprite," she said and pulled the trigger. Then she tucked the weapon back in her bag without looking at whether the shot had hit its mark. She just had to trust that it had. She nodded toward the Ex Natu flying sprite that was detaining Caleb. "Dikaió, take me above that Ex Natu rider, fast."

Mallory's flying sprite flew above the Ex Natu, faster than the rider had time to react. "Dikaió, dump the rider below me!" She yelled, while moving one leg over her own sprite, so that she was sitting side-saddle, hovering over an upside-down flying sprite that was shaking itself left to right. The Ex Natu rider was desperately hanging on to one of the handlebars, but the effort was useless, as the Dikaió shook the rider loose into the darkness of the trees below. "Dikaió, catch me," Mallory said and pushed herself off the flying sprite.

She fell faster than she expected, but the police sprite moved up under her, offsetting her speed just a little bit, so Mallory slid onto it like a feather touching the grass. Then she looked all around her, trying to spot Caleb and the other Ex Natu. She heard him before she saw him. Caleb started screaming.

Mallory looked in the direction of the scream, and she spotted Caleb on his flying sprite. The other Ex Natu police sprite that had been chasing her was next to his. The Ex Natu rider was trying to attach another hook to his handlebars, but Caleb had grabbed hold of it. Sparks shot from Caleb's hand, as he held the hook at bay.

"Dikaió, dump the other Ex Natu rider!" Mallory commanded.

The Ex Natu police sprite pitched left than right, and the rider let go of the hook, trying to regain a grasp on the sprite's handlebars. Then the police sprite rolled upside down and started jumping up and down. Mallory thought it looked a lot like how her father used a pepper shaker at the dinner table. "Why do they only put three holes in these things?" he would always yell. And in about the time it took her father to get a decent amount of pepper shaken loose from its container, the police sprite dislodged the second Ex Natu. Mallory's attention turned back to Caleb's sprite. It was empty.

"Caleb!" Mallory screamed. She moved her hips on the sprite and kicked her feet on it, trying to urge it to go, just like Caleb had when the police had him hooked, but nothing happened. She cursed herself and grunted. She realized that out here with the Ex Natu, she was as dependent on the Dikaió for survival as the people of Hoffen City had been her whole life. And right now when she needed to act fast, she hated having to take the time to formulate words and thoughts. "Dikaió, take me to those sprites," she grunted. "And turn off these stupid lights!" The flashing lights on the police sprite tuned off as it flew up to the other two flying sprites hovering riderless in the air in front of her.

As she got nearer, she heard a male voice calling from a distance. "Mallory! Mallory!"

It was Caleb. She looked around and could not see him anywhere.

"Down here!" The voice came again, followed by a scream: "Arrgghh!!!"

Mallory quickly looked over the edge of the police sprite and saw her husband dangling far below her just above the tops of the trees. He was hanging on to the hook of the police sprite, still attached by a long cord that was stretched taught.

Electric arcs were still spitting from the hook, shocking him in waves.

"Help me!" He managed before screaming again.

"Dikaió," Mallory ordered. "Stop shocking Caleb." The electric arc of the hook immediately ceased as did Caleb's yelling. Her husband's body slumped a little, and he looked like he was about to let go of the hook. "Dikaió, sprite catch Caleb, quickly," she.

Caleb's flying sprite swooped quickly down and slid under him just as he let go of the cord. He was sitting on it awkwardly though and was beginning to slide off. Mallory expected him to right himself, but he did not. His slide slowly continued. Mallory bounced on her sprite slightly, biting her lips. She did not know what to do. The Archivist was going to escape with her son, but her husband clearly needed more help than they had time to waste. She looked back up at the police sprite still hovering with its lights on, and an idea came to her. "Dikaió, make a bed with both the sprites for Caleb."

The other police sprite and Mallory's former flying sprite swooped down beside Caleb's sprite and caught him just as he was about to fall. The sprite he was riding dipped and shimmied to get both of his legs on it. Caleb's body flopped about like a marionette on a string while the three sprites tried to position him between them to fulfill the command to be a bed. Caleb head shot up, and his arms began to flail, and his legs kicked at the sprites. Pinocchio was alive. "Hey! Hey! What's going on?" he yelled in the darkness.

Mallory laughed at the group fighting each other. And for a moment, she forgot the seriousness of their quest. But the laughter made her full breasts ache and reminded her of baby Kirk. Her laughter ended. "Dikaió, take me up to Caleb." Her police sprite flew up to her husband. "Knock it off!" she ordered. "We've got to get moving; just sit down and let's go."

Caleb looked at her in desperation. "I'm trying, Mal. Every time I move, these stupid sprites try pull out from under me, so I fall back down."

Mallory shook her head. "Dikaió, stop being a bed." The sprites immediately stopped jostling Caleb around.

His eyebrows dipped, and he looked at her with irritation. "A bed?"

Mallory shrugged. "You were hurt. Electrocuted. How was I supposed to know you would wake up so easy?"

Caleb swung a leg over his flying sprite and huffed, "Let's go."

"Take the new one, Caleb," Mallory pointed to the police sprite.

He looked at the police sprite still floating between them with disdain. "I'd prefer not. That one hurts."

Mallory bit her lip and mused, "That electric hook might come in handy with the Archivist. Besides, it's got more charge than yours."

Caleb looked at the handlebars of the police sprite and sighed. He swung his far leg off his sprite and onto the police sprite, and then hopped over to it. Then he looked around it until he found the cord attached to the electric hook. It was attached to a handle and spool which he began to slowly wind, pulling it up from wherever it was dangling down in the darkness before them.

Mallory sighed. "Use the Dikaió, Caleb. We're in a hurry."

His blue eyes glimmered briefly in the darkness, and then he sighed again. "I forgot I could. Sorry." He pulled his wrist up toward his mouth and spoke into the Dominus bracelet. "Dikaió, wind up the hook, and take us to Emily Carpenter!"

If Mallory had not been holding the handlebars, she might have fallen off backwards, as her police sprite shot forward along with Caleb's. The spool on his sprite was winding fast of its own volition, and soon, the hook sputtered into place. But the motion must have triggered something on the sprite, as sparks started shooting out of the hook again. Caleb did not notice until he shifted his leg and brushed against it. His body convulsed, and Mallory saw Caleb shakily reach his wrist up toward his mouth, and though she could not hear what he said in the wind, the sparks stopped. Caleb's body convulsed a few times, and then leaned forward into the wind, as if nothing was wrong at all. Mallory shook her head, marveling at how the nano sprites had protected Caleb from electrocution. With the Dikaió, how could anyone stop him?

Her thoughts turned to Omaha, the creator of the Dikaió. Caleb had one of his Dominus bracelets. Alex had taken another from Reddy Lamarr before disappearing. Mallory could only hope she had made it safely back to Hoffen City. According to *The Chronicles of the Matriarch*, the third bracelet was out there in the world, unaccounted for somewhere. But what she knew for certain was that Omaha had the fourth one. He had taken it from the Archivist after defeating her at the Library. And if Omaha had a bracelet, there was no reason he could not use the Dikaió to track Caleb, and even the Archivist, in the same way she and Caleb were following her. All he would have to say was, "Dikaió, take me to Mallory Aiworth," and it would.

There really would not be much she and Caleb could do against him either. Neither of them had been effectively trained in the military aspects of the Dikaió. Omaha literally created the military aspects of the Dikaió; plus, he had an army at his disposal. Every success anyone had ever had against him so far had been because of the element of surprise. His greatest weakness seemed to be his hubris. He could not seem to imagine his plans failing or someone opposing him, and considering everything he had done over the centuries, Mallory worried that he was right and that eventually their luck would run out. A ball formed in her stomach as she began to regret not killing the man when she had the chance. At least that would have been one danger off the table.

But she was not a killer.

She wondered if that was something she would have to change. What if it came down to protecting her child or having to kill Omaha, or the Archivist, or anyone? Would she be able to save her son's life if that were the only choice? She shook her head. She did not want to be boxed into these sorts of absolutes even in her own mind. But the question would not go away. She came from a long line of warriors. Surely, there was a part of her soul that would aim the weapon in her bag at someone and pull the trigger: a black darkness somewhere deep in her soul.

The wind was cold, and Mallory shivered.

She had her backpack in front of her now, and there were some extra shirts in there. A double layer sounded very cozy. She unzipped the main pocket, and then hesitated, imagining how she would try to get another shirt on without falling off the police sprite. She was about to zip the bag back up when she noticed the paper and pen she had taken from the Ex Natu couple. She could not really see in the darkness, but she wondered if there was a way to start the process of writing the section of *The Chronicles of the Lost* that Reddy Lamarr had insisted would show the Archivist's betrayal, even while they were flying. She figured it would be smart to start a few pages behind so that she could get the full picture and not some incriminating blip taken out of context.

She pulled the lip of the bag up so it would block the wind, and spoke to the paper and pen. "Dikaió, copy *The Chronicles of the Lost*, starting on page ninety." The pen jumped up and began to etch onto the paper. Mallory squinted her eyes trying to see what it was writing, but it was just too dark. She held the bag up with one hand, so the pen could do its work. She kept her other hand tightly on one of the handlebars, not knowing when the sprite would unexpectedly start to land again. Every now and again the bag would shuffle in her lap as the Dikaió tucked a completed page to the side and started writing the next page.

Mallory's various aches and pains were all dull in her mind compared to the desperate desire to sleep. She looked ahead of her and saw Caleb sitting upright on the police sprite. He was scanning the trees and horizon, seemingly unfazed by tiredness even after battling the Archivist. She half wished she had nano sprites, so she wouldn't have to worry about falling if she fell asleep. The police sprites had a little bit wider seats with black leather satchels on the sides, but there was still no way she could fall asleep and not die with just this sprite. Her attention turned to the flying sprites they had taken from the Ex Natu citadel, which were trailing after Caleb sans riders. She wondered if the bed scenario would work for her so she could take a nap. "Dikaió, bring those flying sprites back there to me," she said.

The flying sprites slowed and began to float back to her, but they only made it halfway before the glow on one of the flying sprite's handlebars disappeared. The sprite fell out of the air into the darkness below. Mallory sat up straighter. Fear replaced her tiredness. She looked down at her dashboard, and it showed four bars. The flying sprite pulled up beside her. It had two bars, and she had no way of knowing if this was the one she had pushed to outrun the Ex Natu. She could only hope they were getting closer to wherever the Archivist was going to stop for power, and that she had less charge than they did. Either way, there was no way Mallory was going to fall asleep on these sprites even if they could form a bed—not when one of them was going to drop out of sky, taking her with it.

The bag in her lap shifted again as the Dikaió finished writing another page of *The Chronicles of the Lost*. It was probably just as well that Mallory did not fall asleep while the Dikaió was copying. Her hand holding the lip of the bag was getting tired, so she decided to stop the process and stretch. "Dikaió, pause copying." The pen laid down inside her bag.

It was impossible to know how many pages the Dikaió had written, as much as it was to know when she would ever get a chance to read them. Mallory sighed. She missed the Library. She missed Hoffen City. She missed her parents. She missed being warm and asleep.

She looked past Caleb toward the horizon expecting to see nothing but darkness and stars in the direction they were heading. But instead, she saw a faint white glow. They were flying toward another city.

The cityscape approached fast. Even from a distance in the dark, Mallory could make out the glum silhouettes of Ex Natu citadels. She tensed. Was the Archivist taking them back to the Davis City Metroplex? Maybe she knew that there was no other place to charge her flying sprite but back in the city? But as Mallory studied the cityscape, she noticed that it looked much smaller on the horizon than the Davis City Metroplex. This city looked to be roughly the size of her own Hoffen City. In fact, there might have only been twelve or fourteen citadels in the whole place. Mallory wondered if the city was made up of bootjack thugs like the ones she had encountered in Davis City, or if the people were more like those she knew in Hoffen City: normal people like the

Ex Natu couple that had accepted the nano sprites as a way to survive a serious illness. Of course, they were living in what looked like a normal house too. The citadels certainly suggested jackboots. She wondered if they were some kind of government buildings.

The police sprite below her dived suddenly. Mallory looked down in terror at her dashboard, expecting to see that she was out of power. There were two bars left. She looked in the direction the sprite was traveling expectantly. There was a small building with a lit-up portico in the distance, similar to the station where they had last encountered the Archivist. The charging station was surrounded by tall pines, sitting in a tiny clearing in a forest just outside the small city. The Archivist must be there, charging her flying sprite. Mallory sat up in her seat and looked toward Caleb. His police sprite was flying just above and to the left of her. He had seen the station and was leaning forward tensely. That was not good. Mallory did not want to spook the Archivist or have Caleb attack her. She wanted to get her son back alive and unharmed. "Dikaió, take me up beside Caleb," she said.

Mallory's police sprite sped up slightly and rose up and to the left until she was parallel with her husband. She shouted into the wind. "You go past her." Mallory waved her hand forward. "If she tries to run, use the hook to stop her sprite."

Caleb looked at her suspiciously and shouted back, "what are you going to do?"

Mallory looked toward the station and yelled, "I'm going to try and talk to her and get our son back."

"What if she attacks you, Mal?" Caleb shook his head.

"You could die."

Mallory shook her head pretending not to hear him and pointed ahead past the station. Then she said quietly, "Dikaió, take me down to Emily Carpenter, quietly." The roar of the police sprite cut out, and she began to fall toward the station, picking up speed as she descended. "Gently, Dikaió!" she gasped. "Gently!"

The nose of the sprite pulled up slightly, and her descent slowed a little, but she was still moving faster than Mallory wanted. Her heart was in her throat, as the ground shot up to meet her. Then a puff of air pushed her legs away from the sprite, and the sprite's momentum vanished. Mallory's momentum, on the other hand, kept going. Her head jerked forward, and her aching body slammed into the handlebars of the sprite. "Oof!" she exclaimed. She worried the fall had taken her breath away, so she inhaled sharply took a deep breath and found that she was able to breathe without any trouble: a small wonder considering how hard she had landed.

She looked up and saw the Archivist hurriedly disconnecting her flying sprite from the charger. The older woman was still holding baby Kirk. Mallory was close enough to hear her son weakly mewing. "Emily!" Mallory cried matching her son's weakness. "Please!"

The Archivist froze and looked up at Mallory. Her face was twisted in fear, which slowly dissolved into confusion. "I saw you die," she shouted.

Mallory reached out. "My son, please!"

The Archivist's confusion began to shift back to fear. "This is a dream, or I'm going crazy." She shook her head. "Maybe you're haunting me?"

Mallory shook her head too. "No, no! I'm alive!" She swung her leg over the police sprite and dismounted. However, she had not realized the sprite was hovering on its cushion of air about two feet in the air, nor did she remember that one of her ankles was injured. Mallory hit the ground on her feet, felt her ankle roll under her weight, and collapsed in screaming pain. She tried to force herself to concentrate on the Archivist and her baby, but the nerve endings in her ankle would not be ignored, sending white hot pain signals into her brain, all but blinding her to anything else around her.

Mallory didn't know how long she laid there in agony, but suddenly she was aware of something small and warm on her chest. Tiny, desperate movements grabbing at her clothing made Mallory open her eyes. Kirk was there. His eyes were closed, and his mouth made suckling motions as he rooted around on his mother. The backpack that she had turned around was in the way. Mallory tried to sit up to take it off, but the searing pain pushed her back down. She screamed.

Kirk startled and screamed too.

"Be careful, little Matriarch," the Archivist's voice was tender. She knelt beside Mallory. "I'll help you. Here," she shoved one hand under Mallory's back and put the other under Mallory's armpit. "Let's get you sat up." Mallory pulled with her exhausted core muscles to try and sit up, but the heavy lifting was mostly the Archivist. Once Mallory was sitting, the Archivist helped her get the backpack off and get Kirk situated and feeding. The Archivist shook her head. "If I had known you survived the fall …". She didn't finish the sentence. Her sad eyes stared down at the ground, not wanting to meet Mallory's.

Mallory repositioned Kirk. "You wouldn't have tried to blow up my husband? You wouldn't have contacted Zane and offered my baby to him?"

The Archivist fell back like she had been slapped. "How could you know that? How could you know any of that?"

"Caleb brought me to the room under the city. The one with the little screens," Mallory looked away from her. "I almost died."

The Archivist looked bewildered.

"And you've offered up my child multiple times," Mallory snapped. "First to Omaha! Then to Zane! Why? Why do all these people want him? What is happening, Emily?"

"It's complicated, Mallory," the Archivist sighed. "That baby will determine the future of the world."

Mallory clutched her suckling child closer. "That's what Omaha said too. Why? Tell me why!"

Suddenly, a roar sounded from behind the Archivist and both women's head snapped toward it. Caleb's police sprite swooped into the station, and Caleb screamed, "Get away from them! Don't touch them!" He pushed hard with his feet and jumped several feet in the air off the sprite. The sprite spun out of control toward the women nearly taking their heads off. Caleb landed on the ground in a run, heading toward the Archivist. "I'll kill you this time!"

"Caleb, no!" Mallory yelled. "You can't!"

The Archivist used her powerful legs to spring out of her crouch in a back flip several feet away from Caleb. She landed standing; her legs spread wide for stability, and her arms cocked close to her sides at right angles. Caleb ran past where she had just been standing, and his arms windmilled as he tried to stop his momentum. His legs slid out from under him, and he fell, but he twisted as fell, landing on all fours. His head quickly pivoted toward the Archivist, spittle flying from his mouth. Mallory was horrified. The Archivist's eyes were fixed on the raging man, but her face was devoid of any emotion. She waited for him to make the next move: Apparently, she was done running. Caleb roared in rage and flew off the ground. His hands were curled, not in fists but in claws, as he swiped at the Archivist. The old woman moved deftly and quickly, parrying each swing. When openings presented themselves, she would quickly jab at Caleb with hard punches, but they seemed to barely register. At one point, she punched him squarely in the nose. Caleb did not blink even as blood spurted wildly from his nostrils. He clawed at the Archivist again.

Mallory held baby Kirk close. Her body tensed as the battle raged, the suckling child had at least helped ease some of her pain. But it had also left her incredibly thirsty and hungry. She regretted not having joined Caleb in getting some food and water at the last market, at least pack it in her bag as rations. She looked toward the building standing by the charging stations and wondered if there was any food inside this one. Mallory clutched Kirk tightly and tried to push herself up. Her ankle throbbed, and she slumped back to the ground. She looked up at the police sprite still hovering a couple of feet above her. "Dikaió, come here and help me up," she said, and the police sprite slowly descended to her. It tipped itself at an angle, so she could get a good grip on it. Mallory dragged herself up slowly, trying not to jostle her baby. She stood on her good leg and put her other knee on the seat of the police bike. She shifted left and right, and it seemed like the hovering police sprite would make a decent substitute for a crutch. She looked back toward Caleb and the Archivist trading blows and figured the two of them really could not do much damage to each other, at least not enough that their nano sprites would not heal them. They could probably fight forever and never get seriously injured or die. She and baby Kirk would starve to death long before they were finished. It was better to go check for food than wait for that to happen.

Mallory turned away from the battle and said, "Dikaió, walk with me." Her gate was unsteady, and she could tell that the muscles in her good leg were going to get tired quickly, but it was just a short jot over to the building.

There was a large window in the building that was tinted black. She held her baby to the side and leaned over the police sprite to press her nose up against the glass. Kirk snorted at being pulled away from his mother even for a moment, but he did not cry. Instead, he yawned and blinked at the lights of the portico above the charging station. Those lights' reflection made it difficult for Mallory to see into the building, even with her nose pressed up against the glass. All she could see in the window was her reflection and the wondering face of her son looking at the lights. Mallory pulled away from the window and looked around for a door. There was not one on that side of the building, so she hobbled farther along the wall of windows. She paused before turning the corner and looked back to check on Caleb and the Archivist. The Archivist leapt off the ground and wrapped one leg around Caleb's neck, then threw her body hard backward in a swivel, flipping the man and smashing him hard, head-first into the trunk of a pine tree. Caleb bounced off the pine and fell to the ground. The Archivist quickly somersaulted away from him and stood to her feet.

Mallory's eyebrows arched up. She had not expected the fight to end so quickly. She shrugged. The Archivist had been trained to fight her whole life, probably by General Knenne and Mari Nelson themselves before the plasma shield had locked her and her husband out of Hoffen City. It made sense that she would be a better fighter than Caleb. But, and Mallory smiled at this thought, Caleb had a much thicker skull than the Archivist. Surely a little thing like bonking his head on a tree would not keep him down for long. And just like that, Caleb sat up. He shook his head wildly, and then just sat there for a moment as if he did not remember exactly what activity he had been engaged in before bonking his head. But then he remembered, and his head pivoted quickly toward the Archivist just as she was delivering a roundhouse kick to his cheek, sending him back into the dirt.

Mallory sighed and hobbled around the corner to look for the door.

Her screams echoed off the trees and the station, startling baby Kirk who also began to wail. Around the corner, there were three wilding wolves waiting for her. They hesitated in attacking just long enough for Mallory to drag the hovering police sprite between them. Two sank their teeth into hard sprite steel, but one of them tore into Mallory's kneecap. She tried to pull away, but the wilding wolf's jaw muscles clenched shut. It began to shake its head back and forth. Mallory felt bone crack and muscles tear. The movement made her lose her balance, and she fell hard. She twisted her body on the way down to keep her baby safe and landed awkwardly on her elbows and her other leg. There was probably pain in those places, but nothing could overcome the raging fire of the wilding wolf's teeth sawing through her kneecap.

A blur flew over her, and suddenly, the wolf's grip let go in a yipping howl. The Archivist flipped back over the police sprite and grabbed it by one of the handlebars and the seat. She wielded it like a club, bringing it down hard on one of the wilding wolves' heads. But another wolf circled around behind them, and Mallory felt its hot breath on her neck just before it flew into the air away from her. She looked back and saw her husband toss the beast away with superhuman strength. The wolf bounced across the pavement of the charging station, lay for a moment, then slowly rose and shook its head. Then it focused back in on Mallory and Kirk, crouched low, and growled.

Mallory heard rustling to their right and looked wildly toward the trees. More wilding wolves poked their noses through the brush, sniffing the wind. Mallory did not have time to count how many there were before Caleb knelt over Mallory and baby Kirk and drew them up to his chest, holding them tightly. He covered them like a shield. The wolves would have to get through his nigh immortal body to get to his family. Mallory shook her head. He might have been nigh immortal, but the wolves would eventually kill him, and then her and baby Kirk. She knew she should use the Dikaió to protect them, but Caleb's weight was crushing the breath out of her, and the pain in her leg made it hard to find the words. She wondered where the Archivist was. Had the wolves taken her down too?

There was not time to answer that question before the wolves were upon them. They growled and snipped at Caleb, but he did not move. Soon the growls calmed, and the wolves began to sniff Mallory's husband. And rather than tearing him to shreds in front of her, they began to circle the couple and their baby, until finally sitting down around them and panting. Caleb's grip softened, and he sat up, taking his weight off Mallory. Mallory lifted her head and looked around at the circle of wilding wolves. She could not help but remember what had happened earlier with Reddy Lamarr and her wolf skins. The wilding wolves had accepted them as their own.

But why?

Caleb leaned back on his haunches. "What is going on?"

As soon as he pulled away from Mallory and baby Caleb, one of the wilding wolves shot forward and snapped at them. Caleb's reflexes were too fast, and his hand shot forward in a claw, tearing four gashes in the wilding wolf's face. It rolled across the ground, whimpering. The wolf lay there for a moment, looking at Caleb as if it had been betrayed. The gashes healed quickly, and the animal slowly and sullenly rejoined the circle. None of the others made any move toward Mallory and Kirk again. Mallory just stared at the wilding wolves: perplexed. She had no explanation for their behavior.

The Archivist called from somewhere above them, "Caleb, bring Mallory and the baby up to me. They're not safe there."

Mallory's eyes shot up, and she saw the Archivist leaning over the roof of the building waving her arm toward them. Caleb sniffed and called back, "You must be mad to think I would ever entrust them to you again."

"Caleb, please!" The Archivist pleaded. "They'll only be docile until they realize you don't intend to share your dinner with them."

Mallory whispered to Caleb. "What does she mean?"

Caleb shook his head. "I have no idea."

One of the wolves stood and walked toward the family. It nudged Caleb's shoulder toward Mallory and the baby and made a whining noise.

The Archivist called down again. "They're giving you deference as Alpha for the kill and first bite, but they'll kill you, too, if you don't share."

"Alpha?" Mallory worried, holding her baby tighter. "Maybe it would be better to be up higher where they can't get Kirk, Caleb."

Caleb growled low in his throat and pushed away the wolf, nudging him. The wolf snapped back lightly with its teeth at Caleb's hand, and Caleb clawed it viciously, sending it sprawling. The pack shifted nervously, and Mallory touched Caleb's chest tenderly. "Please, Caleb!"

Caleb's eyes rolled in his skull, and then refocused when they came to rest on Mallory and his son. "C'mon then," he smiled and gathered them in his arms, crouching low.

The wolves stood expectantly, and then howled in irritation when Caleb scooped up Mallory and the baby and leapt high into the air. Mallory wondered if he would be able to make it all the way to the top of the building, but they soared several feet higher than the roof, and Caleb landed with ease to set them down gently.

Mallory's knee burned in agony, and she laid down on the ground whimpering, holding her baby tightly to her bosom.

Caleb touched her cheek tenderly, but then stood and spun on the Archivist. He growled low. "How do you know what they want?" He pointed to the wolves. "What did you do to me?"

The Archivist looked down at her feet and shook her head. "This is hardly the time to have that conversation." She pointed to the city lights over the trees. "We're just on the outskirts of Abilene. Those wilding wolves gathering below are going to draw an Ex Natu extermination squad to clear them out, and then we'll be discovered. We need to leave now."

Caleb shrugged. "I'd sooner face an army of Ex Natu then follow you anywhere, Archivist. You betrayed us at the Library! You stole my son!"

The Archivist threw up her hands and yelled back. "I tried to save your son! I thought she was dead." She pointed down at Mallory, and then hesitated. "And if we don't get her help soon, she will be. Look at her leg, Caleb."

Caleb looked down at Mallory, and she looked at him pleadingly. The pain was unbearable, and she did not want to go anywhere, but she knew the Archivist was right. She needed medical attention. She could feel her life slowly oozing out through the wounds in her leg, she was going to die very soon if something did not change. "Caleb," she whispered weakly. "We need her help."

He roared in frustration. "And where would you take us, Archivist. Another trap?"

The Archivist looked down again. "Yes."

Caleb laughed and waved his hands at her in an I-told-you-so manner so Mallory could see. "And she admits it so readily."

The Archivist nodded. "For you and I, Caleb. It will be a trap. The Ex Natu are not welcome there—even those of us who came by our nano sprites against our will—but they can help Mallory."

Mallory groaned. "And our son?"

The Archivist sighed heavily. "It's a trap for him as well."

"What does that mean?" Caleb roared again.

The wolves below howled in response. Mallory could not help but imagine that there were many more voices down there than when they made it to the top of the roof.

The Archivist shook her head. "What do you want me to say?" I betrayed you, young Governor—your wife—your son—our people—the Ex Natu—God Himself." She waved her hand in a circle above her head. "I've betrayed you all. Are you happy?"

"I have no idea what you're talking about!" Caleb yelled

back.

Mallory wheezed heavily and felt her strength wane. She fell back on the ground and gasped. Caleb dropped quickly to her side. "Mal!" Without any effort, he pulled her whole body into his lap. "Mal!"

The Archivist shifted her weight. "They can help her, Caleb."

He looked up at her. "That's what Omaha said and look where that got us."

The Archivist snarled back at him. "Don't you dare compare me to that monster."

Caleb bared his teeth at her, but then he turned his face back to his wife and his expression softened. He closed his eyes. "I don't know what's wrong with me. There's this hunger inside of me that just won't go away. I feel like I'm losing myself." He again looked up at the Archivist, and there were tears flowing down his cheeks. "She's the only thing keeping me tethered to who I am. If I lose her," he paused and looked uncertain. "I don't know what I'll become."

The Archivist again looked down. "I need the bracelet, Caleb."

His eyes narrowed.

"If you let me use the Dikaió, I can get us all out of here." She opened her hands palm side up. "I know it's asking a lot after everything you've been through because of me, but I promise I will help you. I will help Mallory."

Mallory's focus was waning, but a warning screamed in her mind. She wanted to tell her husband not to do it—tell him to keep the Dominus bracelet and just have the Archivist tell him what to say. They needed her help, yes, but they still could not trust her. She wished that she had her backpack with the pages from *The Chronicles of the Lost*, so she could read them and know why it was they should not trust her—what it was that Reddy Lamarr had tried to warn them about—but her backpack was somewhere below. Still, she did not think that giving up the Dominus bracelet was the right thing to do. She opened her mouth to voice her concerns to Caleb, but the loss of blood made it all come out as unintelligible moans.

Mallory watched in horror as Caleb pulled the bracelet off his wrist. He weighed it in his hand as if trying to will it to tell him if this was a wise decision or not. The inanimate object had nothing to say on the matter, and Caleb rolled it across the rooftop to the Archivist, who eagerly scooped up the bracelet and slipped it on her arm. She smiled briefly, but then looked down at Mallory and became somber again. The Archivist raised the Dominus bracelet to her lips and said something unintelligible into it.

Mallory heard howling screams come from below them as whatever the Archivist had ordered slaughtered the wilding wolves. When the sounds quieted down, the Archivist walked to the edge of the rooftop and looked over. Whatever she saw down there seemed to satisfy her, and she again lifted the Dominus bracelet to her lips. Then she sat down and crossed her legs.

"What are you doing?" Caleb screamed at her.

"We'll never make it on empty batteries, young Governor. I'm having the Dikaió charge the sprites," the Archivist said matter-of-factly.

"I could have done that," Caleb growled.

"Clearly, you couldn't," the Archivist snapped back. "You said it yourself; you're not thinking clearly."

"But Mallory needs help, now!" Caleb was getting more upset.

Mallory weakly reached up and touched his chest. "Caleb," she whispered.

He looked down at her expectantly, but she had no energy to say anymore. She just wanted him to calm down and stay with her. If it were her time to enter the life after life, she wanted to be with him. She wished he had not given up the Dominus bracelet, but the Archivist had not immediately abandoned them, and the old woman was the baby's only hope if Mallory died. Fighting her anymore would just cause more trouble for their family.

Caleb seemed to understand and sighed heavily.

Mallory did not know how long they sat the on the rooftop in silence. She was exhausted and cold despite her jacket, the warm spot of baby Kirk snuggled up against her, and the raging heat of Caleb surrounding her. The shivering was barely noticeable at first, but then her teeth began to chatter inside her mouth. Mallory knew little about blood loss, but she wondered if she was going into shock. The more she shivered, the more Caleb's face sank into worry. His arms pulled her closer and closer to his chest, as if he were trying to pull his dying wife inside himself.

"She's getting worse," Caleb pleaded with the Archivist. "We have to do something, now!"

The Archivist uncrossed her legs and walked over to them. She reached down and pulled one of Mallory's eyelids open, checking her pupils. Mallory did not like it and tried to shake the Archivist off, but her body was using all its strength to shiver violently. The Archivist grimaced and moved down to Mallory's bleeding knee. The old woman grabbed her shirt and tore a large piece of fabric off of it to use as a bandage or tourniquet. It was filthy from months of imprisonment with the Ex Natu, and Mallory's mother's voice screamed of infection inside Mallory's head. She forced herself to move and shook her head. "Infection. Not Ex Natu," she managed to stammer.

The Archivist paused and looked again at the filthy rag in her hand and dropped it. She looked around the roof and at Caleb and Mallory, who were equally filthy, though Mallory's clothes were cleaner.

"Where did you get these clothes?" The Archivist asked.

Mallory whispered, "backpack."

The Archivist again walked to the side of the rooftop and surveyed the ground. Then she jumped off the roof. She was gone for only a few seconds before she clambered back to the top of the building. She was wearing Mallory's backpack. She quickly pulled it off and unzipped the top. Her eyes widened. Mallory winced. She had forgotten the pen and paper inside of it and the copy of *The Chronicles of the Lost*. It was still dark out, and she hoped the Archivist would not be able to make out what was being written on the pages.

The Archivist pulled out the pages. She held them close, and her wide eyes narrowed. Then the older woman dropped the pages on the rooftop. She turned her attention back to the bag and burrowed deeper inside. She pulled out a gray shirt and quickly began tearing it into strips, which she tied together. She pulled her wrist to her mouth, and glass shattered below them somewhere. A broom floated up over the side of the roof, and the Archivist broke off the bristles. Then the Archivist turned her attention to Mallory's leg.

Mallory couldn't see what was happening, but she felt it. Just above her knee, the Archivist wrapped her leg with the strips of cloth, and she tied the ends of the makeshift bandage to the broom shaft, which she began to twist around like a fan blade, tightening a tourniquet around Mallory's leg. The pain was agonizing, but Mallory knew it would keep her from bleeding out, and it might save her life. But she also knew the clock was ticking. If the tourniquet stayed on too long, she could lose her leg. The tourniquet had not stopped the shock though; she was still shivering violently.

"We need to get moving," the Archivist said. "She's going to have to ride with you. Can you manage?"

Caleb nodded. "I can manage."

The Archivist nodded as well. "I'll carry the baby."

Caleb shook his head. "I can manage."

The Archivist's brow lowered as if she were about to argue with him, and then she nodded acquiescence. She raised the Dominus bracelet to her lips and began to speak softly.

Suddenly, they were surrounded by bright, white lights. Heavy winds seem to blow at them out of the lights. Mallory closed her eyes tightly, not wanting to know what was happening. She pressed her face into Caleb's chest, and her shivering intensified in the cold wind of the white lights. Had the Ex Natu caught up with them? Was it Reddy Lamarr, Zane, or some other, new villain?

Mallory did not care.

She was too tired to care. So, so tired.

And then the lights, the wind, the Archivist, Caleb, and even baby Kirk disappeared.

All was blackness.

10

Mallory tried to roll over, but no matter how she lay, she could not get comfortable. Someone must have turned down the Dikaió climate control in the house, and of course by "someone" she meant her father. He was the only one in the Knenne household who ran hot; The women of the house were colder much more often than they were hot. She grimaced and shivered. Mallory was too tired to even open her eyes much less go adjust the thermostat. Besides, her father was never happy when she messed with the temperature. She had been down that road with him before, too many times to count, and she knew exactly what would happen. "You're cold?" he would ask. "Go stand in a corner." She had only asked "why" once. "Because it's ninety degrees," he had laughed then shooed her away to go find a sweater. Mallory's mother, on the other hand, could get him to acquiesce when it came to the thermostat.

She would hold up her blue hands in supplication and say, "Roger, I'm turning into a blueberry."

Her father would take her mother's hands and rub them to get the circulation flowing again. "I'm sorry, my love. Let's get you warmed up." Then he would don a pair of short pants and a tank top and spend the rest of the day sprawled on the sofa under a Dikaió fan.

In addition to it being unbearably cold in the house, it felt like her father had moved the Dikaió fan into her room tonight. Mallory shivered harder and moaned. Surely, her mother would say something soon. She reached down for her blanket and found it missing. She must have kicked it off in the night. "Mother," she called weakly. "Mother, I'm so cold."

A man's voice answered in the darkness as if coming from out of a long, tunnel. "I know Mal, I know. We're going to get you help."

Mallory knew that voice, and it gave her some comfort. She tried to open her eyes to see who it was, but she was too tired to manage it. Sleep pulled her past the discomfort of the cold for a time, though it was anything but restful. Her dreams were plagued with shifting images, like a living Ex Natu tattoo. Omaha was there, patting her hand in the dirty hospital bed while touching her belly fondly. Ex Natu soldiers chased her through tight hallways. She was falling. Drooling wilding wolves sat around a dining room table, where she lay in a silver bowl filled with ice. At one side of the table sat

Reddy Lamarr dressed in wilding furs. She was repeatedly sliding a carving knife down a honing steel. "Shing! Shing! Shing!" it sang. At the other end of the table sat Caleb, holding a steak knife and a fork. His mouth was full of wolf teeth, and his eyes were hungrily staring at her. "He needs to eat," laughed Reddy Lamarr and lunged across the table at her with the knife.

A small warmth splayed across her chest, and she screamed and squirmed violently.

"Mallory!" the man's voice in the darkness commanded. "Be careful."

Mallory's eyes fluttered open into blurry slits.

Caleb was kneeling beside her, holding baby Kirk just out of her reach. His face was both concerned and irritated.

"He needs to eat," the Archivist repeated. "Hold her down if you have to."

"No," Mallory said weakly. "I can … I'm okay."

Caleb again pressed baby Kirk to her chest, but Mallory had no strength to help with the feeding. She just lay there barely conscious while the baby sucked away more of her energy. There were lights overhead, just like the last two charging stations they had stopped at, but they were all turned off. It was broad daylight, and this time, the only one fighting was Mallory. It was a fight she could feel herself losing. She thought back to the Library when she was being carried away on a stretcher by Ex Natu. There was a moment when she felt like it would have been easy to step out of her body, like the door to the life after life was open, and if she just pushed a little, it would swing wide and let her in.

She was standing at that door again. And once again, all she could think about was her baby. If she were to take that step, Kirk might die. There was no guarantee that Zane and whatever group the Archivist was leading them to would be able to keep him alive. There was no guarantee that was what they intended to do. Who else would fight for a child if his mother would not? But those thoughts were short lived, as Kirk's feeding took its toll, and once again Mallory fell into darkness.

The stops for Kirk were frequent, but Mallory's sense of reality was so blurred that she could not separate them into individual events or tell whether days or hours were passing between them. Some of the stops included bits of food and water that her stomach kept sending back to the kitchen. And her chefs were growing more concerned with every rejected meal.

"I don't know if she's going to make it," the Archivist worried.

"For your sake, she better," threatened Caleb.

The Archivist shook her head. "And then what? You'll feed the baby?"

Caleb growled in his throat. "If I must!" but the old woman's point was made. He needed the Archivist. His wife and son both needed her, and he softened. "I'm sorry. I'm just worried; I don't know what I'm saying."

The Archivist sighed. "She's strong. Fighting runs in her family. If anyone can beat the odds, it's your wife."

Mallory felt those last words pulse through her like a medicine. Death's door might be unlocked; it might even be open, but even though she was balancing on its threshold, someone would have to drag her through it. She would not be making that step of her own volition. Her senses seemed to return with her determination, and then she gasped with a horrible awareness of intense burning pain in her leg. She gritted her teeth and tried to move it, but every attempt was met with horrible shockwaves of pins and needles. The tourniquet was still on, and she was not sure how long it had been there. She might be prepared to beat death, but she was not sure her leg would make the same commitment. She decided not to think about it. She wanted to try eating again. She decided she would keep it down this time because she would need her strength to win this fight.

"Caleb," she whispered.

He was beside her in an instant. "Mal?"

"I love you," she continued even softer.

He leaned in closer to her. His hands hovered over her, opening and closing, as if he was afraid to touch her, but also wanting to pull her to himself and hold her tightly. "Oh, Mal. Don't go!" Deep sobs wracked his body. "Please, don't leave me!"

Mallory was touched by his fear that she was saying goodbye. She smiled weakly up at him. "Can't leave. Wolf ate my leg."

Caleb rocked backward. His sobs mixed with laughs. His arms crossed, and he grabbed his shoulders. And he looked at her nervously. "Ha. Ha. Sniff. Jokes? Does this mean you're better?"

Mal moved a hand toward him, and he took it in his,

quickly kissing it. Her head flopped limply backwards, and she wheezed. "No." She jutted her chin toward the Archivist. "But I'll fight. Give me more food."

The Archivist laughed. "I knew you were the right stuff the moment I laid eyes on you, little Matriarch. You'll do your ancestors proud." She paused, and her mirth faded. "The sprites are almost charged. Give her a little more, but not too much. We need to go."

Caleb nodded and pulled a small bag out of his pocket. He dipped his fingers in and pulled out some bits of dried fruit. He gently put it in Mallory's mouth, and she chewed dutifully. Her stomach roiled, threatening to send the fruit back up, but Mallory furrowed her eyebrows and forced herself to keep it down. How long could one bite take to digest anyway?

Apparently, the answer to that question was a really, really long time.

She dangled uncomfortably in Caleb's large arms as they few high above lands Mallory could have never imagined. There were snow covered hills bigger than any skyscrapers, vast plains without an inch of green, and craters that could have fit a thousand Mason City gorges. The world was infinitely larger than Mallory would have ever imagined, and she wished she could feel some awe or joy in seeing it all, but Mallory found that she could think of nothing else other than the dried fruit trying desperately to claw its way out of her stomach. "You're going to stay down," she told the fruit in her mind.

The fruit laughed at her and replied, "you, can't make me!"

The battle against the nausea-inducing bite took on symbolic meaning in her mind. Her determination to fight through her pain, suffering, and weakness was transferred to keeping the fruit in her stomach, and somehow that seemed to keep her mind off those other ailments, at least until the flying sprite hit some turbulence and bucked wildly. Then the fruit made a break for it, all over Caleb's shirt. Well, not all over. It was only a bit of spittle, and a lot of dry heaving. Caleb looked into her face and grimaced. She smiled weakly back, and then dry heaved some more. When her stomach stopped spasming, her nausea was replaced with vertigo, and her head swooned. She pressed her eyes closed, gritted her teeth, and prayed the feeling would pass.

It did not.

Hours of misery went by, but never once did she lose her resolve to live. Then she felt the sprite begin to lose altitude. It must be time for baby Kirk to eat again. Mallory wondered how long she could go without eating and drinking before her milk dried up. She tried to open her eyes, but the world swam around her, as the vertigo returned. She felt as if she was again teetering in death's doorway. "No!" she screamed inside her own head. "I am going to live."

She could feel herself being moved, and she braced herself for the spot of warmth, the urgent pull of her child, but it did not come. Instead, there were whispered voices: voices she did not recognize.

"You said you were bringing the child. Who are these two?" a whisper asked urgently.

"His parents," the Archivist answered.

"You brought an Ex Natu here?" the whisper's agitation grew.

"He's not an Ex Natu any more than I am, and you know it, Zane," the Archivist shot back.

"You're as Ex Natu as they come, Emily. It was a mistake dealing with the devil," Zane asserted.

"The mother's dying, Zane. She needs medical attention fast," the Archivist urged.

"We don't need her or the father, or even you," Zane said.

Caleb spoke then. "Please, help my wife. You don't have to take me. Just help her."

There was a long pause, and then Zane relented and whispered to someone else. "Okay. Get them on the ship. Put that one in the medical bay. Hurry up! We need to be out to sea before the dock regulators come looking for our port codes."

Ship? Sea? Those were new words for Mallory, and she wanted to know what they meant, but whenever she tried to open her eyes to look, waves of sickness rushed over her. She felt herself once more being lifted and strapped to a gurney of some sort. She was roughly carried and transferred to a bed.

An unfamiliar woman's voice spoke to her in comforting sing-song tones. "Don't you worry, love. I'm going to give you a draught to help you sleep, and then we'll see if we can't get you patched up and feeling better." Mallory felt a prick in her arm and in a few moments the nausea, the pain, the fight all faded away, and she fell into a dreamless sleep.

Mallory woke up in a well-lighted room with huge windows and rich, wood paneling. There were IVs attached to her right and left arms. One IV tube was colored dark red and ran through one side of a large gray sprite, thumping like a mechanical heart. The other was lighter red and ran up to a red-tinged bag of fluid hanging on a pole. Her knee and ankle were bandaged with white cloths that tickled horribly. She started to sit upright, and a hand reached out and touched her shoulder.

"Calm down, Mallory. It's okay." It was the Archivist sitting in a chair next her. "Just let the nano sprites do their work.

Mallory felt her heart stop for a moment. "Nano sprites!" She screamed. "I don't want them." She reached for the tubing to rip it out of her arms.

The Archivist grabbed her arms to stop her, and her strong grip was like a vice. Mallory struggled hard. The Archivist hissed, "Stop it! It's not that kind of nano sprites, Mallory. You're not turning into an Ex Natu."

Mallory stopped struggling and looked at the Archivist with distrust. She fully intended on ripping the tubing out as soon as she let go of her hands, but she decided to play along to get the Archivist to let down her guard. "What do you mean?"

One of the Archivist's eyebrows went up, and she kept her iron-like grip on Mallory's arms. "The Ex Natu didn't create medical nano sprites, Mallory. They just turned them into something horrible." She nodded toward Mallory's leg. "Your leg was horribly infected. You were going septic. These medical nano sprites are clearing out the infection and repairing the damage to your leg. It will be as good as new in a couple of hours, and then they'll be removed." She looked at the pumping machine. "That thing's already filtering out the ones carrying the infection."

Mallory relaxed. "So, there won't be any left?"

The Archivist shrugged and let go of her hands. "They're tiny molecules. There might be some leftover that your body will destroy and absorb, but they certainly won't make you immortal."

"So, you and Caleb can get your nano sprites removed and be normal again?" Mallory asked hopefully, laying back in the bed.

The Archivist sighed and sat back in her chair. "It's been tried. They reproduce themselves faster than the filter can keep up. The Ex Natu designed them so the process would be irreversible."

Mallory sighed and looked around the room. She froze when she looked out the window. There were tall slender trees with what looked like fans for leaves on top. Beyond the trees, water sparkled in the sunlight, but it was not like any water she had ever seen before. She had thought the lake they passed was big, but there was literally no end to the water beyond the trees. It went all the way to the horizon.

"Where are we?" she whispered.

"The East Asian Islands," the Archivist sighed heavily. "It's the only place I knew to go where they could keep a baby alive."

Mallory turned to the older woman and marveled. She had so many questions to ask that they all seemed to get stuck in the doorframe of her mind, and she just lay there with her jaw slack, but one question pressed through all the rest. "Where's my son?"

The Archivist nodded. "He's safe, and as soon as you're completely well, and nano sprite free, you'll be reunited with him. The Ex Natu sprites don't play well with regular nano sprites."

Mallory's head tilted to the side. "What does that mean?"

The Archivist sighed again and reached down to the floor beside her chair. She pulled up a sheaf of papers and flipped through them as if skimming what was written there. "You know," she began, "even the Dikaió can't make a clean copy when you're jostling about on a flying sprite, fighting Ex Natu, and being eaten by wolves." She handed one of the pages to Mallory.

Mallory held the page in her hand and sighed. It was a page from *The Chronicles of the Lost* that she had been trying to copy inside her backpack. There were a few legible words, but most of the copy was full of blots and scratches where the pen and ink and been tossed about during the trip. It was disappointing but did not answer her question. "What does this have to do with my son?"

The Archivist pulled the page out of her hand. "Everything. And after all you've been through thanks to me, you deserve to hear the story written in these pages." She dropped the pages back on the floor." So, I've had the Dikaió write up a clean copy." The Archivist reached down to the other side of the chair and picked up a small book, opened it, and flipped through it, until she found what she was looking for. "Page ninety-six is where that red-headed pest wanted you to start, and it's as good a place as any. So, lay back and relax, and I'll tell you why you're here."

And with that the Archivist cleared her throat and began to read:

The Chronicles of the Lost

Solitude is one of those feelings we were never meant to get used to.

… I don't know how long ago I wrote that line in this journal. It has certainly been a long time. At the time, I thought that maybe if I just wrote the words down, I could stop thinking about them, maybe stop being tempted to turn the communications equipment back on. It did not work though. Now, not only do I feel the cry of loneliness deep in my heart, but for months, the image of that sentence has been burned into my mind.

I am tired of being alone.

It has been fifty-four years since I turned on the plasma generator: fifty-four years since Omaha and the Ex Natu killed my family: fifty-four years since I used the Dikaió to end the life of every living thing inside this prison: fifty-four years that I have been alone. I spent the first few years grieving with the memories of my sons and my husband to keep me company, but over time, memories fade, even for the immortal. Then for several years, I used the Dikaió to build a Library in my fortress. It moved stone, forged steel, copied books, did the work of hundreds of men and machines. It farmed the land for me, but these infernal nano sprites inside me refuse to be satisfied with vegetables and fruits. My stomach is always rumbling no matter how much I eat. It feel like I am being torn apart inside from hunger and loneliness. What I would not give to eat steak and eggs around a dinner table with friends, families, strangers, enemies…

I stopped keeping this journal long ago because there was no one to share it with, and because I had trouble concentrating through the hunger. Writing down these thoughts was driving me mad. And now, here I am writing in the journal again as if I expect someone to see these words. I guess that means I have come to the end of my ability to be alone. Tonight, I am turning on the communication equipment and reaching out into the world. I would rather live forever imprisoned and tortured at the hands of Omaha and the Ex Natu then torture myself in this prison of my own making. If no one answers, I'll turn off the generator and leave this place, whatever may come.

Last night did not go as I expected to say the least. For the first time since I was locked out of Hoffen City, I feel something akin to hope, and not just hope for myself, hope for revenge. I had salvaged two Ex Natu communication screens from the force the Ex Natu sent to eradicate what was left of our people here, and when I turned them on, I reached out to see if anyone was there listening: I received two very different responses about thirty minutes apart.

The first was an Ex Natu priority channel. An operator answered, and I almost cried. It was another human being. However, when I gave my name and explained my situation, the operator was not happy. "How did you get access to this channel? This is a military priority channel."

"I received it from a man named Omaha," I assured him.

The operator briefly turned away from the screen, and I could hear the clacking of his fingers on a keyboard. He turned back to the screen and said, "hold."

He vanished, and I was alone again for several minutes, until a familiar voice startled me. "Emily! How lovely to see you still alive after all these years!" Omaha's face appeared on the screen in high definition, smiling brightly. "Honestly, you look better than I thought you would. Been sneaking outside the generator hunting meat, have you?"

While that thought had been crossing my mind for a long time, it seemed strange for Omaha to ask it so directly, especially considering international laws had limited meat consumption long before the Ex Natu's rise to power. Omaha opening with that comment put me off of the groveling and pleas for mercy that I had rehearsed for this conversation. "What do you mean by 'than I thought you would?'"

Omaha laughed and waved his hand dismissively. "The nano sprites I gave you were not of the ordinary variety. I was testing a theory, and if you haven't been out hunting, I think I know the results of it already. Back to the old drawing board as they say. Thanks for calling, Emily. Bye, now!" He leaned forward as if to disconnect the call.

"Wait!" I screamed panicking. "Please, please, I'm … I need your help."

He leaned back with one eyebrow raised. "My help? What kind of help?"

I paused. If I were to beg and grovel like I had planned, he might just laugh and disconnect, leaving me alone again. However, there was something in the nano sprites he had injected into me at the citadel: something he cared about, and it was tied to my appetite. I decided to press that point instead of trying to rely on mercy. "I'm so hungry. Something's wrong with me; sometimes, it feels like my body is eating me from the inside out."

Omaha grinned and leaned forward. "Really? Oh, do tell me more."

I leaned forward to the screen as well. "Meet me here, alone. I'll lower the shield, and we'll talk."

Omaha's grin widened. "You want to kill me. How diabolical!"

I shook my head and then paused. "Well, yes. Of course, I did. But that was so long ago. Without forgiveness, immortality would be hell, wouldn't it?"

Omaha considered her for a moment and then happily said. "Okay; it's a date." He held up his arm and jangled his Dominus bracelet. "My one condition is that I keep my bracelet, and you don't wear yours."

I looked at the bracelet on my arm and sighed heavily. "Of course. Whatever you say."

He clapped his hands and said, "I will be there tomorrow morning, Emily. Good night!"

He hung up, and I stood up to start prepare for his arrival when the second Ex Natu communications screen began to beep with an incoming call. I sat back down and wondered if Omaha was calling back. I reached forward and touched the screen, and an unfamiliar woman in a nondescript white room sat there staring back at me. "Emily Carpenter?" she asked.

"Yes," I affirmed. "Who are you?"

"My name is Margaret Simmons," the woman responded.

I nodded as if that name meant anything to me, but I was happy to talk to anyone at that point. "Hi Margaret. What can I do for you?"

"I think we can do a lot for each other, Mrs. Carpenter, but first tell me where you are exactly. Your signal seems scrambled for some reason," the woman betrayed no sense of emotion.

The hackles on my neck stood up. "Who are you again? Do you work for Omaha?"

The woman barely blinked. "We need your location, Mrs. Carpenter."

Human being or not, I had spent so much of my pre-Ex Natu life on the run and undercover, I could sense when someone was being evasive. "I think I'm just going to go now," I said.

"No wait!" A man's voice called from off screen. A young man, perhaps in his late thirties poked his head in on the conversation. He had dark brown hair and gray eyes. "Maybe this will help," he said and then stepped fully into view. He was holding a small, blond-headed toddler in his arms. The little girl was wearing a romper and shoving a fist full of crackers into her mouth.

"You're from Hoffen City!" I nearly cried. "How did you find me? Why did you lock us out? Can I come back in?" I stopped and then suddenly started to cry. "I miss you all so much: my aunts, uncles, cousins …" I trailed off, realizing they were all elderly at this point, if not dead.

The couple on the screen looked at each other sadly.

I started in again. "They forced nano sprites into me. I didn't want to be an Ex Natu, but …"

The woman shook her head and stopped me. "Mrs. Carpenter, please. We are not from Hoffen City."

The man nodded. "We're from what you call the East Asian Islands: the last free state on Earth, and we need your help."

The Chronicles of the Lost (cont.)

"The East Asian Islands?" I half asked, half exclaimed. "I don't understand. I thought the Ex Natu had, well, I thought they had …"

"Killed us all?" the man finished.

I nodded.

"They certainly tried," he continued. "Just like Hoffen City, we've been in hiding."

The woman chimed in, "but unlike your people, we're not just giving up and burying ourselves away while humanity disappears off the planet!"

The man shushed her. "Margaret, please! Forgive my wife.

She's a passionate woman. But she's right. Thanks to the Ex Natu, for the first time in its existence, the human race is facing extinction, and we need your help to stop it."

"But the Ex Natu's nano sprites will make them live forever; how could humans ever go extinct?" I wondered.

"Human nature didn't change just because they found a short cut in our biology," the man laughed. "As long as there were enemies to fight, the Ex Natu were united, but now that most of them think they're all that's left in the world, feuding factions have arisen. Civil wars have broken out across the planet, and they're killing each other. Without the ability to reproduce, they're numbers are dwindling: not quickly, but definitely."

The woman broke in then. "They don't know normal humans still exist, which is how we've managed to so easily infiltrate their factions and stir up some of those human failings."

The man's eyes widened. "Margaret, please! We're on an open Ex Natu channel."

The woman ignored him and went on. "The one you call Omaha is the leader of the Progenus faction. Our operatives infiltrated his group two decades ago and that is how we came across your name, the existence of Hoffen City, and the Dikaió."

The Dikaió. Of course that was what they wanted. "And you want my Dominus bracelet?"

Both the adults sneered, and the toddler mimicked her parents' faces. "Icky," she said with a wrinkled nose.

I went back to feeling confused.

The man shook his head. "We have no desire to play God, whether in immortal bodies or magical words. What we want is to return the Earth and all that is in it to its proper state. No more Ex Natu. No more Dikaió. Just human beings, living the way we were created, filling the Earth and caring for it."

I shook my head. "That is the dream of Hoffen City: Having families the way we were intended."

The woman laughed. "Speak, and it shall be," she said sarcastically.

I shook my head, still confused.

"Look," the man interjected quickly. "We obviously can't keep talking about it over this channel. This is what we're proposing. When you meet with Omaha tomorrow, we want to be there. He must be stopped before he ends humanity forever."

I sat back in my chair. "You want to kill him?"

"You admitted to wanting the same thing too, Emily. We can help you! Just tell us where you are, and we will take care of the rest," Margaret nodded encouragingly.

"How do I know this isn't just a trick to find out if I will betray him?" I wondered more to myself than the couple on the screen.

The man again bounced the young girl on his knee as if that were all the answer I needed. It was. There were no Ex Natu children. While I had talked to Omaha about forgiveness, the temptation to take the life of the man who had killed my husband and sons was alluring. I was about to agree to their terms when an old adage came to mind: better the devil you know than the one you do not. I shook my head again. "I don't know you, and if you're so opposed to the Dikaió and the Ex Natu, what about me? I have both. How can I be sure you won't just kill me, too?"

The woman threw up her hands, and the man sighed. "Emily, please! It's a rare opportunity to find him alone and unguarded."

The hair on the back of my neck stood up. I thought back to the interviews at the Ex Natu citadels. While there were guards, Omaha had his own office and had dismissed them, leaving the two of us alone. He clearly was not afraid to be alone unless something had changed since I stabbed him with his own letter opener. But I doubted it. He was too pompous, too sure of his own intellectual superiority to be afraid. There was something off with their proposal. "Your insider has had ample opportunity to assassinate Omaha if that was truly your intent. There's something more you want. What is it?"

The man and woman looked at each other and spoke in subtle body cues: a shrug of the shoulders, a motion with the jaw, staring daggers, fingers poking forcefully at the air. The little girl mimicked their frustration and threw her cracker in the air. It was almost comical watching the family go at it. Finally, the man's shoulders slumped, and he turned away from the screen. It was clear there was something he wanted to tell her, and Margaret did not want to divulge it. She smiled sweetly and spoke to me again. "Of course, there's more, Emily, and we'd love to talk about it in person. Just tell us where you are exactly."

Irritation turned my face hot. "I don't think so," I said and reached up to turn off the communications screen.

"Wait!" the man called. "We have to tell her, Margaret. You'd want to know if it was you."

The woman looked at him angrily and then sighed. "Fine. Tell her."

I pulled away from the screen and waited.

The man handed the child to her and leaned closer to the screen as if he was about to tell me a secret. "The Progenus faction of the Ex Natu that Omaha leads is committed to reversing the reproduction limitations of the nano sprites. However, all the Ex Natu nano sprite research was destroyed to stop themselves from rebelling against the mandate in the future. The Ex Natu world was supposed to be a utopia where humans would live forever in peace and tranquility. All they needed would be provided for them forever. The developers either couldn't (or outright refused) to imagine a future where there might be a need for more people in the world. And some of Progenus's experiments have gotten close. Several decades ago, they were performing experiments on animals, and while they succeeded in creating a nano sprite that can heal, prolong life, and allowed for reproduction; it came with certain problems."

The woman covered the child's ears and began to hum a lullaby that I had never heard before.

The man leaned in closer. "The animals were faster, stronger than natural varieties, and they were viciously violent. Omaha covered for these issues, claiming the animals were a weapon to clear out any vestiges of normal human beings like us and your people. But it became clear, very quickly, that the monstrosities could not be controlled. Soon after their introduction, a few of the nano-enhanced animals escaped and nearly wiped out every other animal on the planet: they are known as the wilding wolves."

"I've encountered them," I nodded.

"You're lucky to be alive," the man nodded. "We've managed to remove them from our islands, but we lost many to their attacks. Other continents have not been so lucky, particularly the Americas. Many of the Ex Natu won't even come out of their citadels anymore for fear of being killed by other Ex Natu or by the packs of wilding wolves. Extermination programs have worked tirelessly to eradicate them, but there are too many places to hide, and the nano sprites have increased their reproductive abilities. However, that increase is partly what leads to their increased viciousness. The constant production of reproductive cells in their bodies requires inordinate amounts of calories. When sustenance is not available, their systems cannibalize themselves: it's a process where the nano sprites act quickly to reverse and repair the damage. Their bodies literally tear themselves apart on the inside, and then put themselves back together."

I heard my own words to Omaha repeated back to me, and my stomach turned in horror.

The man must have noticed the color drain from my face, and he nodded. "Yes, Emily. Our information suggests that he injected you with some variation of wilding nano sprites."

"What does that mean?" I whispered. "I've become some kind of animal?"

"No, of course not." Margaret rolled her eyes but did not

take her hands off the little girl's ears. "You're an experiment. An experiment that escaped just like all the other wilding experiments."

"Margaret!" The man hissed at his wife.

"You want her to know. Now she knows," Margaret nodded toward me on the screen. "You were supposed to be the first Ex Natu breeder."

The man sighed. "I'm sorry you have to find out this way, but you can understand why we were speaking with some discretion."

My head was swimming. If what they were saying about me was true, did that mean I could still have children? I shook my head. My husband was dead. My children were dead. There was no point in thinking along those lines, but the possibility did bring up another question: "What would Omaha do if I went back with him?"

Margaret laughed. "What do you think?"

"So, you want to get to me before him…to what? Stop me from becoming the mother to a brood of immortal children?"

Margaret set the girl down on the floor out of view. "Not just any immortal children. Omaha has injected himself with the wilding nano sprites as well."

I felt sick.

Her husband interjected quickly. "We can help you, Emily. Take you to a place where he can't reach you."

A voice called from offscreen. "A trace has picked up our signal. You have 20 seconds, and I'm cutting the feed."

The man looked pleadingly at me. "Please, Emily."

I wanted more time to make my decision, but the decision

was about to be made for me. After years of isolation and almost nothing of consequence happening, to be suddenly called on to make such a rapid choice was overwhelming. I quickly scrawled my coordinates on a piece of paper and held it up to the screen. A moment later, it went black. There was no look of confirmation: no way to know if they had been able to record them or had even seen them.

Regardless of the response of the mysterious couple who claimed to be from the East Asian Islands, if what they said was true, Omaha's arrival on the following day had suddenly filled me with dread. And somewhere inside my heart, it had renewed my spite of the man. Had he murdered my family to make me have another one with him? I looked down at the Dominus bracelet on my wrist. There was no way that was happening without a fight.

I did not sleep well, anticipating Omaha's arrival, but I had come up with some semblance of a plan—at least to test what I had been told by the Islanders. When the screen flickered with Omaha's incoming call, I answered it immediately. "Hello, Omaha."

"Hello, Emily. How are you this morning? I'm outside if you would like to lower the shield."

I took a deep breath: worried even though there was no reason to worry about his response. He was still outside the plasma shield. "I'd like to, but I do have a question before I do."

This time his smile disappeared completely, and a tick of irritation flicked at his eyebrow. "What is it?"

"Do you love me?" I asked.

"What?" His irritation turned to disgust.

"Do you love me? A child should not be conceived if there isn't love and marriage involved, don't you agree?" I pressed on.

"How could you know anything about that?" He turned away from the screen and addressed someone I could not see. "We have a leak. I want to know who has been talking to her, and I want to know it right now." He turned back to me. "Emily, lower the shield."

"No, I don't think I will," I smiled. "I don't love you. I never will. You took the only man I've ever loved from me. I'm not going to be your guinea pig, and I'm certainly not going to bear your children."

Omaha growled.

"Now, now, calm down." I said softly. "I don't disagree with your idea completely. The benefits to humanity of living forever, but still having family, are hard to argue with."

Omaha softened, and his mouth ticked up in a hopeful smile. "What are you proposing?"

"Find someone else: A Dikaió Chorus that can have children." I said matter-of-factly.

Omaha's smile fell. "There's no such thing anymore."

"We both know they're out there, in a certain location." I winked at him not sure who exactly was listening. "Leave me some of your nano sprites and give me the materials I need to make a home for them here within the dome, and I'll find them and bring them here."

"This is foolish, Emily," Omaha shook his head. "What you're talking about could take centuries."

"Time we both have," I reminded him.

He trembled and pointed at me, exasperated. "Whoever you have been talking to has filled your head with nonsense. You have the chance to be the mother of the future. Why don't you just lower the shield and come out?"

"It's my way or no way," I smiled.

The screen flickered off, ending the conversation, and seconds later, the second screen flickered to life again. The man from the previous night appeared. "Emily, we're here. Don't lower the shield. There are several Ex Natu vehicles in your vicinity."

"Oh, I know. I just got done speaking to Omaha," I shrugged. "Everything's fine."

"You've decided to go with him?" he asked.

"No," I mused. "No, I did not. But I'm not going with you either. I refuse to be anyone's experiment, but what you said last night did appeal to me: a world without the Ex Natu and without the Dikaió. And more importantly, a world without Omaha in it."

"We'll wait here until the Ex Natu leave, and then you can lower the shield, and we'll talk about it," the man said.

"That's not how this is going to work. The Ex Natu won't be leaving. They're considering my proposal. I'm sure your person on the inside will tell you all about it soon." I reached up to the power button on the screen and said, "they also know there's a leak, so you'll probably want to pull your people out quickly." I waited for the information to sink in and then continued. "I will turn this communication screen on again in one month. We'll talk about what I want and how we will proceed then." I did not wait for a response before turning the screen off.

I sat in silence wondering if I had just doomed myself to an eternity of solitude. I had just told off both my chances for contact outside this plasma shield, but ultimately, I was the reason both of them were here. I had something that no other other person on the planet possessed: immortality, fertility, and the Dikaió. But I would have given them all up to have Jacob and my children back. I did not have time to dwell on that idea before Omaha's screen rang again.

I answered it, and his face reappeared, and he looked sad. "Hello, Emily. I've considered your offer, and I am inclined to accept it."

"Really?" I responded, surprised that he had given in so quickly without arguing.

He nodded solemnly. "You may find this hard to believe, but I do understand love. I lost my wife years ago, much the same way you lost your husband."

"You killed her?" I asked sarcastically and at once regretted it. My mouth spoke without my brain having time to weigh in on the wisdom of what I said, but I admit I did not expect what came next.

Omaha looked genuinely hurt. "I'll admit I hurt you and, as you seem to be aware, injected you with some special nano sprites, but I did not kill your husband, Emily. The Ex Natu high command ordered that action; the same way they ordered my wife's death." He became more animated as he spoke. "Injecting you was the only way to save you from sharing their fate."

"You think you saved me?" I was incredulous.

"Saved you? Yes, partly, but what you are—what I am—we're vengeance, Emily." He nodded as if I should understand what he was saying. "If I killed them all without a way to refill the Earth, it would be irresponsible, but make no mistake, I will kill every Ex Natu on this planet for what they did to my wife."

How could I believe a word he said while he sat outside my shields with several Ex Natu in his service? But arguing with him would not give me what I wanted. I decided to pull him back to the task at hand. "So, you're agreeable to my offer. We'll find Dikaió Choruses—just random, ordinary people that you can give your nano sprites to and repopulate the Earth."

Omaha laughed, "I don't know how you expect to do that, but sure." And then he paused and leaned forward. "On two conditions."

My heart beat faster. I did not know how I was going to do that either; I just wanted to buy time to put my other plans into action. "Conditions?" I asked softly.

"Number one, our mutual connection is off limits," he said.

"Our mutual connection?" I asked.

"You know what I mean, and I'm not going to repeat it in front of so many prying ears. Don't go looking for what was lost, Emily." He pointed at the screen to emphasize his point.

I nodded. He still believed his son had lived and had descendants in Hoffen City. They apparently were not going to be part of his new world. That did not factor into my plan for revenge at all, so I nodded. "I understand."

"Good." Omaha leaned back. "The second condition is a timeline."

"A timeline?" I asked confused.

"Yes, a timeline. I'll give you the nano sprites and all that you ask for to perform your search for two-hundred-and-fifty years. After that, you agree to my original plan."

"You mean I agree to marry you?" The words churned my stomach as I said them.

"Yes," he confirmed. "And bear my children."

I swallowed hard and nodded.

Omaha laughed and clapped his hands. "It's a long engagement, Emily, but I'm not so bad. You'll see." He turned away from the screen and barked an order. "Leave the sprites for her, and let's go." He turned back to me. "The sprites I'm leaving for you will provide all you need and protect you. None of my people will come anywhere near this place, but I wouldn't leave the shield down for long because I have no sway over the other factions. You know how to contact me if your little experiment should pan out, and if not, I'll be back to claim you."

The screen went dark.

And I yelled back, "that will be the day you die!"

I turned off the screen and walked out to to the edge of the holographic plasma shield. I could not see what was beyond it. It just looked like more of the overgrown gardens I was having difficulty keeping up with, expanding off into the distance forever. "Dikaió, protect me," I commanded, just in case Omaha and his goons were still waiting outside. A swirl of odd bits of junk flitted about me in concentric swirls, and I breathed deeply. "Dikaió lower the plasma shield."

Beyond the shield was a small forest that had not been there when my husband and children were still alive. The trees were arced in a curve; their branches had long ago learned not to grow too close to the plasma shield. Our people had cleared this whole area for construction, but now it was wild and green. There was no sign of Omaha or any Ex Natu ships. All that remained were about twenty-five silver sprites of different varieties: culture sprites, fire sprites, flying sprites, and construction sprites. But they were all Ex Natu sprites, and I knew that deep in their programming they had no allegiance to me. Still, I had to work with what I had. "Well? Come on then." I motioned them inside the perimeter.

As the sprites lumbered inside, I noticed they had been standing around a black box. It had four silver latches holding a lid in place. My heart began beating faster again. "Dikaió culture sprite," I called, and one of the cultures sprites stopped and turned to face me. "Open that case." I stepped way back. If Omaha had left me a nasty surprise, I wanted to be outside the blast range. The sprite unlatched the case without incidence, and when it opened the lid, icy condensation steamed out. There was not any sort of explosion, so I approached the case carefully. Inside were several small vials full of clear liquid.

Wilding nano sprites.

"Close it up and bring it with you," I commanded and walked inside the perimeter of my fortress. When the sprite was inside as well, I called, "Dikaió, raise the shield." The endless weedy gardens appeared once more.

The next month was a busy one. I dismantled six of the twenty-five sprites Omaha had given me and used the parts to fashion a sprite of my own design, reprogramming its command core so that it would be loyal to me, and then I sent it out to find a Dikaió Chorus for bait. I also sent several sprites out to collect supplies and started building a trap to put my bait in. I had always been partial to the design of the library in the Davis City Metroplex, so I set the sprites to work copying it, brick by brick. I had to make the trap look convincing after all; otherwise, Omaha might not let his guard down.

Eventually, the time came for my East Asian Island friends to contact me.

"Emily," the man's face appeared on the screen. He was holding his blond-headed daughter on his lap.

I stopped him. "Let's not go any further without a proper introduction."

He blushed and then nodded. "Of course, how rude of me. My name is James, and this little beauty is my daughter Zane."

The Relos Hospital

"Zane's the little girl?" Mallory sat up in the bed and immediately regretted it as her head swam. She laid back down. She had so many questions and had managed to not interrupt through all of the Archivist's reading, but this was too much.

The Archivist looked incredulous. "Well, she was when I

wrote this, but that was almost ninety years ago. She has gray hair now."

"No, I mean, I thought Zane was a man," Mallory laughed.

The Archivist shook her head. "I'm sure that will make a good impression on her. Maybe we should keep that between the two of us?"

Mallory nodded. "Right? So, what was the deal you made with the East Asian Islanders?"

"We prefer to use the term Relos," an old woman walked into the room. "I was eavesdropping outside your door and heard my name mentioned."

The Archivist stood. She towered over the woman but held her hand out to her in deference and respect. "Zane, this is Mallory. Mallory, Zane. She is the leader of the Relos people in the East Asian Islands."

Zane nodded politely but ignored the Archivist, pushing past her with more than a hint of disgust. "The deal she made with us was for your son."

Mallory pushed herself up despite the dizziness. "Where's Kirk?"

Zane waved her hand dismissively. "He's fine, fine, having a visit with my older sister Vivian. She has a thing for babies, even if they are abominations."

Anxiety welled up inside Mallory. "If you've hurt him, I'll ..."

Zane laughed. "She is a real mother after all." Her eyes narrowed. "That fire is good, child. Would that all mothers had it centuries ago. We wouldn't have found ourselves in the situation we're in. But I would never hurt a child. You have no need to worry about that. By 'your son,' I didn't mean we targeted you and your family: just the child of the wilding, whoever's son that might have been."

The old woman looked at the Archivist's seat questioningly, and the Archivist who had not reclaimed it motioned for her to sit. She sat down with a sigh and wiggled her rear end deep into the chair to get comfortable. "The part she hadn't gotten to is that when my father and Emily here made their deal to end the Ex Natu and the Dikaió, we had no idea how to do it." She smiled warmly. "But your son holds the key. By studying his nano sprites, we think we can develop a technology that will disrupt all the nano technology on the planet."

Mallory shook her head. "He's not some animal for you to experiment on. I want to see my baby, right now."

The old woman smiled again. "I'm afraid that is entirely impossible."

Mallory's anxiety turned into anger. Her eyebrows furrowed. "If you've hurt him, I'll ..."

The old woman only laughed again. "You said that once before, child. What will you do?"

And the Archivist looked down uncomfortably.

Mallory gritted her teeth and growled, "Dikaió protect me!"

Nothing happened.

Zane laughed again, and this time she had trouble stopping. "Oh, oh!" She wheezed. "Emily here removed your christening before you stepped off the boat. Last thing we need is some Dikaió-wielding maniac running loose on the island—stuff floating around everywhere—it would be pandemonium."

Mallory looked at the Archivist confused and once again betrayed. The Archivist refused to look her in the eyes, and self-consciously covered the Dominus bracelet on her wrist.

"Don't worry. No harm will come to your child, Mrs. Aiworth. You'll see him in due time. Due time," Zane assured her. "There's no need for your Dikaió here. You may not be one of us by blood, but you are one of us in birth. Mothers are in no danger here. You'll see."

Mallory laid back on her pillow, once again exhausted. She bit her lip and tilted her head in thought, trying to decide what to do next. She wanted to get Kirk, find Caleb, and get out of here. It would be harder without the Dikaió, but she had lived most of her life without the mysterious force—so what if she was back to being a Dikaió Chorus? She could figure out a way to escape and get her family to safety. Admittedly, she had no idea where she was even if she were to escape and accomplish the other tasks. She did not even know where they would go if they could escape. Was there a place in this world where they would be welcomed? But those were all problems for tomorrow. Getting her family back was her first priority.

"A young person's curiosity," Zane pointed at Mallory and looked at the Archivist. "Do you see it? When was the last time you pondered the universe like that, Ex Natu?"

The Archivist did not answer or look at Zane.

Zane shook her head sadly and gave her attention back to Mallory. "What are you seeking to understand?"

Mallory could not confide her thoughts to Zane. She did not trust the old woman. She did have a question that was unanswered though. "Why do you need my son to stop the Ex Natu? And what does that have to do with the Dikaió?"

Zane's eyebrows arched. "Do you not know what the Dikaió is, dear?"

The Archivist shook her head. "At some point, Hoffen City burned their books and lost their history. They think the

Dikaió is magic. The Matriarch is more voodoo woman than Syntec now."

Zane looked sad but answered Mallory's question. "The Dikaió is a network of nano sprites—but the Dikaió nano sprites are more complex than the molecular machines that the Ex Natu use to repair their bodies and certainly more complex than the medical nano sprites we have here. The Dikaió sprites are much, much smaller. The man you call Omaha created them out of subatomic particles like quarks and bosons. They're small enough to alter matter at the atomic level. They're also self-replicating and spread every-where, like a virus. We know our entire island is infected, thanks to Emily here demonstrating the Dikaió to us years ago, but our best scientists have never been able to isolate one of the machines to study."

Mallory understood very little of Zane's explanation. She had no concept of subatomic particles or molecules. Her education had been focused on learning about what she needed to do to run the city. And though she was incredibly curious, she did not need to understand it all right now. There was only one thing she wanted to know. "What does any of that have to do with my son?"

Zane looked irritated at having been interrupted, but she obliged Mallory's question. "As I was saying, the Dikaió nano sprites spread everywhere, even in living matter. If not for the protective protocols that your Omaha built into the Dikaió network, the spoken word would affect living things too. There is one exception in that protocol: the wilding sprites. Omaha turned some of the wilding wolves immortal as well—but he also made them capable of reproduction."

Mallory's mind reeled, and she looked at the Archivist. "Like you and Caleb?"

The Archivist shook her head. "Yes, but no."

Zane continued as if the two had not spoken at all. "The Dikaió hard-wires itself into the wilding wolves' chromosomes during reproduction. Theoretically, for a human born with wilding sprites would make them immortal, but something other than an Ex Natu and thus bypass those protocols. In other words, an Ex Natu born with the wilding sprites hard-wired into them would be able to use the Dikaió too."

Mallory gasped. "Kirk?"

"That's what our scientists are studying now," Zane continued.

"What experiments are you doing on my son?" Mallory started to sit up again.

The old woman in the chair shook her head. "No, no. Don't be so dramatic. We're not monsters. But we are taking some blood and tissue samples to study his DNA and to see if it will tell us more about the Dikaió. He'll be fine. At least until he learns to speak; then who knows?"

Mallory grimaced and fell back again. "So why does Omaha want him?"

The Archivist spoke quickly. "He wants to make himself a god. His plan is to wipe out the Ex Natu, spread the wilding nano sprites here and in Hoffen City and create a race of gods—but he needs a proxy to accomplish it all. There are protocols in the system that restrict him, both as an Ex Natu and as a Dikaió user, even with a Dominus bracelet."

Mallory shook her head. "I don't understand. I thought Omaha created the Dikaió. How could he be locked out of using it; can't he just change it?"

"Apparently not. Early in the resistance, his system was overridden and locked down by General Knenne."

Zane's face crinkled in rage. "You dare to mention that butcher in my presence?"

The Archivist's shoulders slumped. "I meant no disrespect, but you've seen all the files; you know what he did."

"I know exactly what he did. Entire generations, millions of people died at his hand. And then he took for himself what he denied to us? If ever a man's generations deserved to be destroyed, it is General Kirk Knenne's." Zane began to breathe hard and wheeze. She pulled on the hand rests of the chair and lifted herself to a standing position. "Hoffen City should have never existed, and once the Dikaió is gone, we will destroy it and blot out his name from history!"

Mallory panicked. This was what Reddy Lamarr had been talking about when she called the Archivist a traitor to her people. She grabbed at the IV in her arm, fully intending to rip it out, jump on the old woman, and stop her. But the Archivist grabbed her wrist and shook her head. "Patience, Mallory." Her face was strained. "Please."

Zane's old eyes were fiery, and then she softened. "I'll see that your son is brought to you." And with that she slowly stood and hobbled out of the door.

Mallory whispered to the Archivist. "You are a traitor—just like the Sprite Master said."

The Archivist sighed and let go of her arm. She sank back

into the chair. "No one here knows your lineage. All they know is that you're from Hoffen City, which is enough for them to dislike you. But if they knew who you were—who's descendant you were—they would kill you and your son. This is not the time for a fight or misspoken words, Mallory."

Mallory's heart was still racing, and it was making it hard to think straight. "Why would you bring us here?"

"It was necessary." The Archivist looked at the floor. "It was necessary. You need your strength. Just rest for now."

"Necessary for what?" Mallory demanded again.

"Necessary to end the Ex Natu. Necessary to end the Dikaió. We were never meant to live like this." The Archivist pointed to the door. "I should have grown old like her long ago and died. My grandchildren's grandchildren should be carrying on my heritage." She held up her arm with the Dominus bracelet. "And if it means the Dikaió has to go too, then so be it."

Mallory recoiled from the Archivist in understanding. "And then it would be easier to get your revenge on Omaha? The trap at the Library, working with Zane—it's all to get revenge?"

The Archivist looked like she had been slapped but did not deny her motivations. She stood up again, turned away from Mallory, and walked toward the door. "Rest, Mallory. We'll talk more soon when you're more rational."

Rational? How dare she! How could anyone be rational when her son, her husband, her family, her people, everything she loved was under threat. But the Archivist was right about one thing: she was exhausted. She would need strength to do anything to help her people. She laid back and closed her eyes, but Mallory could not rest. Her thoughts were going in a million directions, and she had no idea if any of them were on the right path.

Shortly, her eyes flitted back open, and she looked out the window of her small cell. A gentle breeze was blowing, and the tall fern-like trees swayed in it. Their dark green heads contrasted against a light blue sky and wisps of white clouds. She had no sense of how much time had passed since she had lain in a similar bed: a captive of the Ex Natu. Granted, the view here was much nicer, and the room itself felt much, much cleaner than the one in Omaha's citadel. She could even smell the familiar scent of antiseptic cleaner, just like the hospital in Hoffen City, but it was still more a prison than a hospital.

As much as she hated going to the hospital, she had spent a lot of time there growing up, and she wished that she were there now, waiting for her parents to visit. The monsters they had told children about, which lived outside the protection of light, were all too real. Whether Ex Natu or Relos, Mallory wished she could warn them of all the dangers lurking in the outside world. How would they even begin to prepare for attacks from either group? She did not even know the capabilities of the Relos. But the people here on the East Asian Islands were familiar with Hoffen City, and she wondered if that meant that they knew where it was. If she could only get there to warn them, they could surely work together to figure out how to survive.

Her thoughts were interrupted when a nurse wearing

light blue scrubs walked into the room carrying a sleeping baby. White gauze bandages were wrapped around his arms and legs, and a large one around his head. Blood seeped through all of them, turning them dark crimson. Mallory's chest tightened, and her teeth bit hard on her lower lip, sending a sharp pain through her mouth, but she barely noticed. "What did you do to my baby?" she screamed.

The nurse looked at her sorrowfully as if on the verge of tears. "I … I …" She could not get the words out and quickly placed the child in Mallory's arms before running out of the room.

Baby Kirk was sleeping deeply. Mallory shook his little hand to try and rouse him, but it was no use. Her baby was completely unresponsive. Had they drugged him? And why were there so many bandages? She took hold of one of the smaller bandages on his arm and gently tugged it loose. Underneath was a smear of still-wet blood, but there was no wound that would have emitted it. She tugged another bandage off and found the same thing. Soon, she had her child completely unwrapped and found him perfectly healthy without a single scratch. Had they wrapped him in bloody bandages as some kind of sick joke?

The baby's eyes moved in rapid jerks under his eyelids, and his stomach growled, vibrating Mallory's chest. She watched in amazement as his belly roiled and moved while it rumbled. Then his eyes fluttered open, his eyebrows pinched together above his nose, and he wailed for food. Mallory quickly adjusted herself into a seated position and began to feed her child. He acted like he was starving, wolfing up her milk supply faster than she would have thought possible. He smacked his lips, and once again his belly roiled as it digested the milk. Then he cuddled close to his mother and fell back to sleep. As he did, Mallory tasted blood in her mouth. She pulled one hand away from Kirk and touched her lip.

It stung.

The wound she had caused when she saw Kirk wrapped in bloody bandages was still oozing blood. She used her tongue and licked at it, trying to stem the flow and get it to start the healing process. That was when she realized that the blood on the bandages really was Kirk's: The wilding sprites were in his chromosomes, and they had healed him. They were what caused him to waken from his sedation. Healing took a lot of energy and left him insatiably hungry.

"Miss!" she called. "Miss!"

The nurse who had delivered Kirk to her poked her head sheepishly around the door jam, still looking like she was on the verge of tears. She said nothing.

"He's fine," Mallory said, lifting Kirk slightly, so she could see the baby.

The nurse walked timidly into the room and inspected him closer. She gently picked up his arm and stared at in disbelief. Then his leg. Then she pulled him from Mallory's arms and began to flip him over and over looking for damage. Her timidity gave way to a look of horror and then disgust.

"Hey!" Mallory yelled. "Be careful!"

The nurse's eyes blinked, and she looked at Mallory—the look of disgust still lingering. "It's true then?" she asked coldly.

Mallory could assume what she was asking but played dumb. "Is what true?"

"That you had a baby with one of those monsters." The nurse dropped Kirk unceremoniously into Mallory's lap. "I can't believe anyone would do such a thing. It's sick."

Kirk screamed in protest at being wakened so rudely.

Once again Mallory's chest tightened. She could feel her pulse in her forehead, and the room seemed to be slowly turning red. For months, she had been a prisoner of the Ex Natu, she had fought sprites and won, she had been attacked by wilding wolves, blown up, buried in rubble, impaled, left to die in the woods, burned, and survived it all to get to this moment, to this baby now in her arms. And now this nurse thought she could come in here and judge her? "How dare you?" she hissed. "You don't know anything about me or what I've been through."

The disgust on the nurse's face faltered, and she backpedaled away from the bed a step. "I ... I ..."

"Now, don't start that again," Mallory commanded.

The nurses nodded and froze in place. "I'm sorry."

"Don't be sorry." Mallory softened. She did not want to be nice to this woman, but she needed her. "What's your name?"

"My name is Navarro. Jennifer Navarro," the nurse said, a little pride returning at the sound of her own name.

Mallory laughed. "Navarro? Really?"

The nurse's pride stiffened. "What is wrong with Navarro?"

Mallory continued smiling. "Nothing whatsoever. My doctor back home is Doctor Navarro." She shook her head.

"We saw a lot of each other. I was always managing to get myself hurt as a child." She shrugged and petted Kirk's small, perfect head. "And as an adult too, I guess." She looked up at the nurse and tried to look grateful, though it was pushing her acting abilities to pull it off, even if there was some truth in what she was about to say. "It's a little comforting to know a Navarro is caring for me now, you know?"

The nurse softened immediately and put her hand on Mallory's arm. "We'll take care of you, as long as you're here. You don't have to worry about that. What did you need when you called me in?"

"I'd like to see my husband. Can you find him and send him in, now?" Mallory asked cheerfully.

The nurse's countenance fell again. "I'll ask, but I don't know if they'll allow it."

"You mean Zane?" Mallory wondered.

"I'm not sure who that is," the nurse answered.

"The old woman who was just here," Mallory clarified.

"I think she's the former Prime Minister, but she's been out of office for years. Long before my time. If she weren't so old, you might even wonder if she was an Ex …" The nurse shook her head. "But no, not her, I meant the BENI."

"Benny?" Mallory was confused.

"The Bureau of Ex Natu Investigations," the nurse looked at her suspiciously. "They have your husband locked in a room down the hall with guards posted at the door. I hate when they bring prisoners into the hospital. It always gives me the willies. Though it's rare that we get an Ex Natu admitted. People are usually sick or injured when they come here. Not many Ex Natu in that group, if you know what I mean." She looked suspiciously at baby Kirk again. "And it's certainly the first time we've had an Ex Natu baby here. At least the first one I've ever seen. I thought it wasn't possible."

Mallory looked at her with pleading eyes. "Can you ask someone if I can see him?"

The nurse looked at her and sighed. She lifted her hands palm up in resignation. "I can ask." Then she turned and left the room.

Mallory laid in the quiet of the room. Kirk had fallen back to sleep as Mallory petted his head: a warm bundle breathing lightly on her chest. The baby's heart beat rapidly, and his eyes darted back and forth beneath his lids. What was he dreaming about? What did any child dream about at this age? If he was anything like his father, it was food. Mallory smiled at that thought, and then her heart ached. She desperately longed to see and hear her husband. She wished someone would tell her everything was okay.

The light in the window had begun to grow dark before anyone entered the room again. Mallory looked hopefully toward the door and was immediately both disappointed and ecstatic as a man came in pushing a cart with a silver cloche on it. The man smiled at her and pulled over a dining tray that crossed over the top of her bed. "Hope you're hungry!" he chimed with a smile then moved the cloche to the tray and lifted the lid.

Mallory gasped.

Four steaming red bugs, each about the size of Mallory's hand, lay on the plate. They were cuddled up next to each other, as if they were spooning. Their giant eyes stared up at her, and their mouths looked like they had sprouted tentacles. They had tails that were segmented and curved. There were various green and multi-colored vegetables around them for plating, but nothing about them looked appetizing at all.

"Don't like prawns?" the man asked suddenly concerned. "Or do you have a shellfish allergy?"

Mallory looked up at him in horror. "You eat these things?"

The man laughed. "Of course. But not regularly. Only new moms and VIPs get a dinner like this. Hey, but if you have an allergy, I can bring you a pirok like everyone else is getting instead."

"What's a pirok?" Mallory asked, still eyeing the prawns warily.

"What's a pirok?" the man's eyes got wide. "What island do you hail from to not know what a pirok is?"

Mallory looked at him quizzically. "I'm sorry. I just don't know."

The man quickly threw the lid back on the prawns. "Forget all about these little beauties. If you haven't ever had a proper pirok, I'll bring you two." He whisked the red bugs out of the room. "You're going to love them!"

The aroma of grilled onions hit Mallory's nostrils moments before he reappeared with another cloche on a cart. On the plate he set in front of her were two small steaming loaves of bread. She picked up a fork and broke the crust on one, steadying herself in case more bugs poured out. But what she found instead made her mouth drool. "They're meat pies!"

Mallory exclaimed. "I love meat pies."

The man laughed. "Pies? You must be from one of them distant islands that calls everything by the wrong name. At least you're not as strange as I thought. 'Never had a pirok.' Can you imagine?"

Mallory looked up at him as if asking permission.

And he nodded. "Go on then. Enjoy yourself. Get your strength back!"

The first bite was incredible. Bursts of onion, cabbage, oregano, beef, sang out around the crispy puffed pastry. Mallory had not eaten since the dreadful Ex Natu meatless meatloaf, and before that since the sparse meals in Ex Natu captivity. Real food tasted utterly divine. Her stomach did flips with every bite. She tried to go slow and enjoy the piroks, but far too soon, it was all gone.

The man who delivered her food looked at her with satisfaction. "How do they compare?"

"To the prawns? Much better!" Mallory said smiling.

"Nah, nah," he laughed with her. "To your meat pies back home?"

"Oh! So much better," Mallory raved. "Is there any more?"

The man laughed. "Of course, sweet one. Of course. Just you wait right there." He collected her plate and loaded his cart then headed for the door.

Just as he disappeared, there was a loud crash outside her room and multiple people began screaming. A red light that she had not noticed above her door started flashing. Shots sang out somewhere in the building. Mallory clutched Kirk closer to her chest. She pushed her tray away and swung her feet out of bed on the side where her IV was connected. She was once again dressed in one of those green, paper hospital gowns that did not close in the back. She tried to use her IVed hand to close it behind her, but the screaming and shots were coming closer to her room. This was not the time for modesty. Mallory stepped to the window and looked out. She was on the ground floor, there was only a single plane of glass, and there was no screen to deal with either. She had planned to get her strength back before making a break for it, but she did not want to be here when whatever was happening in the hallway made its way to her room. There was a small latch, which unlocked with ease, but when she pulled up on the sill, the window did not budge.

She was about to put Kirk on the bed when the cloche that her food had been delivered in flew through the door, clanging loudly when it landed and skidded into the leg of her bed. Kirk's eyes popped open in fright at the noise, and he began to scream. Then the man who had delivered her food flew into the room behind the metal lid. He bounced on the floor once and rolled against the bed, laying there limply. A heaving shadow enveloped him, extruding from the doorway. Mallory barely had time to look up in terror before the heaving bulk of the shadow's source hit her, wrapped its arms around her in a protective embrace, pulled her from the ground, spun her around, and jumped backward through the window in a shower of glass and twisted metal.

13

Mallory lay on top of the shadow that had defenestrated her, looking up at the bright blue sky. Sparkles of light danced about a dark vignette in her vision, and she realized she was not breathing. She tried to take a deep breath, but the stunned muscles in her chest refused to comply. There was a sound in her ears like a mosquito was buzzing past her head, but it lasted longer and was more incessant. Somewhere beyond the annoying mosquito noise, almost as if underwater, sirens were blaring, and a baby was screaming. Then below her a voice called up from a deep well.

"Get up, Mal. We've got to move!"

It was Caleb. Just hearing his voice made her body relax a little, which was just enough for her lungs to pull in a hard, rasping breath. Mallory started coughing and instinctively started to put her arms out to roll to her side, but the small bundle squirming in them summoned up deeper instincts. She had to protect baby Kirk. She tucked him into one arm and held the back of his head gently. Then she rolled off Caleb onto her other arm, being careful not to jostle the baby's head.

Caleb jumped to his feet. "C'mon, Mal! We've got to get out of here!"

Mallory could hear him a lot better, though that weird buzzing was still sounding in her ears. She lifted the baby to him. "Here. Take Kirk, so I can get up."

Caleb looked nervous, but he carefully took their son. Mallory pulled herself to her feet and said, "where do we go?"

Caleb paused and his nervousness intensified. "I hadn't thought that far ahead."

Mallory looked around. They were in a small courtyard with some benches. Behind them and to their sides stretched a small beach that led out to so much water, she could not see the end of it. Behind them was the white stucco hospital building they had just exited. There was nowhere to go but back through the hospital or around it. The building was not that big. There were just six windows on this side, including the one they had exited. In the window, the nurse that had brought Kirk to her stood with her eyes wide and mouth agape. She was holding Mallory's IV stand. Mallory looked down at her arm and saw that the IV needle was still in her wrist, though the tubing was torn. Fluid was flowing out into the grass. She carefully pulled the needle out of her arm and applied pressure with her thumb when the hole started to bleed. The bleeding stopped much faster than she thought it would. In fact, the hole healed up almost instantly.

"Oh no!" Mallory gasped.

"What is it?" Caleb grabbed her arm.

"The medical nano sprites. They didn't take them out." Mallory felt like her world had dropped out from under her. "They were supposed to take them out."

Caleb's brow knitted tighter. "So, you're like me now?"

Mallory shook her head. "I don't know. They said they were different than Ex Natu nano sprites, but I don't know."

The nurse staring at them out of the broken window yelled, "they're over here!"

Mallory looked up and saw her eagerly pointing at them and looking to their left. Mallory followed her gaze and saw three men in uniform carrying long, rudimentary looking magistrate weapons. Caleb handed her the baby. "We'll figure it out later." He ran toward the men, and they all froze, quickly raising their weapons. One even managed to pull the trigger before Caleb reached them, but Caleb spun just before the shot rang out. As he spun, one hand quickly swiped all of the weapons' muzzles to the right, away from Mallory and Kirk, and then followed his whirlwind spin with a quick back hand that threw one soldier into the other two. While they were off balance, Caleb planted his foot hard into the pit behind the middle attacker's knee, and the man's leg buckled. As he tottered, Caleb used the man's calf as a springboard to jump and kick the last man hard in the face, which sent him flying several feet back. Caleb landed with both elbows on the heads of the other two faltering men. It all happened so fast, Mallory barely had time to duck to not get struck by any stray shots before the three attackers were laying flat on the ground, not moving.

She stood and ran to Caleb. "Where did you learn that?"

Caleb shrugged. "Fighting the Archivist, I guess. They move a lot slower than she does."

"Caleb! Mallory! Stop!" As if she had heard her name called, the Archivist rounded the far southern corner of the building. "You don't know what you're doing!"

Mallory yelled back. "We'll never let them destroy our city, traitor!"

Caleb's eyes went wide. "Wait! What?"

Mallory saw one of the men's weapons on the ground and picked it up. It was too awkward to control while holding baby Kirk, but she got her finger on the trigger and pointed it in the general direction of the Archivist.

The older woman lifted her wrist to her mouth to use the Dikaió, and Mallory pulled the trigger. The Archivist flew off her feet and fell backward.

Caleb screamed, "Mal!"

Mallory dropped the weapon in horror. "How? It was supposed to be a warning!"

Caleb walked toward the Archivist. "You're a terrible shot, Mal. That's how I ended up an Ex Natu in the first place, remember?" He touched his shoulder tenderly.

Mallory walked behind her husband. "But she's an Ex Natu, too. She'll be fine. Right?"

Caleb knelt down next to the Archivist. Her wrist was

still at her mouth, but there was blood everywhere. The small cone on the Dominus bracelet was shattered. Mallory's stray bullet had hit it dead on, and then the Archivist behind it. Caleb grabbed her other hand and checked her pulse. "She's still alive." He nodded. "She might survive if the nano sprites can put her neck back together fast enough. Let's not be here if she does."

Mallory sighed in relief. "We still don't know where we're going."

A roaring noise sounded in the sky above them. Mallory and Caleb looked up and saw the largest sprite they had ever seen. It was entirely black with windows in front, and an open door on the side. In some ways, it reminded Mallory of the hovering grocery carts they used to use at market day, except it was about fifty feet long, and instead of four sets or rotors on each corner, there was just one giant rotor on top. It was shaped like a flying fish, with wings on the side and a small, sideways rotor on the tail. As it moved to hover over them, a windstorm whipped about them. Mallory's curly hair slapped around her face, and her paper gown whipped about her body. She struggled to maintain her modesty while keeping baby Kirk safe from the sand being blown about.

A voice boomed out of the giant sprite: "Freeze! Do not move, or we will open fire!"

Caleb grabbed her arm and pointed toward the hospital window. He yelled something, but Mallory could not hear.

She might have protested and given up to protect her son, but Caleb again picked her up and sprinted toward the window. A familiar high whirring noise sounded above the rotor roar. It sounded just like the small box sprite that chased them into the woods outside the Library. The Archivist had saved them from it then, but Mallory doubted she would help them now. She looked over Caleb's shoulder and saw the old Ex Natu still lying on the ground. The whirring continued above them, and Mallory tucked her head against Caleb's chest and pressed baby Kirk up against his father too, hoping that his enhanced Ex Natu body would shield them from what was coming next. Caleb sprinted hard toward the open hospital window, and the whirring noise shifted.

WHHIRRR! . . . CRAKETY-CRACK-CRACK!!!

Caleb jumped through the window once again just as its frame exploded in shards of glass, wood splinters, and chunks of white stucco. On the way, Mallory crashed into something soft and landed on top of it, as Caleb huddled over her and the baby. The soft thing squirmed below her, and Mallory realized it was the nurse. Caleb had pinned her down with Mallory and the baby to protect her from the weapon fire as well. Every muscle in his body was tense, and he was grimacing through clenched teeth. Then the firing ceased, and he pulled himself off the group on the floor.

Mallory looked at her husband and saw that his legs were covered with blood. "You've been shot!" she pointed.

"I'll heal." He picked her up and yelled, "let's go!"

Mallory rubbed baby Kirk's head as if he were a lucky charm and nodded, following her husband's lead. As they ran out the door to the room, Caleb nearly collided with six men in uniform with weapons drawn. They stood there staring at each other for what seemed like an eternity before Caleb grabbed the weapon of the nearest man and ripped it out of his hands, smashing it across the face of the next, which sent him sprawling into the rest. They scrambled over each other trying to get a clear shot, but Caleb again picked up Mallory, cradling her in his arms and leapt over the whole pack, sprinting around a corner to the left. He did not set her down when they were clear of the shots firing behind them. "It'll be faster if I just carry you," he comforted without even breathing hard.

"Your legs!" Mallory insisted.

"I can't even feel the pain anymore," he reassured her. "They're fine."

Then he turned sideways and barreled through a pair of double doors with his shoulder. They emerged into a large waiting area. Mallory was amazed how much the hospital here in this foreign place resembled the hospital in Hoffen City. The same white tiled floors, the same too-bright lights, the same uncomfortable wooden waiting chairs: It was as if there were some form of a hospital out there in the ether that every human being built their hospital to resemble—well, every human being but the Ex Natu, who did not need them anymore. At the far end of the waiting room was a set of glass doors. Caleb sprinted toward them, and just like Dikaió doors back home, they recognized him approaching and slid to the side. Mallory wondered about the conversation with Zane. How could they have Dikaió doors here and medical nano sprites, but be so adamant that the Ex Natu and her people in Hoffen City needed to be destroyed for having them? There was much she did not understand.

There was no time think about it though, as the moment they exited the building, Mallory could hear the roar of the large sprite. It was still on the other side of the building, but it would only take a moment to rise over the top and be upon them. Ahead of them on this side of the building was a very small city. The buildings were all covered in plants. Mallory imagined that from above, one would not even be able to see the city at all. She pulled herself up to look over Caleb's shoulder at the hospital and found that this side too was covered in vegetation even though the backside had been white stucco.

Caleb ran forward with Mallory and their son in his arms, down the streets of the foreign, plant city, looking for a place to hide. The first open door they found was a small café. There were several families in the building with children of all ages, even a couple of mothers holding infants just like Kirk. Their clothes were bright and colorful. The men wore slacks with pastel button up shirts, and the women were all dressed in bright floral dresses that showed off their bare shoulders and legs. A waitress was leaning over a table setting down plates. Just past the window into the kitchen, cooks busied about making orders. The place was abuzz with conversation and laughter. At least it was, until someone noticed Caleb carrying Mallory and their baby. Then everything stopped.

Caleb set Mallory down. He walked around her to the nearest table where a man sat with his wife and three children. A light blue sports coat hung on the back of his chair. "May we have your jacket?" Caleb asked quietly and nodded toward Mallory.

The man looked back at Mallory, barely covered in her hospital gown and then looked at his wife. She looked utterly terrified and gave him no help. "Oh, uh, of course," he stammered and leaned forward.

Caleb pulled the jacket free. He carried it to Mallory and held baby Kirk while she put it over her gown. It was much too large for her, but that made the jacket hang low enough to cover up the open parts of the gown. She took back the baby when she was situated. Caleb turned back to the crowd. "How do we get off this island?" he asked.

No one answered. They just stared at him in terror.

Caleb sighed deeply. "Please, someone help us."

Mallory bounced her baby on her hip. And looked at them pleadingly.

A red door behind the counter swung open and a large man wearing a white cap walked out. His white apron looked like a modern art painting, splattered with grease, gravy, and a kaleidoscope of other colorful fluids. He was holding a meat cleaver. "I don't know what kind of trouble you folks are in, but this is a respectable establishment. I've called the authorities, and they're on their way. So, you can take a seat and wait for them nicely, or you can leave."

Caleb growled.

And Mallory touched his arm tenderly. "We'll leave. Sorry to have bothered you." Then she tilted her head and bit her lip. "Can we have some food?"

The man with the cleaver raised his eyebrows. Then he shrugged. He turned to the window behind him and grabbed two round sandwiches off plates sitting on the sill. "Give me another couple of cheeseburgers, Henry." He turned back and offered them to Mallory. "Sure. No one will ever say Danny Sanders wouldn't help a new mother. You look like you need it more than any of us, anyway."

Mallory pushed Caleb's shoulder toward the man. "My arms are full with the baby."

Caleb looked at her, tenuously controlling his rage, but went and took the cheeseburgers from the cook. "Thank you," he quietly snarled and then walked back toward the door. "C'mon, Mal. There has to be someone here who will help us."

They left the café and were once again greeted with sirens. The large sprite with the whirring weapon was circling over the city and facing away from them for the moment. The streets were empty and still. Caleb looked wildly around, and Mallory again touched his arm. "Eat the sandwiches."

Caleb looked back at her, his eyes slightly glazed and winced. "We should save them for you. You need your strength to feed the baby."

"I just ate, and right now, I need my husband thinking clearly, not hunger raging. Eat the sandwiches." Mallory insisted.

Caleb's face looked strained and hurt, but he tore into one of the cheeseburgers. His eyes brightened as he chewed. "This is amazing. We don't have anything like this back home. You should try a bite." He held it up to Mallory.

She took a nibble. Caleb was right. She had not tasted anything quite like this. It was beef with some kind of creamy cheese and bacon. "Mmm ... that's really good." She nodded.

"Can you eat and run?"

"I can run and chew." Caleb shoved the rest of the cheese-burger into his mouth: the whole thing. His cheeks bulged out like a chipmunk's, and he slowly moved his jaw up and down like a cow chewing its cud. He held out his arms to pick up Mallory. "Muh, rum, muh ruh," he mumbled.

Mallory shook her head. "Too suspicious." She looked down the streets and noticed that many of the building had awnings over their windows and doors just like the shops and skyscrapers back home, except that the vines and vegetation had overgrown these awnings. "If we stay under the coverings, they won't be able to spot us from above."

Caleb nodded and chewed, and the three of them moved quickly to the next awning on the street. Mallory still did not know where they were going, but it felt good to be moving, not laying in a hospital bed waiting for some unknown end. They ran to the next awning, and the giant sprite's circle was now facing in their direction, so they pressed themselves up against the building. The sun, which had started to set while Mallory was in the hospital bed, was now completely below the horizon, and twilight spread quickly over the city. The giant sprite turned on four spotlights which it was using to work over the streets looking for them.

Caleb swallowed and said, "it's just a matter of time before they find us out here. We need to find a place to bunker down until we can find a way off this island."

Mallory tilted her head in confusion. "You said that earlier. What do you mean by 'off this island'?"

Caleb's eyebrows lowered and then raised. "Oh, that's

right, you were out of it when we got here. The whole place is surrounded with water. So much water. The Archivist called it the 'ocean.' Apparently, most of the world is covered in the ocean. I wouldn't have believed her except that we spent hours flying over water to get here. Hours."

Mallory thought about that for a moment. "So we need to fly over the same water to get home?"

Caleb looked confused now. "Home? We don't have a home. I'd be happy to go somewhere safe. We can't stay on this island though; I'm pretty sure they intend to kill us."

"Us and everyone in Hoffen City," Mallory confirmed.

"Hoffen City?" Caleb's confusion deepened.

"They want revenge for the war with the Ex Natu, and they especially hate that General Knenne had a family." Mallory bounced the baby. "The Archivist's friend Zane got real angry when his name came up, and the Archivist said it would be better if they never knew I was his descendant."

"That's not good, Mal." Caleb looked more worried now. "I need to get the two of you out of here."

"And we need to get back to Hoffen City," Mallory insisted. "Hoffen City is General Knenne's legacy, and they intend to destroy it."

"Do they know where it is?"

"I think so," Mallory nodded.

Caleb took a bite of the second cheeseburger and grabbed Mallory's free hand. The sprite had circled away from them again, and they ran to the next awning and then to the next. By the time they got to the third awning, Caleb had finished the second sandwich, and the giant sprite was circling around toward them again. They pressed up against the doors to what appeared to be some sort of office building; the words "Michaels and Oliver At Law" were stenciled on the window. Caleb sighed. "But we don't know how to get off this island. We don't know how to get to Hoffen City."

Mallory felt her chest tighten and she whispered, "I know, but we have to figure it out. Our people are in danger."

"Pssst! Pssst!" A hissing noise came from between two buildings just a few feet ahead.

Caleb put his arm protectively over Mallory and Kirk. "Who's there?" he whispered urgently.

A hooded figure leaned out from the nook between the buildings. "Someone who can help. Quick, follow me!"

Mallory looked up in the sky and saw that the giant sprite had once again turned away from them, and she nudged Caleb's shoulder.

He looked back at her in disbelief. "How do we know that we can trust him?"

Mallory shrugged. "You were just ready to trust a diner full of strangers, but not a stranger on the street? Besides, what choice do we have?"

Caleb rolled his head on his neck. "You said it yourself. I was hungry then and not thinking clearly."

"Caleb!" Mallory hissed.

"Okay, okay." He relented.

They ran to the alcove, and the hooded figure led them through a door in the alleyway. The building was a warehouse of some sort, full of large wooden crates, including one that was nearly as big as the giant sprite flying around outside.

The hooded figure walked to the largest crate and placed his hand on a red square painted on the wood. The red square lit up, and a laser scanned the figure's hand. The side of the large crate clicked open with a hiss. A white fog issued out of it that was too heavy to float up into the room. The white mist just hovered around their feet near the floor.

The hooded figure slid the side of the crate aside, and as it moved, it folded into itself. The room was too dark for Mallory to tell whether it was hinged like a set of folding closet doors, or if it was somehow disobeying the laws of physics and getting smaller. Inside the crate was blackness. The hooded figure turned toward them and motioned for them to follow. As they walked into the crate, lights began to flicker on around them.

It was a huge flying ship, much like the one Omaha had attacked the Library with. A crescent moon with four small stars were painted on the side of the ship—the same crest on the fire sprites they had repaired in Hoffen City—the same crest Reddy LaMarr had replaced with Omaha's family symbol when she was the Sprite Master. Mallory paused. She bit her lip and tilted her head, wondering who this hooded figure could be.

Caleb did not stop at first, but he seemed to sense that his wife was no longer beside him. He turned back to her. "Mallory?"

She did not say anything.

The hooded figure stopped at the sound of Caleb's voice and turned back toward them. The lights of the ship illuminated his face slightly. He was an older man with a strong jaw line. His peppered gray hair and thick mustache were curly but well-groomed. His eyes, which flashed with authority even in the shadows, were stormy gray. But most strikingly, just above his starched shirt collar where his jaw met his neck, several moving tattoos danced.

Caleb threw himself at the hooded Ex Natu, but as Caleb swung his fist, the hooded man feinted left and then slapped Caleb's neck. When he moved his hand away, Mallory saw a small black circle stuck to Caleb's neck. Then electric arcs erupted out of the circle. Caleb screamed and dropped to his knees. He tipped to the side, all the way to the floor, and started convulsing.

"Caleb!" Mallory started to rush toward him.

But the hooded Ex Natu stepped into her path. "You would be wise not to touch your husband, Mrs. Aiworth. That is an adhesive taser on his neck, and there's enough amperage pumping through him to kill anyone without nano sprites."

Mallory paused and looked at the Ex Natu. "You're

hurting him. Please stop."

"He'll be fine. He'll wake up with a horrible headache, but he'll be fine. Now, come with me." He grabbed her by the arm and started pulling her towards the ship.

At first, Mallory felt somewhat dazed and stumbled forward with the man. She had been through so much: the world seemed out of control. It was like she was out of her body watching everything happen to someone else. But then, baby Kirk stirred in her arms and routed about looking for food. Suddenly, motherly adrenaline flooded her. This was not happening to someone else. It was happening to her, and her child was in danger. She looked the hooded man over and saw that he had a weapon holstered just inside his cloak. With a quick jerk, she shook loose from his grip and dove her hand inside his cloak. He moved fast, tossing her aside like she was a pillow that had been thrown at him.

She stumbled and fell.

The world slowed down, as Mallory twisted her body hard to keep from landing on Kirk. Instead, she landed on her elbow and white fire shot up through her shoulder and into her chest. She tried to scream, but all that came out was a timid yelp. Baby Kirk had no such difficulties and began to wail at being shaken so much in the fall.

"Shut that kid up!" The Ex Natu looked nervously at the roof of the building. "They're searching for you, and they'll have audio sensors deployed, specifically tuned for a baby's cry."

Mallory sat up and pulled her baby closer. The pain in her elbow was already subsiding. Maybe it was the medical nano sprites, or maybe it was the adrenaline pumping through her. She did not try to calm baby Kirk down. Instead, she held up her free hand and pointed the weapon at him. "Take that thing off my husband, now!"

The Ex Natu's expression changed from nervousness to surprise. He tilted his head to the side and regarded her. Then he threw his head back and laughed. And laughed. And laughed.

Mallory grew frustrated. She was about to fire a warning shot when she remembered what she had just done to the Archivist. She waved the weapon at him more threateningly. "I mean it. I've shot people before!"

"Ho! Ho!" The Ex Natu tried to catch his breath and act serious. "Oh, yes, I know. Shot your husband." He pointed to Caleb still convulsing on the ground. "Shot poor Emily." He waved over his head to some random point where the Archivist might be. "Yes, I've been following your story for awhile, and you've shot some people, Mallory. But let's face it, you have more of Eva's blood running in your veins than Mari's: more Matriarch than Administrator. Don't you think?"

She did not know what he knew about her or about the chronicles of Hoffen City's founders, but this was not the time to try to figure out any of that. She waved the gun again. "You're going to take that contraption off my husband, and take us somewhere safe, or you'll find out how much damage even a poor shot can do."

The Ex Natu waved her threat away. He turned his back on her and bent down to check Caleb. "He doesn't go down easy; that's for sure." He cocked his hand back and punched

Caleb hard in the jaw. Caleb's body stopped convulsing and fell slack.

Mallory yelled, "Hey!" She aimed the weapon right at the Ex Natu, and she pulled the trigger.

CLICK

Nothing happened.

"Wow!" The hooded Ex Natu exclaimed and looked back at her. "You really did it. Thank goodness for biometric safety features. Maybe there is some of Mari's blood in you after all. You can keep that spirit in check for now, young one. I'm not going to hurt you."

Mallory looked at the weapon in disgust and threw it to the side.

The Ex Natu pulled the adhesive taser off Caleb's neck. Then he stood up and grabbed him by the scruff of his collar and dragged Mallory's large husband toward the ship as if he weighed little more than a child.

Mallory pulled herself up off the floor. Baby Kirk was still screaming about all the excitement and not having any food. "I'm not going back to Omaha. I don't know what he'll do to my child."

"I wouldn't dream of taking you to that psychopath." The Ex Natu passed his hand over a small square, and a panel popped open with a hissing sound then lowered itself to form a boarding plank. "I should have killed him centuries ago, but his megalomania is useful sometimes." He paused and tilted his head to the side. There was a soft knocking noise coming from somewhere, and upon hearing it, the Ex Natu moved a little faster. "Of course, you're not going to get much love from the Relos either. If they knew who you were, they would kill you and your whole family." He paused and looked back at her. "Are you coming?"

Mallory hesitated and looked down at her crying baby. Did she have a choice?

Suddenly, the warehouse was flooded with lights. They were coming from a large semi-circle window above a row of loading bays. A booming voice filled the room. "We have you surrounded. Surrender yourselves peacefully and no harm will come to the mother and child."

The hooded Ex Natu shrugged and resumed walking up the plank into the ship, dragging Caleb behind him. "It's now or never!"

Mallory bit her lip and tilted her head. Then she ran after the man and her husband. The plank lifted behind her sealing them all into the ship. The interior of the ship was dark with an array of colored lights blinking above various panels and readouts. Mallory had no idea what any of it meant. The Ex Natu dropped the still unconscious Caleb into a seat and pulled down two straps across his chest. The straps had buckles that he inserted into slots at the bottom of the seat. "There's a chair over there for you. Buckle yourself in like this. You'll have to hold the baby tight. It's not going to be a smooth ride, and they don't make fighter craft with baby seats."

Mallory climbed into the seat and used her free hand to pull one of the straps down, buckling it just as the Ex Natu had done with Caleb. Then she passed Kirk to her other hand and secured the other strap. The Ex Natu had sat down in a seat at the front of the ship. Six windows appeared in front of him. Three were clear, two had illuminated targets projected on them, and the last one had numbers that were counting down. When the numbers got to one, she pulled the baby tight to her chest.

She was not sure what to expect: an explosion, a roar, a whine.

But there was no noise at all, just an instant feeling of weightlessness. Outside the window, she could see that they were moving. In fact, they crashed straight through the roof of the warehouse. Pieces of wood and roofing tile were falling all around the windows, but Mallory neither felt nor heard the impact. Baby Kirk had become enamored by the flashing lights in the window and had stopped crying, and the entire interior of the ship was utterly silent. The two windows with targets started flashing red, and Mallory saw the giant sprite with the rotor approaching. On the sides of it, two large weapons with multiple barrels in a circle began to spin. Mallory expected to hear the whirring noise that came with that spinning, but still there was nothing but silence inside the ship.

The hooded Ex Natu moved his hands in front of the screens like a conductor in front of an orchestra. In beat one, he patted the air with his right hand, and the ship rotated slightly, beat two the giant sprite was centered in the targeting window, beat three he tapped the center of the window with his left hand, and on beat four, the giant sprite exploded in a brilliant, orange fireball. Then he threw both hands forward, and the ship shot through the burning debris of the giant sprite. Mallory averted her face, afraid some of the debris might blow through the windshield, but it seemed to bounce off the glass harmlessly. The silence of the pieces hitting the ship made her feel sick.

Or maybe the sickness was due to the motion of the ship? The weightlessness Mallory had felt when they first took off ended as they accelerated. Now, instead of feeling no weight, it felt like she was ten times heavier, being pressed hard into her seat. Even her eyelids seemed to be under pressure, so much so that it was difficult to blink. She looked down at baby Kirk, and he looked up at her, terrified. She pulled him to her chest, and nuzzled the fine, fuzzy curls on top of his head. When she looked back up at the windows. The sun had completely set, and she saw nothing but darkness and stars.

"That's strange," Mallory thought. It looked like the stars were moving toward them, quickly.

"Here comes the bumpy part," the Ex Natu pilot yelled. "Hold tight!"

One of the stars hit the windshield and exploded in a fire blast. The gravity holding Mallory to her seat suddenly shifted and tried to throw her against the roof. She almost let go of the baby, but her hands reacted fast, gripping him tighter. The windshield did not even have a crack in it, but both the target screens were flashing white then red, white then red. Another star hit the side of the ship and sent them into a spin, but the Ex Natu pulled them out of it with little effort. He began to drum the target screens in a paradiddle pattern—right left right right, left right left left—faster and faster. Red beams began to streak away from the ship, colliding with the white stars. Explosions of pink plasma filled the skies. Mallory could not help but think of the rain back home when it hit the light. Something that seemed so safe when she was young looked utterly deadly outside the ship's windows.

The fireworks outside the ship continued late into the night, but the Ex Natu pilot never seemed to tire: weaving in and out of explosions, tapping the windows, lost in the rhythm of survival. Even the ship's jerking took on a rhythm, to the point that Mallory could anticipate every drop and roll. Caleb never woke up through it all, just flopped about in his straps like a life-sized rag doll. Mallory grimaced when she thought about how angry he was going to be when he woke up.

And then the tapping on the screens stopped, the explosions stopped, and the ship leveled off. There was nothing but darkness and silence. Mallory looked at the Ex Natu pilot, but he never looked back. He just kept his attention on the windows and screens in front of him. She looked down at baby Kirk and found him sprawled out like a rag doll over her arm, breathing calmly. He looked like a tiny version of his father, and he would probably wake up just as angry. She smiled at the thought of her two hungry fellows. But she also wondered if she would ever get her jovial giant back.

She had seen glimpses of his old self—a passing joke, a smug smirk, but she had not seen the cool diplomacy with which he used to handle people. Everything was rage and fists. She could not imagine the suffering Caleb had been through over the past few months at the hands of the Ex

Natu, nor could she imagine what it must be like to carry the wilding nano sprites and have your body unmake and make itself while it starves. Could he ever recover from such psychological torment?

She hoped so.

She had not fought and nearly died over and over to raise a child without his father—all of his father. Somewhere inside the rag doll strapped to his seat was the heart of the Governor of the Triad—the man who had been bred and trained to lead the government of an entire people. Somehow, she needed to resurrect that man. If only they could sit still long enough to catch their breath, she could figure out what it would take to get him back. But they had been on the run, pretty much since the moment of little Kirk's birth. And as that thought hit her, Mallory felt the exhaustion of the past few days wash over her. She was supposed to have laid in a nice bed recovering after giving birth, not fly all over the world trying to stay alive. There was not any pain per se—the medical nano sprites had taken care of that. The tiredness was deeper than that—bone deep, as her grandmother used to say. As a child, she never really understood the expression, but now, well now there was nowhere she could go, nothing she could do. The night was quiet. The ship was dark. And she was strapped in, unlike when she was riding the flying sprites. She slumped in her chair and carefully repositioned Kirk, so he would not fall. Then she tilted her head back, closed her eyes, and fell asleep.

When she woke up, the sun was shining through the windows of the Ex Natu ship, but the hooded Ex Natu was no longer sitting at the controls. Outside the windows, Mallory could see that they were back inside some sort of building, and there was a large doorway in front of the ship that looked out over a massive city. It made the Davis City Metroplex look small, and unlike that city, there were no Ex Natu citadels in her view. Most of the architecture looked ancient, carved from stone with spires reaching toward the heavens like the building where she had sought refuge when hiding from the Sprite Master. Mallory looked over to where Caleb had been sitting. He was still strapped to his seat and unconscious. Then she checked baby Kirk.

He was gone.

"Not again," Mallory thought as she tried to jump up. Two strips of pain burned her neck and shoulders, and she fell hard back into the chair. She panicked and looked wildly around: She was still strapped into her chair. Between her legs where the straps connected was a large red button. Mallory pressed it, and the straps came loose. She untangled herself from the chair and again leapt up. The ship was still closed, and she had no idea how to open it. She looked around at all the buttons and dials scattered in random places. Everything was written in some strange code she did not understand. It had the same letters that she was used to, but they were jumbled and made very little sense. She growled in frustration, surprising herself.

Were her medical sprites making her go feral like her husband?

Mallory again looked at Caleb strapped to his chair. Would he be any help figuring out how to get out of here if she woke him up, or would he fly into a rage and tear the ship apart and her along with it? Still two heads were better than one, even if one of those heads was full of wilding nano sprites.

Mallory knelt down in front of Caleb and began to gently caress his face. "Caleb? Caleb?" she cooed softly. The large man moaned and began to take more shallow breaths. She crawled back a foot and began to shake his knee. "Caleb!" she said with more vigor. "Wake up!"

One of Caleb's eyes slowly rolled open and then the other. He yawned deeply. Then his pupils came into focus on Mallory's face. He smiled. "Oh hey, beautiful! It's nice waking up to see your face."

Mallory sighed in relief. "It's good to see you too." She reached out and touched his knee again. "Can you do something for me?"

Caleb's smile curled up on one side flirtatiously. "For you? Anything."

Mallory smiled back as her heart beat a little faster. She could not help herself, but she needed to stay on track for Kirk's sake. "I need you stay calm and help me find a way out of here."

Caleb looked around the ship, and slowly his memory of what had put him to sleep began to rush over him. His flirtatious smile vanished, quickly replaced by anger. He tried to stand up, but the straps pulled him back down. His anger began to shift to rage. Mallory touched his knee, and she calmly said, "Caleb, please. There's a button right here." She pointed to the release. "It will let you out, but I need you to be calm, to think."

He looked at the button and then at her. The rage rolled back to anger. "I'm calm, Mal." He pushed the button and stood up as the straps released. Then he looked around the ship. "The Ex Natu?"

It was a rhetorical question, but Mallory nodded her affirmation.

"Where's our son?"

Mallory bit her lip and tilted her head.

"You don't have to think about how to answer me, Mallory," Caleb snapped. "I'm not a problem that needs to be solved."

Mallory straightened in embarrassment but smiled. That keen observation of human behavior was a sign that the Caleb she loved was still in there somewhere, and it was what she needed to help them get their son back. "He's not here. I woke up just like you, and he was gone. I can't figure out how to get out of this ship to find him."

Caleb's eyebrows tilted lower, but he did not explode in rage. Instead, he turned to look around the ship with Mallory.

Mallory pointed toward the area of the ship wall that had no seats. "I think this is where the door is, but all of these buttons are in some kind of code."

Caleb examined the code with her. "Have you tried pushing any of them?"

Mallory shook her head. "This thing is packed with weapons. What if they blow up something out there? Kirk's out there somewhere."

Caleb's eyebrow went up, and then he turned his attention

back to the ship's buttons. Then, in frustration, he punched one.

"Caleb!" Mallory yelled, but to her amazement the ship unsealed, and the ramp began to lower. "What? How?" Mallory stammered.

"That's where I would have put it if I were putting an open button somewhere," Caleb said matter-of-factly. Then he grabbed her and pulled her behind him protectively away from the descending door.

"Oh! Thank goodness, you're awake!" a voice called from outside.

Mallory peaked over Caleb's shoulder and saw the Ex Natu who had rescued them from the Relos island sitting in a white, wooden rocking chair, rocking baby Kirk vigorously. The Ex Natu was no longer wearing his hood, and in the light of day, he looked much older than the other Ex Natu Mallory had seen. His hair was salt and pepper and was cut very short, like a magistrate. He had a thick, bushy mustache that twitched wildly as he made faces at the baby. Her son would have none of the man's attempts to quiet him and was screaming his head off. The Ex Natu held the baby out to her in desperation.

Mallory ran to baby Kirk and took him gingerly from the man. He stood and motioned toward the rocking chair, and Mallory sat down with her baby, who, upon smelling his mother, immediately began looking for breakfast. The Ex Natu turned away from her to Caleb, who looked like he was going to kill him. The Ex Natu laughed. "No worries, my young friend. I have your breakfast too." He walked over to a table with several covered dishes. "What's your pleasure? Eggs? Bacon? Sausage? Bread? Fruit? The fresh berries are amazing here this time of year."

"Is it real meat?" Mallory called. "I thought Ex Natu didn't eat meat."

The Ex Natu laughed. "Only the ones dumb enough to have stayed in the Americas with Omaha and his ilk. The wilding wolves ate most of the other animals. Those abominations had a harder time getting established here, and we were more proactive in clearing out the ones plaguing our shores."

Caleb was looking at the food in desperation but also not taking one step toward it. Quietly but firmly, he said, "Ex Natu are Ex Natu. They all need to be wiped out."

The older Ex Natu laughed. "Where does that leave you, Caleb Aiworth?"

"You think I want to stay like this?" Caleb shot back. "I'd rather be dead."

Mallory, who had just gotten Kirk settled, yelled, "Caleb!"

Caleb's eyes flicked toward her and baby Kirk, and he nodded toward his family. "They're the only thing I've got that's worth living for."

The Ex Natu nodded. "And worth fighting for?"

Caleb growled. "Are you challenging me?"

The Ex Natu laughed heartily. "Son, we've already established how that would go. I'm just asking the question. Are they worth fighting for?"

Caleb nodded. "Clearly."

"Good! Then go get some food. Soldiers can't survive on an empty stomach."

Caleb looked him over warily and then moved toward the table. There were two plates sitting next to the covered dishes. He grabbed one and was just about to serve himself, when he paused. He looked back at Mallory. "Can I get you anything?"

Mallory nodded greedily. "Yes, please. Everything!"

Caleb sighed, but quickly loaded her plate for her as the Ex Natu watched. When it was heaped full of food, he grabbed a fork and spoon and carried the plate to Mallory. She reached up and took the plate from him. "Thank you!" She smiled. Caleb turned to go back for his own food, but Mallory called out. "Caleb?" He turned around and saw her holding the plate with a concerned look on her face. Her other hand was busy helping Kirk get his breakfast, and she had no way to get the food into her mouth. Caleb growled a little as he walked back to Mallory's rocker.

The Ex Natu laughed again. "Oh, for pity's sake. Go get your food, man. I'll help your wife!" He pulled another rocking chair over to Mallory and sat down, taking the plate from her. Then he handed her the fork and held the plate out in front of her.

Mallory looked at him, then at Caleb, and then at the plate. She shrugged, picked up the fork, and dove into the eggs first. They were delicious!

Caleb walked slowly back to the table with the food and picked up the second plate. He stood there staring at it for a moment and then set it down. He turned back to the Ex Natu. "Why are you helping us? What's your game?"

The Ex Natu laughed. "My game?"

Mallory nodded and started talking around a piece of

sausage she had just shoved into her mouth. "Everyone's got a motive. What's yours?"

"Can't it be the kindness of my heart?"

"No," Caleb said, still resting his hand on the unfilled plate at the table. "It can't. You know all about us. You knew my name—my last name."

Mallory nodded again; this time talking around some berries, "You knew I shot Caleb. How could you know that?" She swallowed. "You also knew about Mari and Eva in *The Chronicles of the Matriarch* and the Administrator. You even knew who the Archivist was. How do you know any of that?"

Caleb tapped the plate. "Who are you?"

The old Ex Natu smiled and nodded to Mallory. "Let's just say I'm a distant relation."

Caleb threw the plate off the table, and it shattered. "Just answer the question!"

The old Ex Natu's smile vanished, and he threw the plate he was holding to the ground, shattering glass and food everywhere. He stood up and puffed out his chest. "I am President Kirkland Knenne, commander-in-chief of the Ex Natu armed forces, and ruler of the Quad-Continental Alliance." He paused to let the introduction sink in.

Mallory sat holding her empty fork and looking sadly at her food spread across the deck. Then she looked up at the Ex Natu as his words sank in. "Knenne?"

He looked down at her. "Yes." He lowered himself back into the rocker slowly and looked sadly at Mallory and the baby. "The chronicles as you call them are part of my story too. In those days, the people of Hoffen City referred to me as General Knenne."

15

This time it was Mallory's turn to laugh, which made her son choke a little on his breakfast. She patted his back to help him out but did not stop laughing. "No. No. No! That's just too much. General Knenne died centuries ago, inside Hoffen City. There's no way."

Caleb nodded his head and grabbed a piece of sausage. Mallory's levity had apparently alleviated his rage enough to eat. Around a mouthful of savory meat, he added, "Even if you had faked your death. No one could get in or out of Hoffen City until Mallory broke the light."

Mallory huffed. "That was Reddy, remember. We broke the Dikaió."

Caleb whirled his sausage in a circle. "My point still

stands."

The Ex Natu waited patiently for the pair to quiet, and then answered, "What are you two talking about?"

"It was in *The Chronicles of the Matriarch*," Mallory answered. "Eva Knenne specifically mentioned you being dead."

The Ex Natu's eyebrows went up in surprise. "My Eva? I don't think so."

Mallory shifted in her chair. "No, I remember. It was just before the fire sprite attacked Hoffen City, and Mari activated the shield."

The Ex Natu's face darkened. "I have a copy of *The Chronicles of the Matriarch*. I can get it if you want."

"What would it prove?" Caleb said while spooning eggs out of the serving dish directly into his mouth. "You having copies of the chronicles would be a great way to assume a dead man's identity. Reddy Lamarr did it for years in Hoffen City."

"Reddy Lamarr? Why is that name so familiar?" the Ex Natu asked.

"If you don't know, how could you possibly be the real General Knenne?" Mallory reasoned.

"I've known a lot of people in my lifetime," the Ex Natu said. "Does me not immediately recollecting one name mean that I'm not who I say I am?"

Mallory tilted her head and bit her lip. She looked at Caleb. "What we've read of the chronicles didn't say anything about her. If he knew who she was, would that prove anything?"

Caleb shrugged while finishing off the bacon. "He doesn't, so it doesn't"

"Should we give him a hint?" Mallory asked. "Also, can you bring me some sausage before there isn't any left?"

"Sure," Caleb shrugged again, but he made no move toward Mallory.

Mallory scowled. "'Sure' to the sausage, or 'sure' to the hint?"

"The hint. You had your sausage already." Caleb used the pair of tongs to grab two sausage links and throw them whole into his mouth.

"My sausage got thrown on the floor." Mallory nodded toward the ground. "C'mon, Caleb. I've got to get my strength back."

"Look," the Ex Natu interrupted. "Give me the hint, and I'll make more sausage."

Caleb's eyes widened. "You have more sausage?"

Mallory shook her head. "Reddy Lamarr was part of the resistance. She used an Ex Natu medical kit after she was injured and accidentally made herself an Ex Natu."

Their host closed his eyes and thought out loud. "The resistance. Reddy. Reddy. Lamarr." His eyes popped open. "Oh, I know. The redhead Omaha had as an assistant. She's still alive?"

Mallory held up a hand with her palm up. "Well, Caleb?"

"It's a start. Now, let's see the part of the chronicles that says you're not dead," Caleb said, having run out of food. "And you owe us more sausage. Mallory didn't get any."

The Ex Natu laughed out loud. "It's been a long time

since I've laughed. C'mon in and I'll get you all the proof and sausage that you need." He walked toward what looked to be a large window on the deck and waved his hand in front of it. The entire wall next the window collapsed inward on itself just like the crate had in the Relos warehouse, creating a black hole in the wall. The Ex Natu walked in and disappeared.

Baby Kirk had finished eating, but now, he was squirming and crying as if he were uncomfortable. Mallory hoisted him over her shoulder and patted his back until the gas passed, seemingly from both ends. Mallory's nose wrinkled. Nope. One of those evacuations was not just gas. She smiled and held the baby out to Caleb. "Would you mind holding him for a minute, so I can get my sausage?"

Caleb was all ready to walk into the hole with the Ex Natu, but he froze and gingerly took his son from Mallory. "I guess so."

Mallory smiled, kissed his cheek, and followed after the Ex Natu. As she exited the black space of the wall, she froze. The interior of the building they had landed on was a massive atrium. There looked to be an entire rainforest inside the building. Birds were singing, filling the space with music. Mallory could not identify a single bird's song, but she half suspected that even if she could pick out one of the multitudes, she might not know it. The plant life was certainly too exotic for her to identify any of the trees and flowers inside the building. Trees? Yes, there were whole trees inside the Ex Natu's abode, so many that she could not count them, or even see around them. The trunks were wider than the twin oaks outside her home. The air was thick with an unnatural amount of humidity, and yet not as hot as it was outside on the landing. The brick walls rose up about two-thirds of the way to the top, and beyond that, the entire roof was a dome of glass. The cupola was decorated with stained glass, which featured the crescent moon and stars crest from the Ex Natu's ship. Above the cupola, Mallory saw the distinct pink haze of a holographic plasma shield. The place was massive enough to be a city on its own.

The Ex Natu stood on one of what looked to be an intricate system of rope bridges with wooden planks that traversed among the trees, leading to several small bamboo huts. There were no doors on the huts, and each one seemed to have the furnishings of a small house, with couches, chairs, and dining tables. But as near as Mallory could see, they were all empty. The Ex Natu patiently waved to them both to follow him. Mallory thought they had better hurry, or they would certainly get lost in this place—though it did not look like they would have any trouble finding a place to stay if they did. Her natural curiosity urged her to go explore, but she had been promised more breakfast, and she was starving. "Caleb, hurry up!" she yelled behind her.

Caleb did not move immediately. Instead, he stood sniffing the air. Then he pulled baby Kirk up to his nose. His head whipped away quickly. "Mal!" he bellowed. "Mal, the baby needs you!"

But Mallory was already bounding down the rope bridge after their host. She felt amazing. The medical sprites the Relos had injected her with seemed to have healed up all of her ills, including those from giving birth. She did not know how many days she had been out of it after the wilding wolf bite, but in all her experiences with pregnant women back home, running across a rope bridge atop an indoor rainforest was probably one of those abilities that needed a bit more rest than what she had managed, and yet here she was.

Suddenly, the bridge beneath her feat lurched violently upward, and she nearly lost her footing. She grabbed the rope railing and looked behind her. Caleb was galloping toward her holding the baby out to her. She giggled, but then got stern. "You be careful, Caleb Aiworth! You know very well that's not how to carry a baby!"

His face immediately grew sheepish, and he pulled the baby back protectively to his chest.

Mallory giggled again and sprinted away from him after the Ex Natu.

"Mal!" Caleb whined after her, but he walked slowly and carefully this time, holding baby Kirk close to his chest as if carrying a very fragile antique vase. "C'mon, Mal! He's really stinky!" He called. Then quietly he mumbled. "Kid, don't take after your mother, okay?"

"I heard that!" Mallory yelled back at him, but she did not turn around to take the baby. She was starving, and besides, the boys needed some bonding time.

The Ex Natu who claimed to be General Knenne stopped at a sliding glass door at the end of one of the rope bridges and opened it for Mallory. "Welcome to my humble home."

Compared to the atrium outside, what lay inside the glass door was actually quite humble. It was a three-room apartment: a bedroom, a bathroom, and the kitchen, dining room, and living room were all one giant open-room concept. If it were not for the appliances in the kitchen, the table with one chair in the dining room, and a single recliner in the living room, it would have been impossible to differentiate between the spaces. The kitchen had three upright freezers and one refrigerator. From the latter, the Ex Natu pulled a package wrapped in paper. Inside were several more sausage links. He plugged in a square box on the counter, put a dirty skillet on the box, and within seconds the grease in the skillet started to sizzle. "How many would you like?"

At first, Mallory wanted to ask him to wash the skillet, but then she wondered if it was just dirty from this morning's breakfast. The Ex Natu were not a clean people in her experience, except for that couple on the outskirts of the Davis City Metroplex—their home had been tidy. She looked around the room and realized that not only did everything have a place, the abode was also incredibly clean. The white, tiled floor was so shiny, she could see her reflection in it. "All of them!" she smiled.

The Ex Natu laughed. "You're not a shy one, are you?" He stepped back and motioned toward the pan. "If you cook them, I'll go find my copies of the chronicles."

Mallory did not know what to say and took a step back. "I … well …".

The Ex Natu looked concerned. "What's wrong?"

"I've never cooked anything before," Mallory admitted with some embarrassment. "There were always sprites and the Dikaió to cook for us. It was the same at the Library."

The Ex Natu's eyebrows furrowed, but before he could say

anything, Caleb burst into the room still carrying a screaming baby Kirk. "Mallory!" he bellowed.

Mallory giggled. "Oh, alright. Give him here." She took her smelly son from Caleb and turned to the Ex Natu. "I don't suppose you have extra cloth that could be used for a diaper, do you?"

"I do, actually. You," the Ex Natu pointed to Caleb. "Do you know how to cook sausages?"

"I know how to eat sausages," Caleb assured him.

"Come here," the Ex Natu said with some irritation. "It's not hard. Start them on one side, count to ninety, turn them one quarter turn, do that again and again, until you get back to where you started. Then put them on this plate. Save some for your wife." He handed Caleb a pair of tongs. "Use these so you don't burn yourself."

"Won't the nano sprites just heal me if I get burned?" Caleb shrugged.

"Yes, but no one wants to taste your burnt fingers on their sausages," the Ex Natu pushed the tongs into his hand. "There's a right way to do things, and nigh immortality doesn't change what's right and wrong."

Caleb took the tongs and looked at them with curiosity. He squeezed them together twice, and they made a satisfying clicking noise. He smiled and started picking up sausages and dropping them into the hot skillet, where they immediately began to sizzle and pop.

"Mrs. Aiworth, you and your baby follow me," the Ex Natu beckoned her back out the glass door and closed it behind them. He led her out across three more rope bridges to the center of the atrium.

Here, Mallory was surprised to find that the center tree was not a tree at all. It was tall rectangular structure covered in vines, all except for a sliding metal door where the rope bridge met it. She glanced over the edge of the rope bridge and whistled. She briefly had a flashback to the Aiworth Bridge and then to dangling atop the skyscraper in Hoffen City. She could not see the bottom of the atrium, but she could see that the center structure went down several floors, and everywhere it intersected with a rope bridge, there was a metal door.

"An elevator?" she asked.

The Ex Natu smiled and waved his hand in front of a small box on the side of the metal door. It took a few moments, but soon there was a ding, and the metal door slid open. It was an elevator. Inside was what looked to be a skyscraper of buttons to choose from: 162 whole numbers and 10 numbers with a "b" after them. The Ex Natu pushed 6b, and the elevator door closed. Mallory's stomach shot into her throat as the elevator descended. It was so fast. Not quite free falling, but about as close to it as one could come without making a splat at the bottom.

When the door opened, they were no longer in an atrium: They were in the hallway of a concrete bunker. The ceilings were twelve feet high and lined with Dikaió lights. The Ex Natu exited into the hallway and motioned for her to follow. Baby Kirk was still unhappy about his soiled clothing and screaming for relief. The hallway opened into a spacious open room full of shelves. Large concrete pillars were stationed strategically around the room for support. The Ex Natu led them to several shelves stacked full of plastic bins. He grabbed one, pulled it off the shelf onto the ground, and popped the top off of it. Inside were hundreds of cloth diapers. "Here you go!" he smiled at her. "They're adjustable." He picked one up and pulled a cloth tab that cinched up the leg holes and waist. "Just put it on, pull this, and twist the tab to keep it from sliding back."

Mallory took the diaper and laid baby Kirk gently down on the remarkably clean concrete floor. There was not a speck of dust anywhere. As she began to undress Kirk, the Ex Natu sprinted a couple of rows over and came back with some moist paper towels, which he handed to Mallory so she could clean the baby. The Ex Natu's diapers were a wonder, fitting perfectly.

When she was finished and the baby was quieted, the Ex Natu grabbed the whole plastic container and the wipes, threw them on one shoulder, and motioned back toward the elevator. Mallory nodded and followed him. He did not immediately return to his room, instead pressing 2b on the elevator.

"What about breakfast?" Mallory asked.

"As long as we're down here, I thought maybe you'd like to cover up a bit more."

The Ex Natu nodded toward her legs, and Mallory looked down. She was still only wearing the hospital gown and the Relos man's jacket. She felt her cheeks blush. Things had been so hectic and out of control, she had entirely forgotten that she was barely covered.

The elevator stopped, and the doors opened on another storage room. "Stay here," the Ex Natu said and sprinted down the row of shelves, turned right, and disappeared.

Mallory sat down on the plastic tub and waited. Every time the elevator doors tried to close, Mallory pushed the doors-open button, and they sprang back open. After about 15 near closes, she was starting to worry that the Ex Natu was not coming back. She wondered if Caleb could resist eating all the sausage upstairs. She doubted it. But she also doubted that he would be successful at cooking them. She would just leave the Ex Natu and go find breakfast, but she had no idea what floor they had started on, and she was not sure she could find her way through the maze of rope bridges and forest up above even if she made it to the right floor. There was no choice but to wait here. She drummed her fingers on the tub in impatience. At least Kirk had fallen asleep in her lap.

Then the Ex Natu came around the corner, carrying another tub. He was beaming. "Sorry, it took so long. I figured while we were here, I'd grab some stuff for your husband and baby too."

Mallory stood up and pressed up against the elevator wall with baby Kirk to let the Ex Natu squeeze in with his tub. "Can you press 112 for me? My hands are full."

Mallory scanned the numbers and found 112. Once again, her stomach was in her throat, or maybe it was the other way around as the elevator shot upward just as quickly as it had dropped. It was so quick, she almost dropped Kirk, but instincts kicked in, and she pulled the baby tightly to her chest. The elevator door opened, and the Ex Natu picked up the plastic tubs. "C'mon, let's go see if your husband ate all the sausage."

"I would just assume he did. We shouldn't have left him alone with it for so long. Hopefully, you have more; I'm starving," Mallory said following the elderly man out.

"I'm the president of the Global Alliance. I can get more sausage," he assured her as they made their way across another bridge.

"What is this place?" Mallory wondered out loud.

"I'll tell you everything; just as soon as you believe I am who I say I am. And first, you need to eat, shower, and change clothes."

Mallory laughed.

The man glanced back at her. "I'm not sure why that's funny."

"Oh, that's just what the Archivist said when we first got to the Library. 'No, explanations until you shower. You stink.'"

The Ex Natu nodded. "I'd have to agree with her on that one."

"Gee thanks." For some reason, Mallory felt more embarrassed than when the Archivist had said it. She did not have time to explore that feeling before the smell of sausage distracted her. They had reached the Ex Natu's home.

He threw all the supplies up on one shoulder and opened the door with his free hand. Mallory did not expect what they found when they walked into the room. Caleb was laying on the floor moaning in pain. Both hands were on his stomach, which was distended. He looked up at them with puppy dog eyes and moaned, "so much sausage."

Mallory looked at the table and saw that not only had he not eaten all the sausage, but there was still a huge pile of uneaten sausage sitting on a plate on the table. The Ex Natu set down his tub and walked around Caleb to the refrigerator. "How many did you make?" he asked, opening the door.

"All of it," Caleb moaned.

The Ex Natu confirmed. "All of it."

Mallory sat down at the table, rested baby Kirk in her lap, and grabbed the fork off of Caleb's plate. "We'll have to eat our way out of this mess. There's no way around it." And without any sort of ceremony, she did her civic duty. The sausage was delicious—maybe the best she'd ever had. It could be because she had not had sausage in over a year, or it could have really been the best. The only way she was going to figure it out was to have another bite. "Something's been bothering me about you," she said to the Ex Natu between bites.

"Oh?" The Ex Natu had popped the lid off the plastic tub and was pulling out assorted clothing. "About whether I'm really General Knenne?"

"No—well, yes—but something you said back on the island." Mallory shoved a full sausage into her mouth and chewed thoughtfully.

"What's that?"

"Was this before or after he nearly killed me?" Caleb moaned from the floor.

"During," Mallory chewed. "He knew that I had shot you. How could you know that? Were you talking to the Archivist at the Library?"

"Oh no, certainly not! It's better that Emily Carpenter doesn't know about me just yet." The Ex Natu shook his head and then grew serious. He stood up and threw some clothes at Caleb. "These should fit. Shower's in there." He pointed towards the bathroom door.

"Can't move." Caleb moaned. "So full."

The Ex Natu moved across the room very fast and put his face down in Caleb's, then screamed. "I said 'move'!" Caleb rolled over in terror, grabbed his clothing, and stood up. He started to walk toward the bathroom door, then turned back as if to argue again, but the Ex Natu was too fast. As soon as Caleb's body started changing direction, the Ex Natu was in his face again. "Move!"

Caleb stumbled into the bathroom and closed the door. A moment later, water started running.

Mallory's stomach was starting to get full, but there must have been forty links of sausage left on the plate. "I don't know if I can finish it," she groaned. "But I can try!"

The Ex Natu grabbed the plate off the table just as Mallory was trying to spear another sausage. "That's enough. These will keep until tomorrow. Last thing I need is two of you on the floor moaning."

Mallory sighed and set down her fork. "So, how did you know about me shooting Caleb?"

The Ex Natu closed the refrigerator door and leaned up against it. "Back in the 21st century, they used to say that information was power. On the other hand, they also used to say that curiosity killed the cat."

Mallory tilted her head inquisitively. "What's a cat?"

The Ex Natu's eyes widened and then he nodded. "No pets. I forgot about that rule of Omaha's. Too much liability in the food supply if Hoffen City had to be sealed off."

"What's a pet?" Mallory asked.

"Never mind."

"You still haven't answered my question," Mallory insisted.

"True. That's because I'm waiting for something." The Ex Natu tilted his head and listened.

Mallory tensed. What was he waiting for? Was this another trap? Were they in danger. Suddenly, the water in the bathroom shut off.

"There it is," the Ex Natu laughed. "Men never take that long in the shower, no matter how dirty they are." He picked up a stack of clothes and set them in front of Mallory. "Your turn, and then I'll attempt to address all of your questions."

The bathroom door opened, and Caleb exited wearing dusky brown military fatigues. His hair was spiked and wet, and he was holding a towel, wiggling the tip of it in his ear. "What did I miss?"

"Nothing yet," Mallory said. "Can you take the baby?"

Caleb looked at her suspiciously. "Does he need changed again?"

She laughed. "Not this time, but I can't shower myself if I have to hold him too."

Caleb scooped up his son gingerly, trying not to wake him. He looked him over as if seeing him for the first time. "You know. I have a sudden urge to bite his toes and wake him up."

Mallory picked up her clothes, which were the same dusky brown as his and said sternly, "you do it, and I'll have the Ex Natu electrocute you again. Let our son sleep."

Caleb's eyes widened in surprise. "I'm shocked, Mal. Shocked!"

Mallory was immediately reminded of her father and his terrible puns. There must be something that happens in men's brains when they hold a baby. Some instinctual response to teach their children to pay attention to the meaning of every word or miss a joke. Maybe it helped protect children from getting deceived by people that meant them harm. Or maybe having children just made men annoying. She was not in the mood to figure it all out right this minute. She turned to the Ex Natu without even acknowledging Caleb's pun. "When I get out, I want to see the chronicles to see that General Knenne is not dead, your proof that you're him, an explanation for how you know what happened at the Library, and finally, I want a nap."

"Are you sure you don't want that last one first?" the Ex Natu joked.

Mallory did not acknowledge his humor either. Her belly was full, and her body was going to be clean. She was so tired, she could probably lay down on the floor right now and sleep, but she was so curious about who this man was, that she knew there would be no way she could actually sleep, even if she were to lay down. "Move!" she yelled in response.

The Ex Natu roared with laughter. "Yes, ma'am," he saluted as she closed the bathroom door.

The steam and water felt amazing, though having the luxury of cleaning up did make her aware of things she had not thought about for months. For example, when she tried to wash her hair, she realized that she had not used a brush for all of her months in captivity. Her normally wild curls were now impossibly tangled in horrible little nests. They were so far gone, she knew that she was going to need help cutting them all loose if it were even possible to rescue them. When she was little, she had gone a few weeks ignoring her mother's advice about brushing her hair every day and ended up with a huge ball of matted hair on the back of her head. It hung on her head uncomfortably for days. It itched. At times it hurt. And it made it hard to lay on her pillow at night.

When her mother noticed it, she was livid. She dragged her to the salon and initially ordered the sprites there to give her a boy's haircut. "It's easier to take care of." But when Mallory had started crying uncontrollably, she relented and ordered the sprites to just fix her hair instead. Even with the sprites' speed, it took hours of painful pulling and strategic cutting to get that nest free. There were no salon sprites here. How exactly was she going to get the cobweb of nests out, especially with only two men to help? She had no idea. No wonder the women of the Ex Natu just shaved their heads. Eternal baldness would be so much easier to deal with than long hair.

She sighed, dried off, and wiped the fog from the mirror; she did not recognize the woman staring back at her. Her cheek bones were more prominent, and her teeth seemed to push her lips forward, giving her the appearance of a bird bill. Dark craters hung below her eyes. If she had not experienced it, she would have never believed that she had just given birth. She could see the tendons and muscles in her arms. Her skin was stretched like brittle paper over her ribs. The people of Hoffen City had started to look like this when their food rations had been limited, but it was never this bad. She cupped her hands around her mouth and breathed heavily. Sure enough, the acrid smell of starvation lingered on her breath. She leaned in closer to the mirror and thought to herself, "this must be what death looks like."

She slowly pulled on her own khaki colored clothing and walked out of the bathroom to find Caleb sitting at the table waiting for her. He looked her up and down and said, "I liked what you had on before better."

"The hospital gown?" Mallory laughed.

He grinned and then held up baby Kirk next to his face. The baby was awake and staring at her. Caleb spoke quietly and confidentially to his son, "What do you think, kid?" Then he nodded knowingly. "He liked the other clothes too."

"It was literally made of paper." Mallory exclaimed. "And it didn't close in the back."

Caleb's eyebrows bobbed up and down comically.

She sighed and changed the subject. "Where's the sausage guy?"

Caleb feigned shock. "Why Mrs. Aiworth, I'm hurt. I'm the sausage guy. Did you not see all the sausage I made?"

Mallory smiled. It was nice to have the old Caleb back. The crazy wilding man he had become seemed to have been pushed back into the recesses of his mind by a full belly. "All I saw is you laying on the floor, crying that your belly hurt."

Caleb's shock turned to hurt. "You're supposed to care for me, Mal. I nearly died."

"From sausage?"

"People die from eating sausage every day." Caleb nodded as if he had just shared a fact that everyone should know.

"Give me my baby. I don't want him learning to tell fibs from you." Mallory reached out for baby Kirk.

"Don't listen to her, kid!" He pulled Kirk closer to his face and tickled his cheek with his beard. "Stick with me, and I'll teach you everything you need to know in life: self-defense, leadership, and how to cook sausage." Baby Kirk's face scrunched up as Caleb's whiskers brushed his cheek, and he smiled slightly. "Hey, his first smile!" Caleb shouted in triumph.

"That wasn't a smile!" Mallory shot back taking the baby away. "He's just trying not to cry."

"Only because you're taking him away," Caleb said knowingly.

"Seriously, where's the Ex Natu?" Mallory looked around the room.

Caleb shrugged. "He said he was going to go get his copies of the chronicles to prove he is who he says he is."

"Do you think he's really General Knenne?" Mallory sat down on the couch and laid the baby on her lap.

"Would it be any crazier than anything else that's happened to us since we left the city?" Caleb leaned against the back of his chair and whipped his legs up onto the table.

Just then, the Ex Natu walked back into the abode carrying an old book that was falling apart. "Found it!" he exclaimed. He walked quickly over to the table and with a swift motion brushed Caleb's feet off.

Caleb grunted as he nearly fell onto the floor. "Hey!" he yelled.

The Ex Natu set the book down and touched it tenderly. "Let's see," he said opening the book. "It was just a few months after the tragedy of Mason City. Oh yes, here we go," he said handing the book to Caleb.

Caleb started to read quietly to himself.

"Caleb, do you mind?" Mallory snipped.

Caleb looked up. "Oh, sorry," he said holding the book toward her. "You want to read it first?"

"I'm holding a baby!" Mallory rolled her eyes. "Just read out loud so I can hear too."

Caleb looked nonplussed, but he complied.

The Chronicles of the Matriarchs

It has been a long time as the Matriarch since I have had anything meaningful to record in these chronicles. This record is supposed to be for future generations to remember who we are, where we came from, and how we came to be, and not some sort of diary or record of Eva Knenne's personal life. Neither is it supposed to be notations of the daily activities of Matriarch as a leader of the government. However, in my opinion, the absolutely uncalled for, foolish resolution of the City Council warrants an entry in the chronicles so that when they are proven wrong, future generations will forever remember their shame, especially my daughter's, whose vote as Administrator of the City overruled all reason.

Our disagreement started seven months ago when my husband, General Kirk Knenne, led an exploratory expedition back to Mason City to examine the ruins and look for clues as to what went wrong with their holographic plasma shield so that we would not make the same mistake when we turn ours on. It had been three years since the explosion that took Omaha and Melody from us, and there was a general consensus that the Ex Natu were probably no longer watching Mason City.

But the exploratory expedition did not return when they were expected.

Governor Aiworth called the special council meeting

this week and imagine my surprise when he announced the topic: "It's been months and General Knenne's team has not returned. I think this council needs to hold a vote on their status. The consensus is that they were mostly likely killed or captured by the Ex Natu, with some notable hold outs." He nodded at me and rolled his eyes.

This was not a new conversation. He had been trying to pull this maneuver for several weeks, but it had never been officially brought before the City Council. I interrupted the bombastic fool. "Of course, anyone who knows Kirk knows how ridiculous that is. The man has survived multiple wars, his skill as a fighter and leader knows no parallel, and besides, he has a family to come home to—he has me to come home to."

"Mother," Mari said. "I want him back too, but we have to accept the facts!"

This was a new turn. Mari had been on my side until this point. "What facts? Has something new happened?"

Mari sighed. "No, and that's the problem; isn't it? If he were out there, he would have come back by now."

"Your father is a master strategist. If he hasn't come back yet, it's to keep us safe."

Aiworth butted in again. "The best way for him to keep us safe would have been to not to be taken alive."

"You're a horrible man!" I shot back.

Mari patted my hand patronizingly. "He is, Mother. But he's also not wrong. We have to put father's memory to rest and move on."

The Governor shook his head. "We're going to have an

official vote and go from there. We need someone in charge of our military assets. I motion to rule General Kirk Knenne deceased in action and to appoint his daughter Mari Nelson head of the city's defense forces."

Another council member seconded the motion, and Mari's vote carried it.

"This is a mistake. You'll all see," I warned them.

When Kirk comes back, they will be sorry they dismissed him so readily.

The Atrium

"They were both right," the Ex Natu interrupted. "I led a team of sixteen people to Mason City under the cover of night. My daughter Mari wanted to come along, but after what happened on our first expedition with the loss of Alexander—and who knows how many others—to the Ex Natu in the subway bunker, I was not about to risk more than myself and a small team.

"It was too dark to see much when we arrived, but it was clear that the holographic plasma had mostly dissipated over the three years since the explosion. There were isolated patches of glowing pink, but it was drastically better than the science types in Hoffen City expected. Given the fact that Omaha had created the stuff with an internal electromagnetic field, powered by nano-atomic energy, they calculated that the half life of the plasma would be at least 5,000 years. Needless to say, they forecasted the place being a glowing, pink ecological disaster for millennia. But it was pretty clear their calculations were off. You've been to Mason City recently, right? Is all the pink stuff gone now?"

Mallory nodded, "Yes, but there also aren't any plants. It's pretty barren."

The Ex Natu shrugged. "Well, maybe there was something to their predictions, but that night, it looked like everything was going to be okay. We set up camp next to a crater of pink goo and got a small fire going to cook a quick meal before turning in for the night. The idea was to get a better picture of what had happened in the morning.

"But morning didn't come.

"When I woke up, my head was pounding. I was no longer in my tent. I was laying on a cot in an Ex Natu prison cell. I knew from experience, the headache meant they had gassed us in the night for easy extraction. I also knew that as soon as they knew I was awake, I would be dragged into interrogation. The disorientation and the headache of the gas was the first step in getting prisoners to spill information. I did not sit up but lay still pretending to still be asleep with my eyes closed and breathing deeply of the well-oxygenated air. Slowly the headache began to fade.

"The conundrum I faced then was that my team, while trained for combat, was not properly trained for being interrogated by an enemy, and they knew the way back to the city. If they broke—and they would break—my family was in danger. That's when a plan began to form in my head for how to protect the city. I sat up quickly and put my hands on my temples, feigning pain as if the headache were still there. The door swung open, and two guards rushed in, grabbing me under my arms and dragging me out of the room. I did not struggle against them, but I didn't help them by walking either. Instead, I let my weight hang on them. The building was a standard military outpost, which was helpful because I was familiar with the layout. As we moved down the hall, I could tell that we were in fact heading toward the interrogation room, and these structures only had one. That was good news. As I suspected, I had awakened first. The more we walked, the more their breathing became shallow and fast. My weight was straining the oxygen out of their muscles.

"With Ex Natu, speed is an imperative. I knew that their muscles would recover and repair as soon as they weren't holding me up any longer. So, when they stopped in front of the interrogation room to open the door, I waited for one of them to loosen their grip and reach for the handle. As soon as the three of us were slightly off balance, I planted my feet and pushed up hard with my legs. The one still holding onto me with both hands stumbled backward, releasing my arm, and the one who had loosened his grip, turned his head toward me in surprise. I punched him in the throat, collapsing his trachea, and then let my torso's momentum follow the punch forward, and brought my foot around across the other's cheek bone. He slammed hard into the wall and bounced off of it. He was surprised, but hardly down. I stood up straight and drove my palm upward into the bridge of his nose. His eyes crossed, and he dropped to the floor next to his gasping partner.

"I did not wait to see if either of them would survive the fight. There was no time for that. Instead, I took off running.

"My goal was to reach the commander's quarters, which

I did relatively quickly without sounding any alarms. The door was locked with a biometric lock, and I took a bit of a risk with this next part. It had been a couple of decades since I left the Ex Natu for the Resistance, but I hoped that since the war with the East Asian Islands was over, they had not updated much in their systems. I bent over and let the scanner read my retina. Then I spoke, 'Authorization General Kirkland Knenne, Alpha Thirteen Zed Twenty-Seven.' Somewhere in one of the Ex Natu databases on the globe, my metrics matched up, and the door unlocked.

"Inside the room, the commander was sitting with his boots up on his desk trying to dislodge some food from between his teeth. The inside speaker announced my name as I entered. 'Attention! General Kirkland Knenne has entered the room.'

"The commander through his feet down and snapped to attention saluting me. 'Sir!'

"'At ease, commander,' I waved him down. 'Take a seat.'

"He immediately sat down and began to sweat. 'What is the purpose of your visit, sir? We don't get many high-ranking officers here these days.'

"'My visit?' I leaned forward. 'My visit? Your boys gassed me last night.'

"'Gassed you? You mean that camp in Mason City?' The commander rubbed his hand over his bald head. 'I don't understand. No one in the camp tested positive for nano sprites.'

"'Of course not!' I shouted and stood up. 'Just because we won the war with the Relos, doesn't mean we wiped them out. I've been undercover for years with a group of them, trying to protect the world and our future. I was finally coming home with my team to retire and get my nanos, when your boys jumped us in the night.'

"'I'm sorry, sir! I wasn't informed of any of this,' the commander stammered.

"'You don't have the clearance,' I waved my hand. 'Look, I'm exhausted. Can you just arrange a transport for my boys and I to Geneva? If I don't get my nanos soon, I'll die before I finish typing up my reports for this mission.'

"'I hope our company won't make it into those reports,' the commander fidgeted in his chair.

"I smiled inwardly. 'I'm not sure how we can avoid it. I left two of your men in serious condition in the hallway. That's going to be hard to explain without reporting.'

"'I'm sure they'll be fine when their nanos repair them,' the commander nodded.

"'And if not?' I tilted my head.

"'If not?' The gist of what I was saying sank in, and the commander squirmed. 'Accidents have happened.'

"I slammed his desk. 'I should have you court marshaled! These are soldiers' lives we're talking about. We can't just discard them as if we were throwing away a piece of paper!'

"His chair nearly flipped over backwards as his arms waved in defense. 'Sir! I … uh!'

"'You'll submit your report directly to me, encrypted and marked security level 34. You will speak to no one about what happened here, and you will instruct your men to do the same. Do you understand?'

"He nodded and stammered. 'Y-yes, sir!'

"'If those men don't survive, they'll be given death-in-the-line of duty benefits.' I looked at his contorted face and softened. 'Don't worry about it, Commander. Any and all reports I submit will also be classified, and you have my word, your command will not be held responsible for this mix up.'

"He immediately relaxed. 'Thank you, sir. Is there anything I can do for you, sir?'

"'The transport, Commander.'"

"'Oh yes, of course, right away, sir.' He grabbed the phone and started barking orders.

"'I'm going to go let my men out of their cells.' I left his office and went to collect the Hoffen City team.

"The cell doors also opened with my authorization code and biometric scans. The men were full of questions, but I ordered them to stay silent, and they obeyed as good soldiers do. One of the Ex Natu soldiers I had overcome in the hallway and the commander met us in the hangar just as the transport ship was landing. 'Sir, you'll be pleased to know one of the soldiers has recovered,' he said saluting. The soldier joined him saluting me though his eyes were wild in terror.

"I nodded and half returned their salute. 'Sorry about that, son. And for your fallen comrade too.'

"His shoulders slumped slightly, but he maintained the salute—like a good soldier should.

"I motioned for my Hoffen City team to head aboard the transport, and they looked about as wild-eyed with terror as the Ex Natu soldier we were leaving behind. In retrospect, I feel bad for all of them, but that's the way things go in military operations. You have to shut off your emotions if you want your mission to succeed, but time never lets you forget how awful that success feels.

"Anyway, to make this long story short, the transport flew us to Geneva, and I reinserted myself into the Ex Natu military as if I had never left. I used my access to the intelligence systems to thwart any discovery of Hoffen City, including that debacle you two had with the fire sprites I sent to guard the city—"

"Guard the city!?" Caleb interrupted. "They attacked us!"

The Ex Natu shook his head. "Someone messed with their internal processors, and they reverted to old protocols and reconnected to the Ex Natu military grid." He tapped his chest over his heart for emphasis.

Mallory's eyes got wide. "What does that even mean?"

The Ex Natu was about to explain, but Caleb held up his hand. "How can we believe any of this?"

Mallory bit her lip and tilted her head. "The fire sprites had the moon and stars symbol that's on his ship. I believe they were his."

"The sprites that attacked us," Caleb reiterated.

"They were two-hundred-years old!" the Ex Natu yelled. "They were supposed to protect you."

"Why didn't you keep them maintained, so someone like me wouldn't have to mess with them to get them working again?" Mallory shot back. "What happened?"

The Ex Natu stopped pacing, and he looked at them seriously. "Omaha and Emily Carpenter happened."

17

Mallory shook her head. She still had not made all the connections to what exactly was going on between Omaha and the Archivist, much less how this Ex Natu who claimed to be General Knenne fit into it. "Maybe you can explain it to us. What exactly is happening with Omaha and Emily Carpenter, the Ex Natu, the Relos, and how much danger is Hoffen City in?"

The old Ex Natu raised his hands. "It's complicated. We're talking about a couple of centuries of politics, wars, betrayals—"

Caleb cut him off. "How about you give us the short version and explain it to us like we're five."

The Ex Natu nodded. "Okay. Let's see. After I returned

to the Ex Natu, there were naturally questions that came up about where I had been for the past twenty years, and why I hadn't received my allotted nano injections. My cover story of working undercover with the Relos worked for awhile, but the Security Council of the Global Alliance wanted details. How significant of a threat were the remaining Relos? How fast could they repopulate? Was more military action needed? I was never very good at creative writing, but on the other hand, it was not hard to imagine what a leader of a band of militarized mortals rebelling against the global order of Ex Natu dominance would do. The little bits of truth I mixed into my reports about what we had done in Hoffen City helped sell the story of a reemerging threat in the East Asian Islands.

"Two of my scouting team even helped sell the story by refusing the injections of nano sprites. I had tried to explain to them why taking the shots was the only way we could keep the secret of Hoffen City safe, but they were younger. They'd spent almost their entire lives believing the Ex Natu were monsters and would rather die than take the shot. They kept the secret of Hoffen City to their grave, but the entire Ex Natu government saw their existence as proof that the Relos's renewed resistance existed, and that they had infiltrated our ranks. The demand for reports from me and my experience fighting the Relos also grew.

"Then one day, while I was sitting in my office writing yet another report for the security council, my secretary announced an unexpected visitor."

"'He will only give his codename and says you'll know

it,'" the soldier said over the communications channel on the other side of the door. 'Omaha.'

"You can imagine how shocked I was. I thought the man had died in Mason City, and yet here he was in one of the most secure Ex Natu buildings in the world asking to see me. There was no way he could have gained entrance unless he had taken the injection. But this was hardly the place or the time to show any concern over his visit. 'Show him in, please,' I said.

"The door's lock clicked, and sure enough, in walked the man himself. He smiled broadly in that way that always made me uneasy, as if he could shake your hand or stab your eye out. No one ever seemed to notice it. My Eva and Mari loved him. But that smile set me on edge. 'General Knenne,' he laughed. 'It's been a long time. Too long.'

"I stood and shook his hand, while waving my secretary out. 'No disturbances or records, Corporal. This is a highly classified meeting.' When the door closed behind him, I motioned toward the chair on the opposite side of my desk. 'I'll admit to being surprised. We thought you were dead. Is Melody still alive, too?'

"His face darkened, and he did not sit down. 'Don't act like you don't know.'

"'I'm sorry?' I stepped back, turning my torso slightly away from him and setting my left foot just in case this meeting were to become something else.

"'So you admit it was you who gave the order!' His teeth were showing now, and it was not a smile. 'When I saw the reports and what you were writing about the resistance, I didn't want to believe it was true after all I did for you. But here you are.'

"'Omaha, I have no idea what you're talking about.' And I did not. How was I supposed to know one of the Ex Natu brass had ordered him to activate the plasma shield in Mason City while Melody was there? How could I know that when he saw my name pop up in Ex Natu military communications that he would assume that top-brass order was mine? What I did know was that he had murder in his eyes. I had seen it enough times in my life. I shifted my weight and slowly reached under the desk for my sidearm, hoping he would not notice.

"'You don't get plausible deniability, Kirk.' He straightened his sleeve and shook his arm. A Dominus bracelet jangled on his wrist. 'Dikaió, kill General Knenne,' he hissed.

"Nothing happened.

"I pulled my sidearm out, flicked off the safety, and aimed it at his head. 'I may not be an egghead like you, Omaha, but I'm smart enough to figure out that you were running the Dikaió's operating system on the Global Alliance's network. And you're unstable enough that I thought it prudent to introduce a few new protocols in the kernel you couldn't access to protect myself.'

"He dropped his arm and looked at me in perplexion and utter hate. Then his lip curled, and he yelled, 'Dikaió, protect me!' My desk flew up into the air, smacking my arm and causing my firearm to go off wildly.

"I pushed back in my chair and rolled under my floating desk, hoping to catch him from below, but the door was open, and he was already out of the waiting room. 'Sound the alarm,' I barked at my secretary. 'That man doesn't leave the building!'

"But it was too late. With the Dikaió, he did leave the building, and within months of that encounter, he started a bloody civil war with the Ex Natu. Needless to say, it's been hard to keep tabs on Hoffen City while I've been battling a maniac across every continent." The Ex Natu nodded and made a toss-the-ball motion with his hands, as if to say, "Now you know."

Mallory and Caleb did not say anything for a moment, mulling over what he had told them, and then Mallory asked, "What about Emily Carpenter?"

The Ex Natu sighed heavily. "One of the unwritten rules of our military engagements has seemed to be leaving the secret of Hoffen City lie. I assumed Omaha did not know that his son Alexander had also died in Mason City, and there was no way I wanted that information to get out to him. There was no telling what he might do if he knew that he no longer had any family in Hoffen City, so I pretty much pretended it did not exist in the conflict. And it seemed that he did too.

"Outside of that one detail, Omaha was ruthless: worse than what the Ex Natu did to the Relos. He started in North and South America, using the Dikaió to systematically hunt and kill every Ex Natu that resisted his rule, and at first, most did. The Global Alliance called on me to lead our forces in the fight against him. My access to the Dikaió's backend made that possible at first, but Omaha quickly figured out how to bypass those systems. Millions died, and the world did not have the capacity to lose that many people. The foolish rush to stop repopulation mixed with a world war left most of our cities nearly desolate, only being maintained against the ravages of nature by automated sprites."

Mallory laid baby Kirk, who had fallen asleep, on the floor. "Is that why I didn't see anyone in central Davis City besides Omaha and his people?"

The Ex Natu nodded. "And that's not the only empty city. Here in Alexandria, the city once held close to ten million people. Now, there are only about 10,000, and nearly all of them are part of the Global Alliance's military or government. Across the globe, the population is estimated to be less than 100 million down from 10 billion at humanity's peak."

Mallory shook her head. "I can't picture that many people, much less what that much death must have looked like."

Caleb asked, "Are you still fighting with Omaha?"

The man's face grew older. "Yes, which is why I had this place built. His goal seems to be extinction, and eventually that will spill into Hoffen City." He sighed and gestured toward Mallory and the baby. "It's already reached my family, but I can protect all of you here."

Mallory leaned forward. "From Omaha, but what about from the Relos? They want Hoffen City destroyed too."

The Ex Natu grimaced. "Oh yes, the Relos and your friend Emily Carpenter. In our first war with them, they were a technologically backward people—it wasn't even a fight really. But now, thanks to Carpenter and her Library, their weapons are nearly on par with us. And with our diminished numbers, projections for the outcome of that war are much dimmer."

Mallory held out her hands. "I don't understand. What is going on with the Archivist and the Relos?"

"I don't understand it all myself, but from what our intelligence shows us, she's spent the last couple of hundred years feeding them technological secrets to develop their military capabilities. Most of their attacks have been aimed at Omaha's forces in the Americas, and while those attacks are designed to appear random, my analysis shows that there's a particular pattern in the heartland of the continent. They're searching for Hoffen City. If not for the holographic plasma shield, they would have found it already."

Mallory gulped. "If the shield were to go down, how fast do you think they would find it?"

"They have access to several satellites, so almost immediately," the Ex Natu said.

Mallory tilted her head and bit her lip. "You knew that I had shot Caleb. How did you know that?"

The Ex Natu also tilted his head. "Our intelligence network. Why do you ask?"

Mallory's eyebrows knit together. "It's just that if you knew about that event with Caleb, I'm surprised you don't know that the light fell."

"The light?"

Caleb nodded. "The plasma shield"

The Ex Natu stood up and yelled. "The shield is down in Hoffen City? Permanently down?"

"Shhh!!! The baby," Mallory hissed holding her hands

near baby Kirk's ears without touching them.

The Ex Natu grimaced, but lowered his voice urgently. "How long?"

Caleb shrugged. "It hasn't been easy keeping track of time, but more than nine months." He pointed to the baby as proof.

The Ex Natu shook his head. "It might already be too late!" He started walking toward the door.

Mallory shook her head as well. "When I was in the hospital, Zane, the old Relos lady who came to see me, said they intended to destroy Hoffen City, not that they already had."

The Ex Natu looked confused. "But why wouldn't they attack when they had the chance?"

Mallory pointed at the baby. "They wanted him, so they could understand the Dikaió."

The Ex Natu looked at baby Kirk in more confusion. "Now, I am the one who doesn't understand. Why?"

Mallory shook her head. "I'd rather not say, at least not until we know more about you. How specifically did you know about me shooting Caleb?"

The Ex Natu took a deep breath and then turned to the framed painting on the wall over the table. He grabbed an edge and pulled it. The painting swung open on hinges. Behind the painting was a metal safe with a 9-digit keyboard. He covered the keyboard and punched in several numbers. The safe's door swung open, and he reached inside. Mallory and Caleb both gasped when he pulled out a Dominus bracelet.

"You have the fourth one?" Caleb whisper-shouted, trying

not to wake the baby.

The Ex Natu nodded, "I've always had it. At the beginning of the resistance, I told Omaha to destroy them all, but just in case he didn't, I kept one. It's pretty much the only reason Omaha hasn't won this war."

Caleb shrugged. "I guess that proves his identity more than anything else."

Mallory's knitted brow did not go away. "Okay, General Knenne, but having a Dominus bracelet can't tell you about what happened to Caleb. We didn't write that down anywhere. How did you know that?"

The General slid the bracelet on and spoke into the air. "Dikaió sprite, come here please."

A few moments passed and the outer door opened to reveal a familiar copper sprite. "Yes, General Knenne?"

Mallory clapped her hands. "But how? I thought it was destroyed in the attack on the Library."

The General shrugged. "Different sprite, shared memory. Emily Carpenter made hundreds of these and sent them all over the world in service of Omaha's search for fertile test subjects. I don't think she ever intended to give him what he wanted. The Relos would have been an easy mark, but judging from these sprites' programming, Carpenter gave the Relos a reboot code embedded in their shared database, which allowed the islanders to escape these sprites if they encountered one. It was pure happenstance that one ran into you two.

"This one tried to kill me in India a couple of years ago, and I reprogramed it for cyber-recognizance. I added an alert in their system to flag any mention of 'Hoffen City' or Omaha." General Knenne looked at the floor. "But I stopped checking the feed all that regularly years ago—what with the war and all. It wasn't until our satellites picked up the battle at the Library that I went to check for alerts, and that's when I discovered what had happened. By then, you were already in Omaha's hands, and I lost track of you. If it weren't for Carpenter and the Relos communicating via old, unsecured channels about your need for extraction, I might never have found you."

Mallory held up her hand. "So, everything the Archivist's sprite saw, this one saw too?"

The Ex Natu shrugged. "Everything the Archivist's sprite is this one is too—except for the little bit of override code I inserted to make them more friendly with us."

The clockwork sprite's eyes flashed. "He is quite correct, Sprite Master. I am one of many, and we are one."

Caleb asked, "What do you mean more friendly?"

The clockwork sprite turned to him. "We are programmed to evade or kill the Ex Natu, and there is a recent kill order in place for you and the Sprite Master, as well as a retrieval order for your baby."

Mallory gasped. "From the Archivist."

The clockwork sprite's eyes flashed. "No. We have had no contact with the Archivist for months. An Ex Natu is using the Dikaió to give us orders."

"Omaha," Caleb growled.

"Yes," the General interrupted. "But much the way I used the Dikaió to subdue this one to attack me, I've also added some protections for you and your family."

"Yes," the sprite said. "General Knenne's code allows us to ignore some protocols in our programming, including those issued by another Dikaió user." It turned back to Mallory and said, "though the General's code is not the only protective measure restraining our compliance. There is also a curious anomaly that was inserted by the unit you saved at the Library, and it seems to be spreading through our database, which includes a protection protocol for you and your child."

"What do you mean by an anomaly?" The General asked.

"Unknown," the sprite answered.

The General did not seem satisfied with that answer but turned his attention back to the problem at hand. "What else do you know about the Relos's plan for Hoffen City."

Mallory shook her head. "Nothing. Zane said they wanted to destroy your legacy because you had destroyed theirs."

Caleb stood up and smacked the back of his hand decisively. "We need to get back there to warn them. Prepare the City for an invasion. Save our people."

General Knenne nodded. "I agree. The defenses here could hold off the Relos indefinitely, since our plasma shield is in place, and if you combine that with Hoffen City's training with the Dikaió, our forces would be unstoppable."

Caleb shook his head and laughed. "Only if you count using the Dikaió to cook dinner and make groceries."

The Ex Natu looked confused. "I don't understand."

Mallory shrugged. "Long before we were born, the council decided that history was dangerous. We had no idea about the Ex Natu or what the Dikaió was supposed to be.

The closest to history we've ever gotten are some portraits in the Administrator's house."

"So, they don't have any military training?" the Ex Natu asked.

Caleb answered, "the magistrates are trained to fight and shoot to keep the peace, but nothing close to what's in the chronicles, and using the Dikaió to harm others is absolutely forbidden."

Mallory nodded but then tilted her head. "Unless Alex made it back. She learned the real history and has a Dominus bracelet."

Caleb grimaced. "We can't assume that. The best-case scenario is returning and moving the people here." He looked at the old General. "You know how to get there I presume?"

"Of course," General Knenne nodded. "Perhaps just you and I should go. Mallory and the baby will be safer here."

"I don't think so!" Mallory hissed. "Besides, my mother and father and your mother and father will be way more likely to hear us if we bring their grandchild with us." She held out her hand palm side up to Caleb for support.

Caleb nodded. "Grandchildren have been known to change even the hardest of hearts."

The General smiled. "I understand that. I only wish I could have met mine." He looked down at baby Kirk on the floor. "A great, great, great, great, great, great, great grandchild will have to suffice. I guess that settles it. We'll all go." Then he paused, tilted his head slightly, and thought for a moment. "Getting past Omaha's defenses won't be easy. I'm going to need a couple of days to prepare."

Caleb's stomach interrupted with a loud growl. "What time is it? I'm starving."

Mallory sniffed the air. "Oh sure, mister my stomach hurts from eating so much." She rolled around in mock agony.

Caleb shot her an irritated look. "Mal, you know how I get when I'm hungry with these nano sprites."

The General laughed. "I've got some hamburger patties in the freezer. It won't take long to make them."

Caleb's eyes widened. "A burger? With a bun and cheese?"

The General nodded. "The works." He turned toward the kitchen.

"Do you have trimmer and scissors for Caleb's beard?" Mallory called to General Knenne.

"I thought you liked my beard," Caleb moaned.

"Yes, trim like that." Mallory pointed to the General. "Yours looks like a wet dog died on your face. It's kind of gross."

Caleb looked at the General and smiled one of his crooked smiles that Mallory had not seen since the Library. "Want to switch beards?"

The General's eyes twinkled, and he said, "everything you need is in the cabinet below the sink."

Caleb winked at Mallory and rushed into the restroom.

It did not take long for Caleb to finish trimming, the burgers to finish grilling, or for Caleb or the General to finish eating. Mallory however was chewing slowly, savoring the flavor. "Is it real cow?" she asked while chewing.

The General nodded. "Of course. While we don't have much in the way of farmers and ranchers anymore, our sprites have filled that role easily. We have way more food than the world will ever need. It's only in Omaha's domain that they have trouble raising animals, what with the wilding wolves and all."

Mallory nodded. "They were the first thing that came through when the light went down. Four of them went after our cows right away."

The General looked surprised. "Only four? They usually run in much bigger packs."

Mallory nodded. "Oh, we've seen those too." And she gestured toward the clockwork sprite still in the room. "If not for the sprite, we would have been eaten by them." She snapped her jaws in imitation. "Ow!" she yelped. "I bit my yip!" A tiny trickle of blood formed on her mouth, but within seconds, the pain and wound healed up. She laughed. "Oh, never mind, the medical nano sprites got it."

"The medical nano sprites?" the General asked concerned. "You have medical nano sprites in you right now?"

Mallory nodded. "Yes, why?"

"How long have they been in?" The General's concern had increased to anxiety.

Mallory shrugged. "The Relos used them, so since yesterday I guess."

The General relaxed a little but not much. "There's still time to get them out then." He jumped up from the table and motioned for Mallory to follow him. "Caleb, you stay here with the baby. Mallory, come with me now!"

Mallory did not stand up. "Why? What's wrong? The Relos said they would take them back out, but they don't seem to be hurting anything."

The General shook his head. "They're not made for permanent use. They'll keep repairing even if there's nothing to repair, which means they'll start damaging things soon. Extended use can lead to cancer, stroke, clots, any number of medical conditions, and in the worst cases, death. There's a reason they were outlawed and replaced by the Ex Natu nano sprites."

Mallory's heart began to race. "Can you get them out?"

The General nodded. "I think so, but we need to go down to the medical rooms and set up an IV." Then he paused. "If I'm honest, I don't have the equipment for it. The best I can offer is plasmaphreisis, which should filter them out of your blood. He looked down at the Dominus bracelet still on his wrist and said, "Dikaió sprite, come assist me. You probably have more info in your databanks about it than I have in my mind." He tapped his head.

The sprite's eyes flashed. "I will assist as much as I am able, General."

Caleb growled. "You better bring her back alive and in one piece."

The General nodded. "You have my word."

And with that, General Knenne and the sprite whisked Mallory out of the room, leaving Caleb with a sleeping baby, and the rest of Mallory's uneaten hamburger. Mallory knew one of those was going to be in Caleb's belly when she got back—if she got back.

General Knenne said little on the way to the elevator. He was clearly anxious, which made Mallory anxious as well. She had a thousand questions about what exactly plasmapheresis was, but she also did not want to add any more pressure, especially since her health was on the line. Instead, she turned her attention to the clockwork sprite following behind them. "How many of you are there, sprite?"

The clockwork's sprite's eyes flashed. "One-thousand two-hundred and eighty-eight."

Mallory's eyes blinked quickly. "And you all share the same memory?"

"Yes, Sprite Master."

"Does each individual sprite add to your memory?"

Mallory wondered.

"Yes, Sprite Master."

Mallory nodded. "That must be a lot to take in all at once." She tilted her head and bit her lip. "Can any sprite access it at any time? Are the other sprites seeing what you're seeing right now?"

The sprite's eyes flashed. "General Knenne has tampered with my connection to the database. I can access the others' memories, but they cannot access mine."

Mallory nodded. "That's a relief."

The group arrived at the elevator, and General Knenne pressed the down button. He pressed 17, which Mallory was happy to note was not underground this time although it was still several floors below them. The drop was still too fast, and Mallory hiccuped after her half full belly shifted upwards, filling her mouth with a sour flavor. She closed her eyes and grimaced as the doors opened.

"Not a fan of hospitals?" General Knenne asked, exiting the elevator.

Mallory opened her eyes and saw that this floor was indeed decorated to look like a hospital waiting room. It was a weird juxtaposition to see the clinically scrubbed white and wood of a hospital set in the middle of a forest, as the atrium's trees still towered over them. Mallory shook her head but then nodded. "No, I mean yes," she corrected, remembering the hospital in Hoffen City, Omaha's filthy hospital room, and her most recent experience with the Relos. "But it's mostly the elevator." She rubbed her stomach. "And the hamburger."

The Ex Natu nodded. "You probably should have fasted before this procedure, but I'm not sure there's time. We need to get those sprites out of you." He motioned for her to follow him and led her through two double doors into the interior of the hospital floor. "Now, where did I put that machine?"

Mallory stopped walking. "Oh, that inspires confidence. Maybe I should go back to Caleb?"

General Knenne scratched his head. "You'll be shocked to know that I haven't needed to use a hospital for quite some time, but I know it's here somewhere."

"You're still wearing the Dominus bracelet," Mallory pointed out. "You could just use it to point the way."

General Knenne grimaced this time. He pulled the bracelet off. "It's such a crutch. I hate using it, always have. You know, I wouldn't even let Omaha christen me back when my Eva was alive." He turned the bracelet over and over in his hand suddenly lost in thought.

"I remember reading that," Mallory nodded. "I'll be honest, on finding you still alive, I thought you didn't take the Dikaió because you always intended this." She waved her hand around the room, indicating the whole set up. "Just in case."

He looked her in the eye and studied her. "I've laid awake at nights wondering that same thing. If I did, it wasn't a conscious decision. I loved my wife and children. It killed me to leave them."

"Or didn't," Mallory mused lightheartedly.

"What?" the General's countenance grew darker.

Mallory realized her pun fell flat. "I mean because you have nano sprites and are still alive. I understand it must have seemed like a hard choice."

General Knenne blinked slowly then he held out the bracelet to Mallory. "Here. You do it."

Mallory hesitated for a moment and then took the bracelet. "I could just use it to order the nano sprites out."

The clockwork sprite's eyes flashed in the hallway. "You would not survive that course of action, Sprite Master."

General Knenne's shook his head. "It's right. That would be…messy."

Mallory nodded. "Dikaió, take us to the plasma free what's it room."

Nothing happened.

"Fur-Reese-Us ," General Knenne corrected.

"Dikaió, take us the plasma fur-reese-us room," Mallory tried.

The sprite floated up off the floor and began to hover down the hallway. "Follow the sprite, I guess," General Knenne sighed. "This is why I hate the Dikaió. Quantum computations should have never been paired with predictive algorithms; it's too wacky."

Mallory shook her head. "I don't know what that means."

"Just that the Dikaió will fulfill the request at any cost, and you can't always tell how it will do it. This time it floated the sprite, but it could just as well have torn the hallway apart to lead us where we wanted to go."

Mallory smiled. "I've seen that happen."

"I'm sure you have," the General sighed. "C'mon, the

sooner we get those medical nano sprites out of you, the sooner we can get to Hoffen City."

The sprite took two lefts and then a right. It stopped outside a door labeled "Storage" and then slowly floated back down to the ground. Its eyes flickered twice, but it made no comments about having been co-opted as a beacon.

"Oh, swell! You'll have to be more specific, Mallory. This is the room," General Knenne muttered. He opened the door to the storage room, and several lights inside flickered to life. The room inside was much bigger than Mallory anticipated—at least as large as the Rookery in Hoffen City or the Archivist's Armory had been at the Library. Rows upon rows of shelving with crates and equipment wrapped in plastic filled the warehouse. The General finished his statement, "but we need the machine."

Mallory laughed. "Dikaió, take us to the plasma…" she hesitated.

"Fur-reese-us," the General prodded.

"…fur-reese-us," machine," Mallory finished.

This time the sprite stayed on the ground, but several pieces of equipment flew off the shelves and created arrows on the floor to point them in the right direction. The General rolled his eyes and followed the Dikaió's arrows. Mallory and the sprite tailed after him. The arrows stopped at what appeared to be a large, white toolbox on wheels. General Knenne unlatched the lid and folded it up. Inside were several dials and a large circular drum. He nodded and turned to the sprite. "Again, you know how to use this, right?"

The sprite's eyes flashed, and it said, "the basic functions are in my database."

"Great!" The General spun on his heel. "Grab it, and let's head to a clean room. I know where those are."

The clean room was a white room with a countertop sink, several cabinets, and drawers on the left. On the right side of the room, there was a second room enclosed in transparent glass, with a glass door. Inside that room was a blue recliner. The sprite wheeled the white box into the glass room. Then it turned and closed the door. General Knenne walked over to a panel near the counter sink and flicked it. The panel lit up revealing a screen with several sliders and buttons represented by lights. General Knenne pushed a large red button, and the glass room's lock clicked closed. Nozzles descended from the ceiling and began to spray white fog into the room. An indicator on the panel slowly filled with red light as the fog poured out. Mallory watched in fascination as the glass room turned completely white, and all she could see were the two circle lights of the sprite's eyes. When the indicator on the panel hit one hundred percent, a motor fired up and the fog was sucked out through vents. When the fog was completely gone, the door unlocked.

General Knenne opened a cabinet and pulled out a familiar green gown.

Mallory rolled her eyes. "I literally just changed out of one of those."

General Knenne laughed. "Yes, and you just showered, but you'll still have to wash up and wear the gown." He pointed to the sink. "You don't want to get an infection."

Mallory laughed. "You sound like my mother."

General Knenne shrugged and handed her the gown. "I'll leave you to the sprite and some privacy," he smiled and left the white room.

Mallory started to undress, but then she looked behind her at the sprite, who was watching her unblinking. Then she imagined the hundreds of other clockwork sprites behind those eyes that could be watching her too. Sure, it said General Knenne had made it so that it couldn't upload its data to the rest, but Mallory could not shake the image. "Do you mind?" she yelled at the sprite.

"No, Sprite Master. I do not mind," the clockwork sprite responded.

"Well, I do. Can you turn around while I get dressed?" Mallory hissed.

"If you wish," the sprite's eyes blinked, and it turned away from her.

Mallory undressed and used soap and water at the sink to clean herself, then she put on the green hospital gown. Much like every other hospital gown she had ever worn, this one also would not close in the back. She held it closed awkwardly and walked to the glass door. "Okay, what now?"

One of the sprite's tentacles slowly extended from its body, and it indicated the blue recliner. "Please enter and sit here."

Mallory sat in the chair, and the cushions barely sank under her weight. One of the the sprite's tentacles gently pulled her arms up on the arm rests, and the other picked up a tube with a large needle attached to it. Mallory winced. "What exactly is about to happen here?"

The sprite's eyes blinked. "This machine will pull your blood out of one arm and run it through a centrifuge, separating and filtering out the medical nano sprites, and then your blood will be pumped back into your other arm."

"Would that work for removing the Ex Natu nano sprites?" Mallory asked hopefully.

"No, Sprite Master. Like the Dikaió, the Ex Natu sprites are much smaller. Parts of their machinery work at the quantum level, using proton tunneling to rewrite the body's DNA as needed, creating whatever protein or cellular composition is required to repair the body—including novel stem cells to repair the damages of aging. Their subatomic components are not affected by most physical forces, so there is no conceivable means to remove them from the body once they have been introduced," the sprite answered.

"But these can?" Mallory wondered. "Why?"

"Medical nano sprites are molecular machines that work with your body's natural processes to facilitate rapid repairs. They are large enough to be influenced by forces like the artificial gravity of a centrifuge." The sprite's eyes blinked rapidly. "Are you ready to begin, Sprite Master?"

Mallory nodded. "Okay, just make it quick." Mallory closed her eyes and laid her head back, trying not think about how awful the procedure sounded.

"I have no control over the speed of the procedure, Sprite Master," the sprite said matter-of-factly.

Mallory sighed but did not respond. The punctures in her arms came quickly and were barely noticeable. The sprite was very good at finding a vein. The machine made a low humming noise with a regular suction sound, kind of like an artificial heartbeat as it slowly pulled the blood from her body. The room grew steadily colder. And after about fifteen minutes, Mallory's body began to shiver. She tried to ignore the involuntary twitching, but it seemed to be getting worse. She opened her eyes and looked toward the sprite, which was monitoring the machine's progress. "S-s-sprite? S-s-something's wr-wr-rong."

The sprite turned toward her, and its eyes flashed, scanning her. "You are experiencing tetany," the sprite said. "Muscle spasms are a common reaction to plasmapheresis because the machine has filtered out too much calcium."

"I-s-s it-t-t dan-dangerous?" Mallory stuttered.

The clockwork sprite turned back to the machine and opened one of the doors in the cabinet. "Quite dangerous, Sprite Master. Calcium deficiency can result in life-threatening seizures and heart failure."

Mallory's mind reeled as she looked in terror at the blood-red tubes coming out of both of her arms. "Sh-sh-should w-we st-st-stop?"

The sprite pulled a vial and a bag of fluid from the machine's cabinet. "Unnecessary, Sprite Master." In a motion almost too fast to follow, it snapped the vial and added its contents to a syringe, which it injected into a rubber stopper at the top of the bag. The sprite hung the bag on the tall metal pole running up the side of the machine and fed a plastic tube toward the arm that was feeding her blood back into her body. It opened a package with a needle and put a third IV into her arm and attached the tube to the new IV.

Then it punched a few commands into the machine and the fluid in the bag began to drip into Mallory's arm.

The spasms did not cease immediately, but eventually Mallory was able to lay still. She was still shivering from the cold, but not so violently as she was without the new drip. "Is there calcium in there?" Mallory asked, nodding toward the drip.

"Yes, Sprite Master, as well as some other essential elements the machine might be filtering from your blood."

"It sure is cold," Mallory said quietly.

"Colder temperatures discourage bacterial growth," the sprite answered without doing anything to address the temperature.

Mallory sighed and closed her eyes. She had been cold before. It was nothing that she could not handle. Her mind drifted for a while, but after a moment she began thinking about what General Knenne had suggested. He intended to take them back to Hoffen City with a plan to evacuate the entire city here. She wondered if they would listen to him, to her, or even to Caleb. They had been exiled on pain of death after all. And for good reason, too. What would they say exactly? "Hi, all! We're here to take you away from everything you've ever known because there's an entire society that wants to kill you all. Why? Because of this guy. His name is General Knenne, and he founded the city hundreds of years ago. Oh yeah, he's also the guy who put the fire sprites outside the light." Mallory almost laughed at that.

They were going to kill her for sure.

Then she thought about showing her mother and father

their grandson. Despite her youth, Mallory had seen many family squabbles between parents and their children vanish as soon as grandchildren were introduced into the picture. Mallory was sure that both her parents and Caleb's would go to bat with the City Council for them if only for Kirk Aiworth's sake. Would it be enough to convince the Council, much less the entire city? Mallory was not sure. She tried to imagine someone like the Smith Guild leader and his wife giving up everything they had spent their whole lives building—add that to the fact that they already hated her and Caleb, and they would almost certainly put up a fight. How many more in the city would side with them?

On the other hand, she was wearing General Knenne's Dominus bracelet and could restore the Dikaió to everyone in the city. That would surely count for something. She would be seen as a savior, not an enemy. But having the Dikaió returned might make them even more resistant to leaving the city, as they might think their lives could just return to normal then. And normal was never coming back, the Relos likely knew where Hoffen City was and they intended to destroy it. As heirs of the Triad of Government, Mallory and Caleb had a duty to protect the city and everyone in it. She was sure of that.

The clockwork sprite intruded on her thoughts: "The treatment is complete, Sprite Master. Scans show that no medical nano sprites remain in your system."

Mallory opened her eyes and blinked. She looked down at her arms and saw three bandages with gauze, then at the machine now sitting quietly with a dark screen. A small vial with about two ounces of silver liquid sat bubbling next to the round centrifuge. Mallory tilted her head and asked, "Are those the nano sprites?"

"Yes, Sprite Master." The bronze sprite replied.

Mallory reached out and took the vial. She bit her lip and held the vial up in front of her eyes, looking at it carefully. The silver liquid bubbled and popped as if it were in a pot on slow simmer. Then she slowly tried to stand up. Her legs wobbled under her, and she grabbed the sprites head to stabilize herself. The sprite flinched slightly when she touched it but held her weight. "Thanks," she said and let go of it. Mallory slowly shuffled out of the glass room and walked over to the pile of clothes she had left on the counter.

"You should rest, Sprite Master," the clockwork sprite whirred over to her. "Do not overexert yourself after the procedure."

"I'm freezing in this gown," Mallory said. "I'd be happy to rest once I'm dressed and warm again."

The sprite made no more suggestions but just stood there patiently waiting for her.

"Do you mind turning around?" Mallory sighed. The sprite complied, and Mallory started the process of changing. Getting out of the gown was relatively easy, as there was not much holding it on, but getting dressed in regular clothing was not as easy as she had imagined it being—particularly getting her arms into her shirt without dislodging the bandages. But eventually, she was dressed and at least slightly warmer. "Okay, I'm ready," Mallory said. "Let's go get that rest you recommended."

The sprite offered her a tentacle to steady her as she walked, and she gladly accepted it. The cold steel immediately brought to mind the near miss she had experienced on the deadly end of the Ex Natu's culture sprite in the field. A clockwork sprite just like this one had saved her, and then she had saved it by ripping out the culture sprite's heart. That was the same heart she had used to fix the clockwork sprite after battling Reddy Lamarr at the Library. Somehow that string of events had started a connection with the bronze sprite that was shared by at least a thousand others just like it. The sprite started to lead her back to the chair in the glass room, but Mallory stopped. "No, I want to rest in a real bed. I want to be warm and comfortable."

The sprite's eyes flashed. "If you will sit here momentarily, I will bring back a means of transportation to accommodate you, Sprite Master."

Mallory sighed and allowed it to lead her back to the cold blue chair. "Please, hurry though."

The sprite's eyes clicked as Mallory sat down, and then it quickly floated out of the room. Mallory looked after it and then saw that she had left the medical nano sprites all the way over on the counter. She tilted her head and bit her lip. Those might come in handy in the future. It would be a shame to leave them here. She slowly stood up and walked to the wall in front of her. Then she steadied herself on the wall and began walking across the room toward the counter. She reached the vial of silver fluid and slid it into her pocket. Then she turned around and started to walk back across the room. Feeling steadier she moved a little faster this time, but almost immediately, the room began to swim out of focus.

There was a spark of light that flashed in the corner of the fuzzy room. Then another in the other direction. And another. It was like silent fireworks going off all around her. And then Mallory realized that the lights were not actually in the room at all. They were just in her vision, and as they flashed, her balance became less and less steady. She remembered her grandfather getting hit in the head by a grocery sprite at the market and how he had complained of seeing saw stars. She thought it was just a funny expression old people used, but here they were, dancing around in her vision like fireflies. She did not have long to contemplate the experience, as nearly as soon as they started the little lights went out, and she fell.

It was impossible to tell how long she had lain on the floor in the cold room, but Mallory's eyes groggily opened. She felt even weaker and colder than before she fell. When she moved, she felt some pain in her side. "That's a bruise for sure," Mallory mused, and then she immediately thought about the medical sprites in her pocket, as they would have fixed the injury already. She reached down and touched her pocket. The medical nano sprites were still there, and the vial felt intact. "Well, that's something," her inner voice sounded relieved. Still, she was afraid of getting up and having another dizzy spell. Looking around the room, she saw that she was just a couple of feet from the door, so she slowly dragged herself across the floor to it, lifted her arm to the handle, and pulled herself to a standing position.

There was no immediate dizzy spell that followed. As she shifted positions, her stomach growled angrily at her. Lunch had been digested, and she was starving. And if she was starving, she was sure baby Kirk was awake and hungry as well. She opened the door and looked out into the hallway. It was completely empty. Where was that sprite? Her head tilted, and her eyes widened. Maybe something was wrong? She stepped quickly out into the hall and immediately regretted the sudden movement as her ears were filled with a whooshing noise, and the floor shifted under her. She grasped at the door handle again and held on hoping to keep from fainting. There were no stars and no blackout, but when she opened her eyes, the floor still seemed to be tilted. It was not her. It was the building. Something was seriously wrong.

Mallory needed to get back to her baby right now! There was no time to wait for the sprite. She looked quickly back and forth down the hallway and realized that she had no idea where to go. "Dikaió, take me to the elevator," she called. The tiles below her cracked in a zigzagging pattern to the right of her room, and she followed quickly after it. After a few moments, she exited into the waiting room of the hospital area, which looked out into the atrium.

The scene that met her was horrifying. The glass dome at the top of the atrium was shattered, and the trees were in flames. Above the dome, two of the Relos ships with the rotating blades hovered. As she stood there staring up in horror, one of them sent a trail of smoke and fire hurtling down into the atrium, and an explosion several floors up rocked the floor under Mallory's feet again. How had they broken through the General's plasma shield? She understood the shield to be unpenetrable, and yet the ships were raining destruction down from above.

Again, her thoughts turned to baby Kirk and Caleb. She needed to get to them and make sure they were okay. She looked forward where the elevator should have been and saw that its shaft was knocked over, and it was leaning against one of the burning trees. Mallory could barely see that there was movement just below the box of the elevator. A bronze blob was swinging itself upward on tentacles branch by branch and level by level—probably heading to the General to protect him.

Mallory could see that she would be getting no help from that route. She turned around and looked at her surroundings. There were several seats in the waiting room, a desk, and a wheelchair. Mallory walked over to the wheelchair. She tilted her head and bit her lip, and after a moment's consideration, sat down in the chair. She slouched down and locked her arms under the armrests, holding on tight. She tried to do the same with the leg rests, but she could not get her legs to bend quite that way. "I guess this is as good as it will get," she said out loud to no one. Then she closed her eyes and said, "Dikaió, take this wheelchair to Caleb Aiworth."

The wheelchair jerked hard to the left, dragging it towards the railing that overlooked the atrium. Mallory knew she should keep her eyes closed, but she could not. Just as she opened them, the Dikaió flipped the chair backwards over the railing. Mallory screamed as the invisible force pulled her chair rapidly upward into the flaming trees. The Relos ships continued shooting trails of fire and smoke into the building, followed by explosion after explosion. One of the walls to Mallory's right blew out, and the Dikaió made no attempt to avoid it. Mallory was pelted by hot rubble, and she felt several hot spots singe her skin. Somewhere near her hip, the burning did not stop. Mallory leaned forward to see a small piece of flaming wood and sheetrock stuck between her and the chair. Her immediate thought was to unwind her arm to flick it off, but the Dikaió was swinging the chair violently around as it flew, and she had to cling to it with all her might.

Mallory's teeth clenched as the small fire chewed through her pants and began to burn her skin. Her eyes squeezed shut and tears welled up. At the point that she could no longer bear the pain and was about to unwind an arm, Mallory opened her eyes and saw that the Dikaió was hurtling her directly toward a wall. She screamed just as the wall shifted out of focus around her, and the chair landed two feet away from General Knenne's ship.

Caleb stood at the open doorway of the ship, holding a screaming baby Kirk away from him toward the interior. Much like her son, Caleb was also screaming into the ship. "I don't care! You take the baby! I'm going back for my wife!"

At first, Mallory felt touched at Caleb's courageous affection, but then the pain in her leg burned away all her sentimentality. She jumped out of her chair and began dancing around the landing pad, patting at her leg and yelling "ooh, ooh, aah!"

The copper sprite appeared at the door of the ship. It had

apparently managed to scale the walls, get to the ship, and was preparing to abandon her. It brushed quickly past Caleb, and a small compartment opened. A nozzle poked out and aimed at Mallory. She clenched her teeth and closed her eyes half expecting a squirt of butane like when the other sprite had started a fire for them, which would have sent the rest of her up in flames. Instead, a cold, moist rush of air enveloped her leg. She opened her eyes and looked down to a cloud of white gas spraying from the nozzle. The fire was extinguished immediately. "Come, Sprite Master. We must flee!" the sprite said, rushing back toward the ship.

Caleb dodged the sprite and wrapped his arms around her. "Mal." That was all he managed to say as heavy sobs rose and fell in his chest.

Mallory touched his chest. "Me, too … me, too." She kissed him urgently then pulled away shouting, "Now, let's get out of here!

Caleb sniffled hard and then his face hardened. He tucked the very indignant baby into the crook of one his arms as if carrying a football then grabbed Mallory's hand with the other and half dragged her onto the ship.

General Knenne was in the cockpit, pressing buttons. "Glad you made it!" he called back when she was aboard.

"You would have left her there to die," Caleb spat. One of his eyes twitched, and Mallory could feel his grip on her hand tighten.

"But he didn't, and I didn't," Mallory said calmly as she pulled their baby away from Caleb. "Let's focus on survival right now, love."

Caleb's head snapped toward her, but he softened immediately and nodded. They both took their seats, and Caleb helped Mallory get her safety harness secured before putting his own on. Mallory clutched Kirk to her chest and cooed to him. "I know your hungry, and this is a lot of stress right now, but everything's going to be okay. I promise."

Caleb touched her leg and called up to General Knenne. "We're in!"

The door did not even finish closing before the General had the ship in the air. It shot straight up over the top of the atrium, spinning to the left as it went. When it cleared the roof, it was directly facing the two Relos ships. General Knenne began to tap the screens like drums again, and the two ships exploded in white fireballs. He punched the acceleration, and the ship flew forward into the wreckage of the ships as they fell. As they passed beyond the smoke and fire, Mallory sucked in her breath. There were hundreds, maybe thousands of the Relos ships, raining fire down on the Ex Natu city. Some Ex Natu ships had managed to get airborne, but while they seemed to be more maneuverable and better armed, they were hopelessly outnumbered.

General Knenne cursed. He flipped a switch between the screens and spoke calmly. "This is President Knenne of the Global Alliance. The capital is lost. Alliance armed forces who receive this message report directly to the Carpathian stronghold. I repeat. All Alliance armed forces report to the Carpathian stronghold." As he spoke, he maneuvered the ship upward at breakneck speed.

About twelve Relos ships turned toward them. Small

engines on their wings erupted in cones of purple fire, and the rotors slowed then folded backward, while their wings expanded outward. General Knenne cursed again. "Clever! It doesn't look like we'll be outrunning this group. Too bad for them." He tapped at his screens sending thousands of white lights toward the enemy ships. Three exploded; the others evaded. Then he yelled back at Caleb and Mallory, "hold on!"

The ship jumped upward, and Mallory felt herself pushed heavily down into her seat. The shock of the motion took the wind out of baby Kirk, and the infant stopped crying, just looking up at her confused. The day-lit sky outside the cockpit disappeared, replaced with the clearest night sky Mallory had ever seen. The force of the upward motion abated almost as soon as it started, and Mallory realized that instead of being pressed into her seat, she was floating above it. Suddenly, the stars of the night sky began to fly by them in trails of white fire. General Knenne began drumming the screens, and the ship spun around.

Mallory gasped. Behind them were several Relos ships, firing white fire toward them, and behind them was a giant blue circle. There were huge swaths of brown and green, and white clouds floating in front of it. It looked like someone had taken the day sky and framed it within the night sky. "What is it?" Mallory whispered.

Caleb shook his head equally in awe. "I think it's the ground."

Mallory wanted to unbuckle herself and get a closer look, but then the wall buckled across from her, and the ship spiraled away from the view of the ground. The General cursed again, and then he paused and breathed deeply. Mallory saw his shoulders relax. He stretched his fingers twice, and then began drumming on the screens. The ship swung back around toward the Relos, and the rhythm of his drumming took on a more musical quality. Four more Relos ships exploded in front of them. But their explosions were different in this night sky: Instead of exploding in a red and orange fireball, the ships erupted in purple rings of gas that expanded rapidly, then collapsed in on themselves, leaving little glowing puddles floating in the blackness. It was fascinating to watch, and she got to see this phenomenon five more times as General Knenne quickly destroyed the rest of the Relos ships following them.

He sighed heavily and stopped tapping the screens. He looked back at them. "Is everyone okay?"

Mallory nodded, Caleb grunted, and baby Kirk seemed to have been lulled asleep by the weightlessness of the ship.

Mallory bit her lip and looked out at the glowing blue disc in front of them. "What is it?" she asked again.

The General turned back to the window and said, "that's the Earth: the planet we live on."

"It's beautiful," Mallory mused.

General Knenne clicked his tongue. "I guess it is. It's been a long time since I thought of it like that, but it is beautiful."

Caleb interjected and changed the subject. "You were going to leave Mallory behind."

Genera Knenne nodded. "Yes. I was." He turned back to them. "Minimal casualties—it was a tactical decision."

Caleb growled. "I would have never left her."

"And you would have gotten yourself and your son killed for that decision," the General snapped back. "But that's neither here nor there. It didn't come to that because your wife is smart and scrappy." He smiled and winked at Mallory. "Just like her too-many-greats-to-count granddad." Then his face grew serious. "But it shouldn't have come to that anyway. How did they get through the plasma shield?"

Mallory bit her lip and tilted her head. "The Archivist knows a lot about plasma shields. Maybe she figured out their weakness?"

The General considered that. "If that's true, the quicker we get to Hoffen City the better."

Caleb shook his head. "Hoffen City's plasma shield is already down, and your evacuation plan just went up in smoke. What difference would it make?"

The General smiled. "A good strategist never puts all his eggs in one basket. The defenses of the Carpathian stronghold involve more than a plasma shield, and there's more room there than in the Alliance capitol; they'll just have to share it with the Ex Natu. It's a global retreat center."

Caleb balked at that idea. "Do you really think the Ex Natu will be okay living with fathers, mothers, grandparents, and children?"

The General shrugged. "They'll have to be. Between the Relos and Omaha's insurgency, there won't be any Ex Natu left soon. Besides, I'm the highest-ranking officer still alive, and I'm making an executive decision." He tapped the nearest screen, and the ship changed course. "Re-entry gets kind of bumpy, so get ready."

As they approached the Earth, the cabin of the ship started to get very warm. Mallory felt her weight begin to increase and was soon pressed into her chair again. She watched in fascination as fire rolled up and over the window. Suddenly, an alarm began to blare in the ship, and red lights began to flash. "What's wrong?" Mallory yelled over the alarms.

"The hull integrity is compromised!" General Knenne called back. "I need to pull up."

A small explosion rolled the ship sideways, and Mallory instinctively caught baby Kirk before he tumbled out of her arms. The ship's sideways roll did not stop, however, and soon they were spinning out of control. The fire was rolling up the window engulfing the ship. Mallory's vision was blurred by dizziness, but she could see that the wall across from her, which had crumpled slightly in their fight with the Relos, was glowing red hot.

Caleb screamed, "when are you going to pull up!?"

General Knenne screamed back. "The engine's out! Steering's minimal! We're going down!" He looked over his shoulder. "Sprite, protect the mother and child!"

The clockwork sprite, which was buckled into a seat at the rear of the ship, unharnessed itself and used its tentacles to pull its way to Mallory and Kirk. "Do not be afraid, Sprite Master," it said, and then pushed its tentacles through the bulkhead and floor, while simultaneously opening its core. Mallory marveled at the inner workings of the sprite. There was the sprite's heart with its tendrils working out to other areas of its gears and motors. Its innards shifted slightly, and it pressed up against Mallory.

Then it exploded.

Mallory gasped—surprised to still be alive. She tried to pull away from the sprite but found that her entire body was covered in some kind of air-permeable, transparent foam that made it impossible to move. She could not move her head down to see if baby Kirk was okay, but she felt his warm body still in her fingers. Mallory closed her eyes and concentrated on what her fingertips were telling her. His chest was still inhaling and exhaling, and she could still feel his small heart beating rapidly in his skin. Her fear for her child dissipated and, after a moment, and was quickly replaced by her old enemy: claustrophobia. She was stuck in a tiny ship and completely immobilized by an unbreakable clear foam. Mallory's muscles tensed, and her breathing became shallow. Just when she thought she was going to pass out, the world turned inside out.

BOOM!

Time seemed to stop, and Mallory watched as the ship's ceiling crumpled over them like paper. The window in the cockpit exploded, sending shards of transparent metal flying everywhere. General Knenne, still strapped to his chair, flew past her eyes and out the back of the ship, which was missing. She tried to look over toward Caleb, but she could not turn her head. The crazy thing was that even though she felt the impact in terms of the instantaneous end of her momentum, the foam around her seemed to absorb all the kinetic energy—both her movement and that of the shrapnel and bulkhead flying around her. As soon as any flying bits would touch the foam, they would fall away toward the front of the ship, which she assumed must be where the ground was. She bit her lip and tried to tilt her head, to no success. What was this stuff made of? She bounced her head from side to side inside the foam and could not help but wonder if it was keeping her head in place or just absorbing the energy of her movements.

And then the sprite's eyes blinked on. They were directly in front of Mallory's eyes, and she felt herself instantly blinded. "Come, Sprite Master. We must exit the craft. The impact foam will become unstable at high temperatures."

When Mallory's eyes adjusted to the sprite's light, she noticed that the entire ship was now in flames. Mallory squirmed against the foam to no effect. "How do I get out of here?"

A small nozzle that extended from the sprite's interior began to spray cold, wet smoke. The foam around her dissolved almost instantly, as did the fire nearest her. "Do not inhale the fumes, Sprite Master. They will be detrimental to your health," the clockwork sprite said. Mallory could not help herself. She inhaled deeply, intending to hold her breath once she had sufficient oxygen, but instead sucked in a bunch of the wet smoke. Her chest immediately began to burn with a strange heaviness, and she started coughing. Without the foam, the coughing shook her whole body forcefully. The clockwork sprite continued to spray the smoke until the hardened foam was dissolved enough to dislodge the mother and child. Then it wrapped a tentacle around them both and floated them up and outside of the wreckage.

They landed about twenty feet away. Mallory coughed hard and long, sucking at the fresh air, trying to clear her lungs of whatever the sprite had sprayed into them. When she could finally breath without long wracking coughs, she noticed that little Kirk was also coughing; his coughs were not hard, and they were getting weaker as he lay in her arms. Mallory quickly turned him upright on her shoulder and patted his little back firmly. The little coughs strengthened, and soon the infant began to wail. Mallory stopped patting his back and tucked him into her arms again. He rooted around looking for food, but Mallory ignored his need for the moment. She was looking around for what she needed first.

They were in a clearing in what appeared to be a forest, though it was not a natural clearing. The shockwave of the ship's impact had knocked down several trees in a circle around it. The closest trees had been torn out by the roots and thrown yards away. Others had their trunks cracked apart but were still holding on by shreds of bark. The nearest trees still standing were almost 100 feet away, and those were leaning over in various states of distress.

And while normally the physics of the scenario she was seeing would have consumed her curiosity, there was only one question on her mind at the moment: "Where's Caleb?" she called to the sprite.

The sprite turned, and its eyes blinked rapidly. Mallory knew it was scanning the area. It stopped and turned to face some of the trees. "There are two human life forms several yards from here to the north."

Mallory looked in the direction the sprite was facing. A

trail of smoking was coming from the tops of the trees in that direction. "Are they alive?" Mallory asked.

"I would not be able to sense them if they were not," the sprite answered.

"Sprite, go see if they need help and bring them back here." Mallory waved a hand in that direction.

The sprite did not move. "My last order was to protect you and your child, Sprite Master."

Mallory sighed. She looked down at her wrist and saw that she was still wearing the Dominus bracelet and that it had not been damaged in the crash. "Dikaió, sprite, do as you were asked." The sprite's eyes flashed, and it floated up and toward the smoking trees. Mallory looked down toward baby Kirk, who was still insisting that this was a great time to eat. "Okay, fine," Mallory said and adjusted herself to accommodate her baby.

She looked up toward where the clockwork sprite had floated off to, hoping to see it returning with Caleb, but all she saw was flattened trees and smoke. She hoped he was okay. All the worries about raising baby Kirk without his father—the same feelings she had tried so hard to bury while in captivity with Omaha—hit her at once. Along with the stress of the past few days, running for her life, protecting her child, being betrayed—it was all too much. She burst into tears. Baby Kirk squirmed irritably while her chest heaved in sobs. "S-s-sorry, little one," she stammered and tried to pull her emotions back into check. It was no use. She cried even harder and clutched the child desperately, as wave after wave of emotional release poured out of her.

A glint of metal in the sunlight finally made her take a deep breath, and she sniffled hard. She hoped the clockwork sprite had found Caleb and was bringing him back to her, but something was off: The metallic reflection was not coming from the direction of the broken trees and smoke. It was about 15 degrees to the right of that. Mallory squinted her eyes trying to see what it was. Then she gasped.

There was a fire sprite in the woods.

Mallory looked around for cover and gasped again. Two wilding wolves exited the trees on the opposite side of the fire sprite, sniffing the air. She looked at the Dikaió bracelet on her arm and then around at her surroundings. She was in the middle of a forest full of organic material that the Dikaió would be useless in, except for the ship twenty yards away, and the fire sprite about 100 yards away, which at least for now was not moving toward her. The wilding wolves, however, had locked onto her scent and were crouching toward her. They slowly parted from each other, looking to hem in their prey. Mallory made a break for the ship.

She called out. "Dikaió, protect me!"

Pieces of the burning ship rolled and then rose into the

air around her. The two wolves yelped and paused in their tracks. Mallory could not be sure, but this pair of wilding wolves acted like they they recognized the Dikaió and that it was dangerous. Mallory slowly moved closer to the ship, clutching baby Kirk firmly to her chest and away from the two animals. She wanted to get close to the ship in case the wolves over came their fear, and she needed to use parts of it to defend herself from attack. The animals fidgeted where they stood, but they did not move any closer. Mallory shook her head and chuckled. If the wolves had been this afraid of the Dikaió in the Davis City Metroplex, it would have made her escape a lot easier and wildly less violent. Her mind turned to the fire sprite opposite the wolves. Like the wolves, it too seemed to be frozen in place.

Mallory bit her lip and tilted her head. There was something familiar about the fire sprite in the woods. Her eyes widened. It was too far away to tell, but she wondered if it might be …

"Mallory!" Caleb's happy voice interrupted her thoughts.

She spun to see him, General Knenne, and the copper sprite walking across the clearing toward her. Her heart leapt into her throat, and she felt like she was on the verge of tears again. The two men's clothes were in tatters, and they were covered with dried blood, but they both were walking fine and smiling—no doubt completely healed by their nano sprites. Mallory was happy that she had not seen either of them before they were healed; she was not sure she could have handled seeing what they looked like after being torn from the burning ship.

"Look out!" Caleb screamed and burst into a run across the clearing. General Knenne froze and immediately began scanning their surroundings. Caleb picked up a piece of the ship that was lying on the ground while he ran and swung it over his head screaming.

It took a fraction of a second to realize what was happening, but Caleb was running toward the two wilding wolves. "Caleb, wait!" Mallory yelled, but it was too late.

Her husband stood over the bodies of the wilding wolves; his chest heaving. He looked up at her with deep concern, and when their eyes met, Mallory felt her heart beat a little faster, but she shook her head. "They were afraid. They weren't any danger to us or anyone."

"The wilding wolves are always a danger" General Knenne said. Then he looked at baby Kirk's feet dangling in Mallory's arms. "Is the baby okay?"

Mallory nodded. "He seems fine, though how would you know. He heals fast you know."

General Knenne shook his head sadly. "I nearly forgot Omaha's experiment. All the more reason not to let the Relos or Omaha get their hands on him."

Mallory tilted her head. "I get Omaha's obsession, but I still don't understand why the Relos need my child."

The General looked serious. "If they truly mean to destroy both the Ex Natu's nano sprites and the Dikaió's quantum sprites, his DNA holds the key to both. Your son's DNA is coded with the the sub-atomic sequence, which connects to both the orbital networks that control them. And if the Relos can follow that connection, they can access the satellite networks above us and shut it all down."

Caleb looked confused. "What are the two of you talking about?"

Mallory smiled and answered, "I have no idea, but apparently everyone wants our son for something."

The General nodded, "And we can't let anyone have him."

Caleb's confusion did not go away, but he folded his arms and gave one of the lopsided grins that Mallory loved so much. "Unless he's stinky, then anyone can have him."

Mallory grimaced. "You're stinky, and I don't want to give you away."

General Knenne looked at both of them with bewilderment, but rather than engaging with their banter, looked around at their surroundings. "I tried to bring the ship close to Hoffen City, but if we were near it, the crash should have attracted more wilding wolves. Caleb and I should never have had time to recover back there before being attacked. Something's wrong. Sprite, do you see any more wolves in the trees?"

The clockwork sprite's eyes flashed as it scanned the circle of felled trees around them. After it completed the circle, it spun a quarter turn counter-clockwise. "There is one more wilding wolf in that direction, but it is a small cub." And as if on cue, a small wilding wolf cub tumbled out of the standing trees, bumbling over the branches and felled lumber, heading right for his parents on the ground. He nuzzled one of them and whined.

Mallory looked at Caleb then at her own little cub, happily sleeping in her arms. She understood exactly what was happening. "They were a family."

The General looked at her incredulously. "A family that would have gladly tore us all apart for supper, including your son. They are a plague on the planet and need to be destroyed: all of them." He pulled a weapon from the holster on his hip and aimed it at the wolf cub.

Mallory shook her head and spoke without biting her lip or tilting her head at all. "No!" she screamed. "You can't!"

General Knenne's voice was low and commanding. "Wilding wolves and humans being cannot coexist." He began walking toward the cub to get a better shot.

"Caleb! Stop him!" Mallory screamed.

Caleb moved from his crouching position in front of Mallory with lightning speed and pushed the General's arm into the air as he fired at the wolf cub. The General almost fell over with the force of Caleb's collision but gained his footing quickly. "Don't be foolish. I know it's hard for a new mother and all her raging hormones, but it must be eradicated."

"Like you had to eradicate the Relos?" Mallory shot back.

General Knenne's eyebrows narrowed. "This is not the same." He jumped away from Caleb, lowering his weapon toward the cub again.

Mallory shouted, "Dikaió, don't fire!"

General Knenne squeezed the trigger, and nothing happened. He exhaled in disgust, holstering the weapon. Then he said quickly, "Sprite, kill that wolf!"

The clockwork sprite's arms extended into long whips and started to float toward the cub, but Mallory quickly shouted, "Dikaió, stop!"

The sprite froze in midair, not moving any further.

The General sighed heavily. "Sprite, override commands from Dikaió user Mallory Aiworth, authorization General Knenne, alpha seven nine zeta three." The sprite's eyes blinked, but it did not continue toward the wolf cub. "Sprite," the general yelled. "I order you to kill that wolf cub."

"I am sorry, General," the sprite said. "The anomaly in our programming does not allow me to ignore commands from Dikaió user Mallory Aiworth."

General Knenne spat and turned to Mallory. "What did you do to my sprite?"

Mallory had no idea, but she set her mouth in determination and decided to use this moment to her advantage. "No one is harming that wolf cub."

The General softened and pleaded with her. "It's just maternal hormones, Mallory. Please, be reasonable." He looked at Caleb and raised his hands, palm upward. "Talk to your wife. Make her understand."

Caleb laughed heartily and walked back over to Mallory. He threw his big arm over her and smiled. "There's no chance I'm siding against her."

General Knenne shook his head and conceded. "I'm too old for his," he muttered. "Sprite, are you sure there are no more wilding wolves in the area?"

"Not that I can detect, General Knenne," the sprite confirmed, still frozen in place.

The General sighed and looked back at the cub. "You'll regret this some day, but at least it won't be reproducing anytime soon."

Mallory handed the sleeping baby to Caleb. "Here, hold him for a minute." She walked over to the sad cub and held out her hand to it. The little wolf sniffed at her hand and then went to bite it, but Mallory bonked its nose, and it shuffled back with a yelp Mallory smiled and patted its head. "No, no little one. You are not going to be doing that anymore." The wolf cub squirmed under her touch, but as it smelled her hand, it slowly began drawing near to her, then it licked her palm and set its head in her hand. Mallory scooped it up and scratched its head behind its ears. "We're taking him with us."

General Knenne threw up his hands. "Now, that's just too much! Hundreds of years without pets, and this Matriarch decides she's going to tame a wilding wolf."

Mallory pretended not to hear. "He's family, now." The wolf cub clambered up her arm onto her shoulder and poked its head through her tangled curly hair. It growled at what it saw behind her. Mallory turned around to see what it was growling at and again saw the fire sprite still standing stationary in the distance. "Hey! Is that one of the fire sprites you left near the city?" she asked the General.

General Knenne's attention shifted from scowling at the wolf cub to staring in the direction she was pointing. "Maybe. It's hard to tell from here." He pulled his weapon from its holster again. "Unlock this again, just in case."

"You'll leave Scout alone?" Mallory asked.

"Scout?" The General asked incredulously, rolling his eyes. "You've named it already?"

Mallory smiled and patted the wolf cub's head. "He scouted that fire sprite over there didn't he?"

The General shrugged and patted his weapon as if to remind her to unlock it.

"Promise me first," Mallory said. "Promise you'll let him live."

The General nodded. "Fine! Just let me protect you."

Mallory smiled. "Dikaió, unlock the General's weapon."

The General started walking toward the fire sprite, and Caleb followed holding baby Kirk with Mallory close behind holding the little wilding wolf. She looked behind her and saw the clockwork sprite still hovering amongst the fallen trees; its whip-like tentacles draping over the ground. "Dikaió sprite, come protect us, but leave this little one alone." Mallory called back over her shoulder, and the sprite flew after them, retracting its tentacles as it did so.

As they approached the fire sprite, Mallory could see that it had been sitting out in the elements for a long, long time. She stopped when they were about fifty feet from it and looked to the right. There was another fire sprite that had fallen over in the impact blast, and another still standing beyond it. "Caleb, do you see them?" she called.

Caleb stopped and followed her gaze. He looked confused. "It can't be the Hoffen City fire sprites, Mal. We'd be able to see the city. It should be right over there." Caleb pointed in the direction the fire sprites were facing.

BOOM!

Mallory squeaked and looked at General Knenne, who was pointing his weapon in the direction Caleb was pointing. "What are you doing?"

General Knenne said, "Watch closely."

Mallory and Caleb looked at the place he was pointing the weapon, and the General fired again. A small spot of one of the trees that was still standing blinked almost imperceptibly with pink fire. The pink fire disappeared almost as soon as it had appeared, and the tree looked completely unharmed. "They got the light working again!" Mallory shouted excitedly.

Caleb smiled. "Alex must have made it back. They're safe!"

General Knenne shook his head. "Not any safer than we were inside the plasma shield of the Global Alliance's capitol."

Mallory and Caleb's happiness faded immediately. Mallory nodded, "we need to get in and warn them."

Caleb bounced baby Kirk to his other arm. "But how? We don't have any way of getting through a plasma shield."

Mallory held up her wrist. "We have a Dominus bracelet."

Caleb shook his head. "C'mon, Mal. Remember when we were kids, and I used to try to open the light with the Dikaió, so we could see what was on the other side? It never worked."

General Knenne nodded. "That was the design. What good would it do to have a defensive shield if people could come and go whenever they pleased? The idea was to have a passcode along with the Dikaió that could turn the shield on and off."

Mallory bit her lip and tilted her head. "But the Archivist was able to open a doorway in her holographic shield using only the Dikaió. We heard her."

Caleb nodded. "Oh, that's right! After we got caught in the net, she used her Dominus bracelet to do it."

General Knenne paused and tilted his head, staring at the trees. "Maybe it was something she added."

"Or maybe it was something Omaha added for her," Caleb pitched in. "When he showed up at the Library, he acted like he owned it."

Mallory shook her head. "According to her, she got the generator working herself and contacted him later. And besides, when Alex shut it off, she freaked out. Remember? And Omaha didn't show up until it was down."

"That doesn't change this plasma shield," General Knenne said. "Whatever Emily Carpenter made; this is Hoffen City. This is different."

Mallory bit her lip and tilted her head looking at the forest ahead of her. It was so realistic that it was hard to believe it was just a generated hologram. She walked toward the holographic tree that General Knenne had shot. "Dikaió, open a doorway in the plasma shield," she ordered.

Nothing happened.

"Well, so much for that idea," Caleb sighed.

Mallory huffed in frustration. "There has to be a way to get in, or to at least let them know we're out here." She looked back at the General. "The Dikaió could still affect things inside the plasma shield, right? I mean, I know the Archivist said there was a distance limitation, but the shield shouldn't interrupt it."

General Knenne nodded. "Theoretically, but what would you do?"

Mallory turned back toward the shield. "I'm going to send them a message."

Alex Nelson stood at the front of a small party, which included her father the Administrator, Mallory's father the Chief Magistrate, the Governor, and the Matriarch. Before them stretched the endless plains of the light, and behind them a city, which was once again running smoothly now that the Dikaió had been restored to all the people. The culture sprites were once again tending the crops, the grocery sprites were once again attending the market, and even the yards were back to being well-manicured. The starvation rations had been reduced after this year's crop had produced a little more than expected: a small feat considering they were still down two whole skyscraper greenhouses in the city center. Meat was still very limited, as the wilding-wolf invasion had left its mark on their herds, but even those were growing. Twenty-one calves grazed beside their mothers in the pasture behind them, which was an increase of fifty-two percent—but that was a long ways from having enough meat and dairy to feed a city of thousands. So, even though no one was starving, some rationing was still a necessity to keep the city alive for now.

The Council was hopeful that in two or three years, those measures could be completely removed—though they calculated that it would be a decade or longer before the city could return to its former glory—if it ever did. The loss of Reddy LaMarr as the Sprite Master had left a hole in the city's leadership, as well as a hole in sprite production, which Alex had not realized was so integral to the city's operations. The sprite steel, which seemed so indestructible, had been recycled many, many times, and its nigh invulnerability only lasted ten to eleven months. Apparently, Reddy Lamarr and the other Sprite Masters had been recycling them under everyone's noses for decades and never told anyone that they were short on materials or that they had such a short lifespan. That short lifespan was growing shorter with every iteration of sprites. Now, sprites were beginning to break down all around the city, and even with a Dominus bracelet, Alex hadn't been able to get the Rookery functioning the way it needed to in order to fix them. In fact, the Rookery was not working at all anymore. Without anyone being able to stop it, the Dikaió had automated the building into utter disrepair, and it had to be shut it down completely. She had used the Dikaió to copy several books on making sprites and fixing a Rookery, but it was taking a long time to teach the population to read, much less to learn the technical specifications of sprite manufacturing. There were concepts in them that probably needed their own books to explain, but she did not know the names of those subjects, and the Dikaió was not intuitive enough to conjure them up no matter what commands she gave. How Mallory had just understood what to do was beyond her when it came to fixing sprites. Add that all up, and Alex was not sure the current crop of sprites would last until the population developed the technical savvy to replace them.

It is a funny thing how short people's memories are. Not even one year ago, Alex was the savior who had slain the wilding wolves, and now there were rumors that her leadership was going to lead them to ruin when the sprites fell apart. But as long as she wore the Dominus bracelet, no one would dare oppose her openly, and she was at least smart enough to not tell anyone that the Dominus bracelet was what gave her complete control of the Dikaió—nor would she tell them how she regained the Dikaió, choosing to only say, "there are some stories better left untold." The wilding wolves were enough to make them fear the outside world. And when she told them that there were evil immortals called Ex Natu who wanted them all dead, they were immediately subdued. And yet, there were still malcontent whispers in secret corners against her.

To make matters worse, over the past couple of days, the Dikaió had started to act strangely. Culture sprites were scrawling messages on walls: "Help us, we're trapped outside the light." Buildings were tearing themselves apart to make arrowed paths pointing across the pasturelands toward the dark forest outside the light. Just this morning, one of Alex's house sprites had arranged the blueberries in her oatmeal to say, "Alex, please! Let us in!" Of course, Alex knew who was on the other side of those messages. It had to be Mallory and Caleb, but so far no one else had guessed. The Council was tearing itself apart, debating whether to lower the light and see who was responsible. The funny thing was that Alex's mother and father opposed opening the light the most— fearful of their youngest daughter's safety, no doubt.

Alex herself was torn on whether to let Mallory back in. On the one hand, if anyone could fix their sprite problem, Mallory could. On the other, she would probably do a lot of damage recounting the city's history. She consulted Omaha's book on holographic shield generators and found that there was a setting to make the hologram only work one way: She would be able to see out, but no one on the other side would be able to see in. She had intended to do it on her own while no one was watching, so she had gotten up at sunrise to make her way there but was shocked to find a good portion of the city already up and bustling about—including the small consortium of Council members standing behind her. They had no idea where she was going or what she was doing; they just had incessant questions about city business to discuss and followed along behind her—talking and talking and talking: "The people are asking if there will be meat at the festival next month. Two more culture sprites have gone offline. There was a small disturbance in the northwestern quadrant last night. Do we really need more magistrate christenings?"

When Alex stopped at the edge of the light without answering even one of their concerns, silence ensued.

"Dominus?" the Chief Magistrate asked.

Alex ignored him. She placed her feet shoulder-length apart and clasped her hands behind her back. She straightened her head and spoke, "Dikaió, open a semi-transparent viewing panel in the plasma shield in front of me."

Immediately, the space in front of Alex was replaced by a rectangular doorway about seven-feet tall. On the other side of the door was the dark forest, or at least part of it. It looked like a good section had been flattened and burned. A few feet away from the window was a small fire. Mallory and Caleb were lying asleep on one side of the fire. Caleb had his arm around Mallory, and she was holding an infant against her chest. On the other side of the fire lay a small sleeping wilding wolf. Staring back at her was a bronze-skinned man with brown curly hair, stormy gray eyes, and tattoos moving just below his neckline. Next to him floated the clockwork sprite. Its eyes flashed, and it began to hover toward the viewing window.

"Dikaió, close the viewing pane!" Alex said quickly, forgetting to camouflage the panic in her voice, and the dark forest was instantly replaced with endless pastureland.

The Matriarch asked, "was that Mallory and Caleb? Did they have a baby?"

Alex did not answer. She simply turned on her heel and started to walk away. The Chief Magistrate grabbed her arm. "We have to help them, Dominus!"

She shook his arm loose. "I understand your concern for

your daughter, Chief Magistrate, but it is misplaced. The man with them is an Ex Natu, and the bronze sprite carries the very disease that turned Caleb into one of them…"

The Governor interrupted, "My son?"

Alex spun on her heel to the Governor. "Yes, your son is an Ex Natu now: an immortal monster, and if Mallory is still alive, she may have joined them as well. We cannot sacrifice the safety of the City for the sake of one."

The Matriarch shook her head. "You can't leave them out there to die. They've asked for help. My grandchild needs our help!"

Alex's eyes narrowed. "You were part of the decision to banish us, Matriarch. Don't forget that. If Mallory dies on the other side of this light, that's your fault, not mine."

"She was your best friend, Alex! Your only friend," the Matriarch persisted.

Alex nodded and then turned herself back toward the City. "Which makes this decision all the harder, but it's the right one nonetheless. We tried the other option, Matriarch — placing Mallory's needs above the needs of the city — and how many died from that decision? That is a mistake I do not intend to repeat. Now, let's address your concerns from this morning. This matter is closed."

"Yes, Dominus," all the leaders except the Matriarch said in unison, and they lowered their heads in submission as they followed after her.

"Roger!" the Matriarch shouted with indignation at her husband.

The Chief Magistrate glanced back at her without lifting

his head, but he did not stop walking. "Not now, Sarai."

"She's our daughter, Roger!" the Matriarch continued.

He rolled his eyes toward Alex. "Mallory is lost to us; we must protect her sister, so she will be the new Matriarch."

With steel in her voice, Alex cut them both off. "Listen to your husband, Matriarch. I said that this matter is closed, and the more you squabble over it, the more I think I made a mistake in restoring your positions. Should I look for a new Matriarch and a new Chief Magistrate?"

"No, Dominus," the Chief Magistrate said quickly and motioned for his wife to follow suit.

"No, Dominus," the Matriarch complied and with one last look at the endless pasturelands behind her, she turned her back on her eldest daughter.

Acknowledgements

We thank God for calling us to finish this project: We owe sincere gratitude to You not only for providing constant inspiration and real joy in the process, but also for hounding us with conviction when we were distracted, discouraged, and ready to quit. We are thankful that You gave us this idea, that You turned our hearts toward our children and their needs, that You blessed our marriage with times of creative bonding, while guarding our words so that we would not mislead or cause harm in the process.

To our parents, thanks for helping us obtain library cards and supporting our creativity. Thanks to Stephen's father, Dale Porter, for exhilarating overnight adventures at the TV studio and encouraging his education. Thanks to Stephen's mother, Terry Porter, for providing his first dictionary and encyclopedia sets. Thanks to Gayle's father, John Gustafson, for trips to the library and teaching her how to operate the microfiche machine and use the Dewey decimal system. Thanks to Gayle's mother, Marjorie Gustafson, for teaching her that girls can learn anything if they are willing to work hard. Thanks to all our parents for giving us a good sense of humor, and for showing us beautiful places to remind us that God is the creative genius who made this vast, gorgeous world.

To our dear friends, Brad and Joy Kroes, Ken and Donna Stucki, and Joe and Susie thank you for encouraging us and praying for our success in our writing. We are grateful for your faithful friendship, for laughter, and for your indelible patience with our incessant puns and sarcasm.

We also thank August, Anne, William and Abigail Thurmer; Brandon and Kaylee Gustafson; and our church family for patiently cheering us on during this endeavor.

Finally, thank you to our readers who give purpose and fresh perspective to our writing. May you be inspired by our words, as you have inspired us to write.

9 781957 907130